RJ CLARK

Homecoming

First published by M4L Publishing 2025

Copyright © 2025 by RJ Clark

All rights reserved. No part of this publication may be reproduced, stored or transmitted in any form or by any means, electronic, mechanical, photocopying, recording, scanning, or otherwise without written permission from the publisher. It is illegal to copy this book, post it to a website, or distribute it by any other means without permission.

This novel is entirely a work of fiction. The names, characters and incidents portrayed in it are the work of the author's imagination. Any resemblance to actual persons, living or dead, events or localities is entirely coincidental.

RJ Clark asserts the moral right to be identified as the author of this work.

First edition

ISBN: 978-1-951762-97-1

Editing by Melissa Prideaux
Cover art by 100 Covers

This book was professionally typeset on Reedsy.
Find out more at reedsy.com

Contents

IV   A Whole New World

Dedication:

With love and gratitude:
    Hank Adams, 5th grade,
    Patricia Lobosco, 7th grade English,
    William "Harry" Rettino, 9th grade,
    Teresa Iacovetti, 9th and 12th grade English,
    Frankie Rella, 11th and 12th grade,
    William Pace, script consultant, ongoing,
    and **Andre and Natasha Gonzalez**.

Teachers.
    Mentors.
    Friends.

All of whom saw my potential long before I did, believed in me when the nights were unbearably long, pushed me when everything told me to give up, that I was not and would never be good enough, and inspired me to always reach higher.

An Extra-Special "Thank You" to:

All the enthusiastic and dedicated
    STAYCATION-*ers* out there.

I have *loved* every minute
    of sharing these stories with you.

You've made this wild ride so much fun.

There are too many of you to list,
    and I would kick myself later
    if I forgot to name someone,
    so just know that I appreciate
    <u>*all*</u> *of you.*

A **"HOMECOMING"** *is defined as*:

1. An instance of returning **HOME**.

2. A person's return **HOME,** often after a long period of absence.

"You Can't Go Home Again."
  · *Thomas Wolfe*

"There's no place like home."

  · *Dorothy Gale, The Wizard of Oz*

"Home is where the heart is."

  · *Pliny the Elder, AD 23–79*

"Home is where the bodies are buried."

  · *Anonymous*

**"Every story has an end, but in life,
every ending is just a new beginning."**

  · *inspired by the writings of Seneca*

"Go then, there are other worlds than these."

· Stephen King, *The Gunslinger*

We Begin: It's Not Usual

"Ladies and gents, won't you please welcome to the Eden main stage, your favorite and mine—and I mean that sincerely, I do. Let's give a warm Garden of Eden Casino and Nightclub welcome to The Strip's number one rated, by your votes and mine, Seventies Tom Jones impersonator, the one... the only... the incomparable... Josh Grooooooo-ban!"

Before Joshy Baby could get out one "It's" of the signature song, his head exploded like an overstuffed burrito. Bits of him blew into the shrieking audience of two. A droopy eye landed in one woman's Manhattan, while a wisp of Joshy Baby's hair plug landed gingerly on top of the other gal's Cobb Salad. They darted for the nearest exit with no one in their way. But as quick as they moved, the thing in the darkness was far quicker. It always was.

I fucking hate that guy, the thing in the darkness thought. *I'll always fucking hate that guy.*

CROATOAN.

I

REQUIEM FOR A DYING WORLD

Through the Looking Glass

Detective Joseph P. Harding didn't know where he was.

Correction: not that he didn't know, but rather he didn't remember. They'd been on the road for days, traveling countless miles in the darkness. At that moment, both their location and destination felt a mystery. Something sitting on the edge of a dream you can't quite recall. Harding wondered if the details had faded because of his own tired brain or if they were being deliberately erased, little by little.

It wasn't just the details of this final ride into Hel that had grown dimmer, but so much of his life before their final ride began. *Til Valhalla!* Somehow, he knew then, when he'd spoken his allegiance to the quest, where they were heading, but now he felt like he had in Mr. Juliano's shop class all those years ago—lost. Where everyone saw bookcases and chests in a pile of wood, Harding saw only a pile of wood. Even though his hands could not create, Harding was skilled at the art of destruction. He may not have been able to build walls, but he could tear them down. Margaret, his ex-wife, knew this all too well.

His tired reflection stared back at him from the broken mirror on the wall of the dingy shit box at the rest stop. He couldn't breathe at first, for the entire room reeked as though the dead were trying to claw their way out of the toilets and the rusty old pipes. A sick feeling swirled in his belly, and had there been anything worthwhile in his stomach, Harding knew it would have exploded onto the tile floor that had more stains on it than Jennifer Hopez had ex-husbands. He pushed the feeling back down and splashed handfuls of the cold, brownish water onto his face.

Christ, is that me? Is that what I look like now? I look like my Grandaddy Paul.

The face staring back at him did not seem to be his own. It was older, much older. Ragged. Wrinkled. This was the face of a man approaching seventy, which Harding was not. If he hadn't been wide awake, he would've sworn he'd fallen asleep at the wheel and had been sucked into another one of his nightmares. The last thing he needed was waking nightmares. That was the first stop on the crazy train that derailed quickly. And there were no other trains that stopped at that station. Once you got there, you were fucked. It was a one-way trip.

In the time Harding hooked up with the Millers, he'd seen enough weird shit to drive any man to the brink of insanity. Andy West's severed talking head was enough to make anyone wonder if they'd lost a few of their marbles. But Harding still had all his intact. Well, most of them. At least, he felt that way until recently. As the concept of time slowly slipped away, he couldn't even say when the feeling first came to him. But it was there now, and he couldn't ignore it. His gut told him to be on guard. Something was indeed rotten in... wherever the fuck it was they were holed up now.

He had the vaguest memory of a busted-out neon sign reading "OTEL" instead of "hotel." The place resembled the infamous Bates Motel from *Psycho*, but it was a place to rest for a while. He'd risk tetanus for a decent night's sleep. Just one night of not sleeping upright in the car with his passengers. Olivia's snoring kept most of them up half the night.

Wait. This isn't a rest stop. It's a hotel. I'm in a hotel. I'm standing in the bathroom. In my room. But... how did I get here? I don't—

Harding glanced over his shoulder and eyed the old-fashioned brass key resting on the dusty desk. It was on a large keyring with a big plastic tag that, once upon a time, clearly had a silver printed image of the place on it, along with its proper name. The image and the name had faded, and all he could make out was Otel. He wouldn't have been at all surprised if the place's proper name was *The Shit Hole Hotel.* A mystery for another life.

He turned and stepped a foot into the main room, seeing if it rang any of his memory's bells. The room wasn't as unappealing as the bathroom, but it wouldn't be recommended by AAA anytime soon. If anything, it would be on a "do not stay unless your life depends on it" list, if any such compilation existed. Still, it would do. It had to. You never knew these days when another oasis in the encroaching wastelands would appear out of the darkness like magic. The wastelands grew larger every second, as though every fragment of life were slowly being devoured by an unseen ravenous mouth with boundless hunger.

The room jostled nothing loose in his brain. Just a cheap hotel room. The curtains smelled like cigarettes. The bed was lumpy and squeaky, and the carpet wore a dozen or more unidentifiable stains. If they hadn't left Vegas behind them, this could have been a room in the pay-as-you-go Sunrise Motel off The Strip on Sahara. It was a place for lost souls and people that charged by the hour for the pleasure of their "company." Harding marveled that technology hadn't yet taken the jobs of hookers. People would always want "the real thing," so that was one business that was tech-proof. Even during the lockdowns, the Sunrise was littered with lonely Janes and Johns looking to either fill a hole or be filled. It's not money that makes the world go around, but random fucking. That people risked catching a life-threatening virus for a little sketchy sex was all the proof Harding needed.

Harding returned to the bathroom and the broken mirror. He still couldn't wrap his head around the face staring back at him. Like he was a dog aging years instead of days. In this brave new world, anything was possible. But if that were the case, how many days lay ahead of him? Ten? Twenty? Fifty? Only time would tell.

The amber bulb flickered above him as the water in the toilet splashed like a fish was swimming laps in it. Harding did not want to see the kind of fish that swam—no, the kind of fish that *lived*—in the 'otel's toilet. Still, he was curious. Despite the approaching end of the world, Harding still thought of himself as a cop. And even though curiosity killed the cat, he couldn't deny the urge to look.

He crept to the bowl, which sat tucked in the corner. In that instant, to Harding, the toilet looked like a tombstone. All that was missing was the epitaph. The burning in his belly told him that if he could read the writing on the bowl, he was likely to see his own name, birth, and expiration dates etched onto the porcelain.

Rust-colored water splashed out of the bowl, landing just in front of his hesitating feet. A gurgling sound came from deep in the toilet—from deep in the pipes, as though something were making its way through them. Pulling itself through. Coming right at him. Or, maybe right *for* him.

The gurgling sound turned into a low moan, followed by a rapid release of bubbles. It sounded like something was drowning in the basin of the shit collector. Drowning, or clawing its way through miles and miles of murk to come and say *good day, asshole.*

Harding readied his revolver, mentally preparing himself for whatever new horror was about to present itself for inspection. Since the quest began, Harding had seen more things than were previously dreamt of in his narrow philosophy—things that made a talking severed head look like child's play. He wasn't numb to the nightmarish visions, but he wasn't so rattled by them anymore either. When you're traveling with a telekinetic, mind-bending family, weird is the staple dish. Everything else is just gravy.

The bubbles came faster. Water sloshed and splashed around the bowl, spilling over the shit-stained brim. Harding grabbed a towel that once had been whiter than that TV game show host's buck teeth and tossed it on the floor, hoping it would swallow the overflow. Harding wasn't about to get on his hands and knees later to mop that shit up.

The pipes groaned. Metal screeched, as though screaming, as they bent into impossible angles and shapes. Something was coming. Something was definitely coming. For a split second, Harding thought he saw the porcelain base stretch like it was made of bubble gum, as though someone were punching their fist through a sheer web of the stuff. Then, the base returned to its usual shape, but the water splashed about more violently. The towel was soaked, and the floor had collected a quarter of an inch of shit water, and it continued to rise as more and more water exploded out of the bowl.

A moan, something akin to a cry, rose beneath the bubbles, the desperate gasps for air. Harding steadied himself. It didn't matter if it was a cat, an alligator, or Old Scratch himself; whatever pulled itself out of that toilet was getting a magazine emptied into it. The gun shook in his hands, despite his best efforts to plant himself in place. Sometimes the fear finds its way in there no matter how resolute you think you are. And though he was loathe to admit it, Harding was afraid. Very afraid of what was coming for him.

Then, as suddenly as it began, the whirlpool stopped. One last splash of water and the bowl grew still. The room hushed, save for a lone dripping sound. That, and Harding's heart pounding in his chest. He took a small step forward, prepared for anything. And nothing. By then, he almost had himself convinced he was going to find one of those nightmarishly oversized rats floating in the bowl, its eyes rolled back in its tiny head and its mouth open wide, frozen.

Harding inched closer. Sweat dribbling down his chin. The shake in his hand betrayed him, and he fought back his fear as futilely as a lion tamer armed with a hairbrush. The fear was getting the better of him. But he couldn't just shut the lid and not know what had crawled its way through the dark to bite him in the ass. And, besides, it might still be alive, as impossible as that was to fathom. Dead wasn't necessarily dead in this new world. Sometimes dead just meant asleep. And life meant asleep at the wheel, because who was really living anymore?

He took a bigger step forward, and his foot slipped in the still water. Harding slid onto his ass with a thud and a moan. The revolver flew out of his hands into the next room. He watched it soar until he lost sight of it. A second later, it landed somewhere on the wall-to-wall carpet.

Fuck, fuck, fuckity, FUCK.

An ache swelled in the small of his back. Harding knew there'd be a big ol' black and purple blotch there in the morning, if not sooner. He'd tweaked something, and that was going to make driving countless hours without stopping a chore. It wasn't like anyone else would offer to take the wheel for an hour or two, a day or two, so he could stretch out in the back. No, he was the chauffeur. The driver. Security. The hired help. And though they hadn't said it, Harding knew they thought he should've felt privileged that they allowed him along for the ride. As he fell onto his back, Harding wondered just how privileged he felt.

"Goddammit," he shouted at the floor. He laughed at his own two left feet, his carelessness. Why hadn't he walked in like he owned the shit box? Strode in like John Wayans in those old westerns. *You looking for me, kid?* Instead, he slid in like a kid wearing his first pair of ice skates. "Mother fuck—"

Bubble. Gurgle. Bubbleeeee.

"Shit," Harding groaned as he slid back until his head touched the wall. He had hoped to make it through the door and onto the cigarette and coffee-stained carpet, however unappealing that thought was to him, but he miscalculated his position and now he was stuck. Caught like a god-fearing Republican slipping his private number to a kid at a barbecue. *For a good time, call... I'll make it worth your while.*

Bubble. Bubble. Gurgleeeee.

Harding kicked at the air, as though he could send whatever it was coming for him back into the abyss. But it was futile. The thing continued to slither its way out of the toilet. A giant wave of dirty water shot out, slapping Harding on his face.

He screamed, wiping his face furiously.

"Son of a bitch!"

Another swell of shit water. Harding dodged and weaved, and it missed him by less than a couple of inches. He felt like a bullseye in one of those cheap carnival games. *Six shots for a buck! Win great prizes!*

Somehow, Harding crawled on his stomach, dragging himself across the tile floor. He thought about burning his clothes later as he shimmied and slithered toward the bowl.

"I'm gonna flush your ass back to hell, whatever you are! You hear me?"

The thing in the toilet gurgled in response.

Shit.

Not literal feces, but the expletive.

The bowl was less than a foot away. He reached for the flusher, and his hand slipped. His fingers were soaked. He reached for it again, and, again, his hand slipped.

"Jesus, Mary and—"

Joeeeeeeeeeeeeeeeee.

The muffled voice came from inside the bowl. It sounded muffled because whatever was doing the talking had a mouthful of water. He almost felt sorry for the thing. Maybe later, after this close encounter was through, he'd take his clothes and it out back and burn them both. It'd be a mercy.

Harddddddingggggggg.

The voice now had a familiar ring.

Help meeeee, Joeeeeeeeeee.

"West," Harding thought.

He stumbled to his feet, using a hand and the sink to steady himself. The ache in his back had turned into a wicked throbbing and burning sensation. It hurt like hell, but Harding ignored it as best he could. No one ever died from a backache, he reasoned. But what about disembodied voices from the beyond? From beyond his shit box? The jury was still out.

"West?"

Joe! Help me!

Harding inched his head forward until his eyes were staring into the shit swallower. And there, as he expected to see, was indeed Andy West's severed head, facing down, drowning in a sea of the 'otel's brownish water.

Don't just stand there, Joe. Help me!

Harding didn't have time to wonder how West knew he was indeed just standing there, looking down into the bowl. Eyes in the back of his head? He almost fell on his ass again as he knelt beside the basin, reached in, and turned West's head so its eyes stared right into his.

"Oh, Joe," West said, puffing at some strands of wet hair that had gathered over his right eye. When they didn't budge, West eyed Harding. "Would you mind?"

"No," Harding said, pulling the hair out of West's eye. "Better?"

"Much," West said, sighing a little. "Thanks."

"Don't mention it. Please... don't mention it."

"Alright," West said, smiling. A shit nugget fell out of his open mouth, leaving a trail down his chin. "Sorry about that, Joe. I'm embarrassed."

"It's fine."

"I'm wondering if you wouldn't mind ripping off a piece of that shit paper and..."

"And," Harding pushed.

"You know... wipe my chin. I feel you won't be able to take

me seriously if I've got a shit tattoo on my face. Come on, Joe. I'd do it for you."

"With what arms, genius?" Harding laughed, rolling some shit paper into his hand.

"Still a comedian, I see," West said, rolling his eyes. Then he continued in a mock announcer's voice. "The 'otel is proud to present, in its shit box theatre, let's give it up for Joseph P. Harrrrrrrrrrding."

West made the roar of the crowd with his voice as Harding moved in with the shit paper.

"JOE!"

Harding recoiled, almost falling back onto his ass again. He also almost lost the crumbled stack of shit paper.

"Christ. What, West?"

"I'm meltttiiinnnngggg, Joe! Meltttinnnnggggggg. What a world..."

"Asshole," Harding said, moving back into wiping position. Before he dabbed at West's chin, he smiled. "I could just flush you, you know. Keep pulling the trigger until you're clogging up someone else's shitter."

"You could, Joe. You could."

Harding threw the soiled shit paper into the toilet.

"Hey!"

"Don't be such a baby, West," Harding laughed. "How'd you get through the pipes anyway? I mean... you couldn't have dragged yourself."

"No, because I have no arms, as you've noted. Well, it wasn't easy, I'll tell you what. I rolled myself like a bowling ball. And then I got a little more creative when I got... stuck... in the muck... and the poo."

"You... rolled?"

West shook himself from side to side.

"Rock and roll, baby. It's here to stay."

"Do I even want to know what 'got creative' means?"

"Uh, probably not, Joe. Best keep some things just for me, you know. I wouldn't want to freak you out."

"That's rich, West. Anyway…" Harding reached for the flusher. "It's been nice seeing you."

"No, don't! Don't you dare flush me, Joe!"

Harding's hand lingered on the flusher.

"Yeah? Give me one good reason why I shouldn't."

"Okay, Joe," West began. "I'll give you two."

Harding withdrew his hand.

"I'm listening, West."

"One, if you send me back down… there, you'll never know what it was I came here to tell you. And that will eat at you. You'll always be wondering in the back of your mind 'what did West want? If only I hadn't flushed my friend down the toilet.'"

Harding shrugged.

"And two?"

"Sandra Miller is standing behind you."

Harding laughed.

"I'm not falling for that."

"I'm not kidding, Joe. Turn around."

The hairs on Harding's neck rose to attention. His blood iced even as his heart pumped furiously.

"No."

Suddenly, her scent was everywhere, surrounding him like a toxic cloud. Her fingers gripped his shoulder, digging into the skin with just enough force to not draw blood.

"Have you missed me, Detective?"

"Sorry, Joe. It had to be done," West said.

Harding tugged at the flusher several times and watched as West's head sank beneath the murky water. He tugged at it several more times, finally grabbing the cleaning brush and poking West's head with it until the wide-eyed, open-mouthed noggin was finally sucked back down into the shitty abyss from whence it had come to torment him.

"Detective?"

Harding tossed the brush aside and rounded on his feet. He was shocked to find no one, and nothing, behind him. But he was sure that Sandra Miller had been there only a second ago. The room still reeked of her perfume and cigarettes. So, where had she gone?

This bitch is gonna be the death of me.

He went to the sink, having finally convinced himself that the bitch was gone, and that she had been there—and West, too. It'd all been real. He wasn't losing what little gray matter he had left. He turned on the faucet, and the sink flooded with murky, musty-smelling water. After his exchange with West's head, splashing a little more shit-stained water on his face seemed almost pleasant. Almost.

He had to admit, the water felt good as it shocked his skin awake. He turned the faucet off and studied himself in the mirror. There was something... odd there. Not with him, but with the mirror itself. It looked almost as though it were moving. No, like something was moving underneath it. No, not under it... behind it.

Then Harding realized it wasn't just the mirror that was rippling with life, but the entire wall. Then, the entire shit box rippled as though Harding were seeing it through a waterfall. It looked like the shit box itself was coming to life. Breathing.

Waking up from a deep sleep.

The broken shards of mirror stretched to him, reaching like fingers, but they did not crackle or break. They just reset, and then reached again. The walls shimmered and rippled. Behind them, it looked as though a spectacular fireworks show was taking place. And behind that, darkness.

So much dark, Harding observed.

Then, without warning, out of the dark, a set of hands reached out and pulled him through the looking glass and into the endless dark that lay behind the mirror.

They were the hands of the beast.

They were Sandra Miller's hands.

Ghost Stories

"Why, Detective," the thing that was Sandra Miller grinned, baring her blackened teeth, "you look as though you've seen a ghost."

Harding's instincts took over. He surveyed the room with the eyes of a seasoned detective. They were sitting in a large dining room, on opposite ends of a long, shiny wood table. It felt like a rustic cabin, given the stone fireplace and walls made up of logs. A series of skulls over the mantle, like hunting trophies. Human skulls. Harding counted a dozen, at least. A fire roared, crackling and sparking, shooting bits of ash into the air. Save for the spattering of candles throughout the obscenely large room, the fire's flames gave off the only light. Shadows danced and crawled along the ceiling, walls, and floor. Moving with ease like ballerinas, pirouetting and spinning madly. Occasionally, Harding noticed a shadow would flash him a grin. His eyes moved to the ceiling, tracking a shadowy specter. A chandelier made up of bones and skulls hung above the table. Candles sat somewhere inside each skull, casting an unholy glow.

Sandra popped a cigarette into her cigarette holder. A moment later, it seemed to light itself as she sucked in its poison. She held it in for close to a minute before blowing it through her flaring nostrils.

"IKEAH," Harding said, indicating the chandelier with his head.

"You see, Joe. That's why I just adore you. You have a wicked sense of humor."

"It drove my wife... ex-wife crazy."

Sandra took a long drag and exhaled slowly through her nose and mouth. Harding thought she looked like a dragon. Either that or a sorceress from one of those cheesy sci-fi flicks he used to watch late at night as a kid, hoping to see a flash of titty.

"And here I thought it was the job that drove poor... Margaret, wasn't it?"

Harding nodded, feeling sick at hearing that name on this devil's lips.

"The job that drove poor Margaret away."

"I have that effect on people," Harding said, moving his eyes from the beast to further inspect the room. For the briefest of moments, just before his eyes left Sandra, Harding could've sworn the table, which seemed to stretch half a mile from end to end, had gotten smaller, bringing him closer to the beast. And he could've sworn he felt something slither about his feet under the table, although he dared not look for fear of what he might see there—West, rolling about, or something far worse. Something foul.

"Don't be so hard on yourself, Joe. You're not all that bad."

"Gee, thanks." Harding laughed as the table shrank more. Her putrid scent teased his nostrils as the heavy smoke from her endless supply of cigarettes hung about his head. The plumes came out of her mouth like smoke from a factory stack.

"I mean it, Joe. In this world, or that, I'd say you were quite the catch, as they say."

"I'm more of a catch and release kind of guy. I gotta ask."

"Yes," the thing said, batting its long, dark eyelashes.

"That coat."

Sandra ran a hand over the fluffy, furry collar.

"What's it made of? Mink?"

The thing that was Sandra Miller cackled. Smoke puffed out of her nostrils.

"Mink, Detective? Mink is for paupers. This is vicuna. Would you like to... touch it?"

Harding wondered if she meant the coat or her. He noticed for the first time that the beast appeared to be wearing nothing, or next to nothing, under the fur coat. Then something caught his eye in a darkened corner of the room. Movement. There was definitely something there. Not there, in the corner, but—

"Something catch your eye, Detective?"

Harding didn't have to look at the beast to know it was smiling. He felt her grin like a dagger to the heart.

No, Harding was sure the thing moving about in the dark wasn't there, but somewhere else. Behind the wall. Maybe even in it. And whatever it was, it was reaching out to touch someone—him.

"You didn't think I was the only one, did you?"

Harding watched as the wall seemed to breathe, expanding as monstrous hands reached out one after another, farther and farther, before collapsing into itself as the hands retreated. The logs stretched like cellophane but did not, thankfully, tear and let those things through.

Harding turned back to Sandra, who now sat less than six feet away from him. The thing under the table, slimy and wet, circled around his ankles, ensnaring him like an animal trap.

"We are legion, Detective," Sandra said, exhaling the longest trail of smoke Harding had ever seen in his life through her nose. For a moment, the smoke ate her face up, concealing it. When she spoke again, it was from behind the wall of smoke, and she over-enunciated each syllable. "Legion."

Harding was no altar boy, but it came to him in a flash like a memory buried in a shallow grave clawing its way through the earth: *And Jesus asked the demon its name, and it replied, "Legion, for we are many."*

Harding felt his blood turn to ice. Something he suspected since their first encounter at the Miller house on St. Augustine Place in the Bronx proved to be true. His infallible gut came through once again. This bitch wasn't just older than she looked. She was ancient. Maybe even older than time itself.

"Mother has many children, Detective. I don't know how she did it, personally. One rugrat seems enough to me. And why have more when your first is pure perfection."

The beast smiled devilishly and the tip of the fresh cigarette in its holder sparked and burned a bright reddish-orange glow as Sandra inhaled.

"You were the first?"

"I am the oldest of her children, yes, Detective."

"How... old are you?"

The beast winked.

"Don't you know, Detective? Never ask a woman her age."

"Ballpark then. Give me something. I think I've earned it."

The beast laughed, taking another drag.

"Earned it? Why, you haven't even begun to pay, Detective."

The table shrank, bringing them nearly face to face. The tentacle-like arm, which Harding was convinced belonged to the monster calling itself "Sandra Miller," tightened, almost to the point of turning his feet blue. He felt his right foot go numb, and then the left. If he had to make a run for it, Harding knew he wouldn't get far. Although he noticed there was nowhere to run. The room itself had grown smaller, along with the table. As his face inched closer to the beast's face, the hands reaching through the wall were nearly at his back. He felt a light breeze on the back of his neck every time a hand swiped at him. Harding didn't know which would get to him first—Sandra Miller or the things behind the wall.

"This isn't going to end the way you think it will, Detective."

"Oh no?" Harding asked, a part of him, a big part, didn't want to know. He'd had a bad feeling in his gut since he pulled out of the diner—however long ago that was. It wasn't so much a nervous feeling, worry about the road ahead, but the feeling that he'd just made the biggest mistake of his life. And as the miles stretched on and on, he'd seen nothing to prove him wrong. *Always trust your gut.*

"I'm going to tell you a story, Detective. A ghost story."

"Should we sit around the fire and toast marshmallows?"

The beast slammed its claws on the table, and the room trembled. So did Harding. For the first time he noticed the meat suit the beast wore was slipping. As though she no longer fit into it. Either that, or whatever it was that hid underneath that leathery skin was finally done hiding and coming out to play.

"Don't interrupt, Detective."

Harding dared not blink. He didn't want to take his eyes off the beast for even a second. The tentacles tugged at his ankles, climbing higher up his leg. Reaching up, setting course for his hardening cock.

Of all the times... this bitch is gonna be the death of me.

"Come, let's sit by the fire. The dining room is not the proper place for telling ghost stories."

Before Harding could respond or react, he was sitting in a comfy, oversized armchair beside the fireplace. The thing that was Sandra Miller sat beside him. The room had not only gotten even smaller, but now the fire was the only light in the place. It didn't slow the shadows in their dark dance, nor did it do anything to the hands reaching out through the wall. They felt closer than ever, but still just far enough away to not grab a hold of him. Harding wondered if that was Sandra's doing or just dumb luck. He looked down and saw that he held a large skewer in his hand, and at the end of it sat a marshmallow burning in the flames.

"What are you?" Harding asked in a gentle, almost reverent tone. He feared offending the beast and losing his head like Andy West, former coroner now a phantasmagoria of Harding's mind. *R.I.P. West.*

"Why, I'm just a girl, Detective. Standing in front of a boy."

The beast howled and shrieked with unearthly laughter. It was more its trademark cackle than a laugh. He imagined all the things she said with that horrid sound. *I'm going to gobble you up and suck out your eyes, Detective.*

A shiver ran up his spine, and his cock twitched in his pants. *Mama always said, "Boys will be boys." And here I am, getting aroused by some otherworldly thing that wants to devour me.*

"I'm flattered, Detective," the thing said as a pair of tentacles poked under the chair from out of the darkness, ensnaring his legs in their powerful grip. The tip of one tentacle slid over his hard dick. "Mine's bigger, Detective. But I guess I still got it, as they say. And don't worry. I don't want to eat you. At least, not in the way you're thinking."

The thing laughed again. Harding got a whiff of its malodorous, rank breath. He wanted to throw up whatever he had left inside of him but knew nothing would come. And there would only be a new, more putrid horror peeking around the corner to tease his gurgling gut.

Harding knew he should have felt relieved to hear the words, that the thing didn't want to have him for Sunday dinner, but he knew that was how they got you in the end. Placated and soothed you with kind, reassuring words, only to move in for the attack, delivering a fatal blow before you could breathe. No matter what the beast said, or did, he wasn't letting his guard down. Not for a second. No matter how hard his cock got. With his luck, the bitch would probably bite it right off and snowball it back to him. Not exactly the blaze of glory Harding pictured himself going out in.

Harding's head whipped behind him. Somewhere in the dark, faint but coming through crystal clear, was a voice. No, voices. It sounded like a wall of TVs all tuned to a different channel like at Krazy Kevin's, the electronics store on the corner of West 57th. Harding wondered for a split second if the place was still there. Not just Krazy Kevin's, but West 57th Street.

Each voice sounded entirely different. Harding noted some weren't speaking in English. Some were male and some were female. Some sounded more adult-like than others, and a few of the voices were clearly children. Young children. Alexandra Miller young. And Toby Miller young, back at the time the events at the house of horrors occurred.

One voice kept repeating, louder than the others. One line spoken by many different tones at once—

Honey, I'm home.

"Tell me, Detective. Do you want to play a game?"

Snow White

Harding awoke in his own bed, sweat seeping through every pore in his body. He practically stuck to the cover sheet on the 'otel's less than comfortable mattress. When he rose to his feet, he noticed he left a perfectly formed sweaty outline of his sleeping form on the sheet. He stumbled into the bathroom. Part of him wanted to make sure it had all been a dream, which he knew to be a lie. And another part of him needed some Mytai-Lenol for his aching head.

The first thing Harding noticed was the toilet seat was down. And he knew he had left it up just in case he had to take a midnight tinkle, as he so often did these days. Old age. A merciless son of a bitch. Do not recommend.

He took his time making his way to the commode. After taking a deep breath, he flipped the seat open, expecting to see... something. Instead, he was shocked to find nothing but the clusters of rust and shit stains lining the bowl. Harding exhaled, his body relaxing as though he'd just dodged a bullet. But when he turned to inspect the mirror, he gasped in horror at the sight that greeted him.

Every strand of hair on Harding's head had turned white as snow, including his brows. His face hadn't aged, but his hair looked as though it'd put on ten thousand miles while he slept.

The funny thing was that Harding didn't remember lying down or falling asleep. The last thing he remembered was looking in the mirror. Then, West making a guest appearance in the shitter. And... *her*. That foul thing that purported to be Sandra Miller. Surely none of *that* had been a dream.

As Harding studied his reflection, he caught sight of something else in the mirror. Something that had not been there before. Something new. Scrawled in blood, the words—*She's awake, Detective.* He turned to examine the bloody message, touching it with his index finger. It was still fresh, still warm.

As Harding stared at the blood on his fingertip, he heard its voice in his head, plain as though the thing were standing beside him in the shit box. He would've sworn there was a tentacle wrapping itself lovingly around his waist, as though pulling him in for a kiss.

See you soon, Detective.

He rounded on his feet, falling against the wall. But the monster wasn't there. The only thing Harding saw was a thick cloud of cigarette smoke. She'd been there, and now she was gone.

As Harding crumbled to the floor, drowning in a sea of sweat, he wondered what else he couldn't remember about his time through the looking glass with the thing that was Sandra Miller. There had to be more, right? He'd been on the other side for more than just a few minutes, at least it seemed that way to him. So why was it all a blank. He hoped it would come back to him. The vision of that bitch riding him in an oversized armchair flooded his mind. Harding crawled to the shitter and threw up until he was as empty as RFK Jr.'s head.

And then, as he watched his pool of vomit circle the bowl and then disappear down the shitter's open, sucking mouth,

Harding wondered who the "she" in "She's awake" was. It meant something. It was a clue. He knew it was. His gut was on fire. But a clue to what, he had no idea. But everything in him screamed that it was important. Inside, something was trying to ignite the engine in his brain, but it stalled. A memory. Maybe? The missing time with the Miller thing. It would come. Surely it would.

It has to.

As Harding rose to his feet, he was overcome with a coughing fit that seemed to come from his toes. It was deep, and painful, sucking every breath out of him. By the time the episode had passed, some five minutes later, Harding noticed a small spattering of blood on his sleeve.

"Well... fuck."

Pussy Galore

"Like, I'm just sooooo boreddddddddd, Imo. Bored. To. Death. For real." Ally laughed, falling onto her back. The squeaky bed sank as though the young girl weighed as much as a bag of gold bricks. "Imo! Imo! Look! It's like I'm on a TRAMP-oline! You're not watching."

Ally sat up and then threw herself back onto the mattress again, hard enough for the momentum to toss her about a foot into the air.

"You're dumb," Imogen Rockwell laughed.

"Wheeeeeee! Come on, it's fun! Come on! There's plenty of room."

"No, I'm good, thanks."

Ally patted the mattress invitingly.

"Are you surrreee?"

"Yeah, I'm sure. How are you even doing that?"

Ally bounced so high that Imogen thought the bed frame was going to break on the way down. She giggled and laughed like a kid in a toy store with daddy's credit card, back when there were still toy stores. Back in the before days—the time before tech ruled everything, including childhood. Before kids became consumers, stealing their innocence.

"Doing... what, Imo?"

Ally played dumb, or maybe she wasn't playing. Wherever she'd gone after her head went BOOM, she clearly hadn't been rewarded with a functioning brain for her efforts.

"Rephrase. How are you here? In the 'otel? I mean, you're… you know?"

A somber expression washed over Ally's pale face. Her dead eyes watered in the corners, and she sank her head into her hands with a loud *PLOP*. The next thing Imogen knew, Ally was sobbing into her hands.

"Dead! I'm dead! I KNOW! Do you have to remind me?"

Imogen rushed to the bed and sat beside the sobbing Ally Cat.

"Aw, shit, Al. I'm—"

Ally rounded on her so quickly Imogen never saw her move. One minute Ally was sobbing into her palms and then BOOM! Their faces were practically touching. Imogen felt the heat of Ally's breath on her face. The smell was not pleasant, nor was the scent Ally wore like a knock-off Alvin Pine perfume.

"It's so tragic. Tell me, Imo. Does this lipstick make me look DEAD?" Ally shrieked with maniacal laughter. "Gotcha, Imo! I knew I'd get your sorry ass on the bed one way or another."

"You so dumb," Imogen said, shaking her head. "How are you… you know?"

Ally leaned into Imogen, so close that the tips of their noses touched. A chill ran down Imogen's spine. Ally's nose felt colder than the grave.

"Here?"

"Yes. How are you here? I saw you die."

Ally threw herself onto the bed so that she lay on her back, staring up at the water-stained ceiling.

"I don't know… exactly."

Imogen lay on her back beside Ally.

"But... you know?"

Ally nodded.

"I'm, like, out, but not out."

Imogen turned her head to look at her recently deceased friend.

"What do you mean... 'out'?"

"Of the game, silly. And you say I'm dumb."

"I don't understand."

"Obvs. So, like, when you're taken out of the game, you're not out for, like, good. Just out of that cycle. I'm waiting for the game to recycle."

"Wait," Imogen said, turning her head back to center so she too was staring at the ceiling.

"Uh huh."

"Everyone that dies in the game, isn't really dead?"

"By George, I think she's got it," Ally laughed.

"They're just out of the game."

"Like in checkers. Once the board is cleared, you reset the chips and start fresh. I'm a chip waiting to be put back on the board. I may not get put back in the same place, so, you know, we may not be friends anymore. Aw, sad face."

"But... I saw you die. I saw it."

"No, you saw me get taken out of the game. Death, like, real death, is rare. Only a Miller can be taken out for, like, good. The rest of us? We just keep recycling, over and over and over again. We're just pawns, Imo. Pawns, here to play their game."

"But... I'm a Miller."

"Uh huh. And that's why I'm here, Imo." Ally reached across and grabbed Imogen's hand. "I've come to warn you."

"Warn me?"

"You will be visited by three spirits," Ally began, but couldn't hold back her laughter. "You should've seen your face, Imo. Shit. You looked as though you'd seen a... ooohhhh... ghost!"

"Fun-ny."

"You knew this was comin', Imo. Somewhere, like, down deep, you felt it. You've known something was wrong, haven't you?"

Imogen did not want to admit that she had known something was wrong since they pulled out of The Greasy Spoon. The numbers just didn't add up, even if you used that new math. The more miles they drove, the more questions she had, and the more evasive Toby became. He and Alex had taken to communicating almost entirely via telepathy, and their minds were locked up tighter than a Catholic nun's girdle. She couldn't open that door no matter how hard she pushed. Imogen had doubts, about everything. Something was rotten in the state of... wherever the fuck they were. Alex and Toby were keeping secrets, and Imogen Rockwell did not like secrets.

Imogen did not speak but nodded. She wondered if being "out" meant that Ally could read her mind. She cleared out her cache of thoughts just in case.

"I want to ask you something, Imo."

Imogen steadied herself and locked down her mind. "Okay."

"Where are you going?"

"To—"

"Valhalla," Ally interrupted. "But... where?"

Imogen hated to say the words, but she didn't see the point in lying. Somehow, she knew Ally would sense the lie.

"I don't know."

"What direction are you traveling?"

"I don't know."

"I'll give you a hint: New York, New York, it's a hell of a town!"

"Okay, so we're going to New York? Why does that matter?"

"It doesn't. Like, not really. What matters is what's behind you."

"There's nothing behind us."

Ally squeezed Imogen's hand so tight Imogen knew it'd leave a bruise.

"Exactly. Almost like it's being—"

"Erased," Imogen said, finishing the thought.

"So, Imo, I ask you this: who's doing the erasing?"

"My Aunt. Sandra. Right?"

"Now, think real hard, Imo. Use that Ivy-League brain of yours. If you're walking into the belly of the beast, if Sandra is the destination..."

The lightbulb glowed above Imogen's head.

"Who's doing the erasing?"

"Precisely. Damn, I told you I'd make a great cop. Maybe in the next cycle. I hope I'm a narco. I wanna, like, go undercover in Miami or some shit like that. Wear skimpy clothes and infiltrate the cartel. Bring it down from the inside. That'd be so fucking hot."

Imogen had already tuned it out. She knew the answer to Ally's question, but she dared not say it aloud for fear that her voice would carry on the wind. Suddenly she felt like there were eyes and ears all around her. She wasn't safe. Even her own mind wasn't safe anymore. She'd have to be careful from now on about what she thought on the surface.

She wondered if her sister knew or had similar suspicions. Imogen knew she'd have to find a way, a safe way, to get to Olivia without alerting the others. Figure out how to get them to their special place and wall the shit out of it so no one could get to them. Their powers were stronger now than when they began the quest, but there was still so much they didn't know. Toby was holding out on them. Showing them just enough. Showing them what he wanted them to know.

No, Imogen realized. *Showing what he* needs *us to know.*

"I have to go, Imo."

"Already?"

Ally nodded.

"My time's up. But don't worry, bitch, you'll see me again before the end."

"Ally?"

"Yes, Imo?"

Imogen took a deep breath and let it out slowly.

"I'm scared."

"You should be, Imo. She's awake, and she is pissed."

"Who?"

Imogen felt Ally's grip on her hand easing, growing lighter and lighter until it was barely there. Lighter than a piece of shit paper.

"Beware the hitcher, Imo. Beware the hitcher."

And with those words, Ally was gone. Again. Imogen knew she'd be seeing Ally again, eventually. But she feared what Ally meant by "before the end." The end of this so-called cycle? The end of the game? Or...

No, Imogen wouldn't let herself go there. She anchored her thoughts, but the pull was stronger, and her thoughts sank to the bottom anyway.

The end of everything.

She's awake. Who the fuck is she?

Wakey, Wakey

Imogen Rockwell did not sleep well that night. She tossed and turned until the sun started to peek through the broken blinds, which served more as decoration than a tool for blocking out the light. Her mind raced in circles, replaying her conversation with Ally. One line stood out above all the others—she's awake, and she's pissed.

Who the fuck was "she"? It couldn't be Sandra. She'd been awake this entire time. Imogen knew it had to be referring to someone else, a player not yet on the board, so to speak. Someone who'd been watching from the sidelines. But what was their role? Referee? Benchwarmer? Or just another random player waiting to be tagged in when the time was right.

Then Imogen had a chilling thought, one that had not occurred to her before: *what if "she" is a Miller?*

That would change everything.

This was the trap that ensnared Imogen's thoughts. Were there other Millers out there she didn't know about? If so, how many were there? Who were they? And where were they?

She was about to reset her thoughts back to the beginning when something caught her eye. A shadow slithering across the ceiling, inching slowly from the darkness at the far side of the room, heading right for her.

As it moved closer and closer to the bed, Imogen saw clearly what it was. A clawed hand, with the longest, sharpest-looking nails she'd ever seen outside of the Timm Brothers' book of fairy tales she'd read as a kid in grade school.

Imogen knew at once that the shadow hand belonged to her. The unnamed thing that according to Ally was now awake, and not very happy to be so.

Imogen didn't know when their paths would cross, but she knew it would be soon.

Very soon.

And she knew something else, too.

Not all of them would live to tell the tale.

Maybe none of them...

What Happens in the 'otel—

Olivia Christine Lovejoy wanted to take a bath. She was up on her tetanus shot, so she was willing to risk soaking her naked body in the ratty-looking, rust-lined tub. It, like the 'otel, had seen better days. The tub reminded Olivia of those "If Monday looked like…" memes. In this case, Monday was a toxic tub.

Still, her body felt worn down. Tired. She needed something more than stretching to release the tension in her muscles. They'd moved beyond sore a week ago. And with the pain approaching critical, Olivia knew a simple shower wouldn't do. It was either sit in a tub of soapy scalding hot water or risk not being able to move in another day or two.

She poured what remained of the anti-bacterial hand soap into the tub and turned on the hot water. She didn't touch the cold water, for now. The water pressure was pitiful. Olivia had expected as much. She thought she'd be able to fill the tub faster by blowing water through a straw. But it would be worth the wait. As soon as she slid into the cesspool, she knew the aching would simmer down. She might emerge from the tub red as a lobster, but she didn't care. There was no one left to impress.

Steam blanketed the too small bathroom. The tub seemed an afterthought and practically abutting the shitter. She reasoned a larger person might actually have to hang their legs over the tub to empty their bowels into the equally revolting shitter. Olivia did not want to guess what the stains that decorated the bowl were. Some things were better left unknown.

She dipped her index finger into the water and pulled it back at once, as though she were a child touching a hot stove for the first time. The 'otel didn't have a lot in the way of amenities, but it had hot water aplenty. A pleasant surprise.

Olivia pulled her sweat-stained shirt over her head and tossed it into the corner. She was about to reach back and unclasp her bra when she noticed there wasn't a single towel in the bathroom—not even a hand towel.

What the hell am I supposed to dry myself with? Shit paper?

Olivia groaned, fetching her crumpled shirt and sliding it over her head. She swore under her breath as one of her arms got stuck in the sleeve. The threads stretched to the point of ripping, but they did not. Olivia was thankful for the little things. Spare clothes were few and far between, and as the group ripened in the car, they'd had to stop every few days to wash both themselves and their musky clothes. Not far into the quest, they'd started driving with all the windows open. That might have been the smartest thing they'd done since they left The Greasy Spoon.

She turned off the water, hoping it would cool down just a little bit while she fetched clean-ish towels from the front desk. She grabbed the room key and walked down the maze of dimly lit corridors, heading for the unimpressive lobby. Olivia wondered if there was anyone still on duty that late into the night. The 'otel wasn't exactly a happening place. They hadn't seen a single other guest since they'd checked in. Like the roads, the place seemed deserted. Forgotten. Or maybe just useless. Who would choose to stay at a dingy motel in the middle of nowhere during the apocalypse? Travelers such as themselves, of course. But tonight, everyone else was tucked into beds elsewhere. The 'otel was a ghost town, and they were the ghosts.

After a while, Olivia felt like a mouse in a maze. She'd lost track of every turn she'd made. The room numbers seemed to go on and on, climbing higher and higher. Occasionally she'd take a turn, and she'd be back in front of a room she'd passed moments before. She swore she'd passed room 217 a dozen times, which she thought odd since she was staying on the first floor. So far, the highest room number she'd noticed was 247.

She didn't feel like she was traveling in circles. It felt like she was always moving forward, even when the numbers weren't ascending or descending in any logical pattern. They seemed to appear at random. She'd been a decent platform gamer for a while as a kid, noticing patterns to clear levels faster than her friends. But the 'otel didn't have any patterns. Everything appeared to be random.

Occasionally, she heard whispers coming from behind the doors. Indiscernible whispers. Other times, she made out the words with ease—*Oliviaaaaa* and *she's awake*. She wondered who, or what, was whispering in the empty rooms since they were the only guests in the place. But clearly, there were plenty of other ghosts staying in the 'otel.

Olivia was ready to give up and just sit in place, waiting for the gang to come and rescue her, when she noticed a bright light at the end of the hallway. Bright by 'otel standards. Her brisk walk quickly turned into a gallop as she realized the lobby was only twenty feet away.

Fifteen... ten... five...

"Can I help you, hon?" the haggard woman behind the desk asked, eyeing her from head to toe. "Why, your face is so white. You look as if you've seen a ghost."

"No, I just," Olivia said, cutting herself off. She couldn't imagine how she'd explain the 'otel's labyrinthine hallways to the strange lady behind the desk.

"You just... what, hon? Don't be shy. We're all... friends here."

"Excuse me?"

The woman pointed over Olivia's shoulder. Olivia turned slowly to see a faded poster for the 'otel, showing it in what must have been its glory days—although they weren't too glorious. She noticed the saying beneath the 'otel's generic block lettering and logo.

"That's our motto. 'We're all friends here'."

Olivia turned back to the woman, who now wore a grin on her face that made Olivia's blood run colder than a microwave dinner; the kind her father used to love sneaking behind her mom's back. *Garbage,* was what her mom had called them. To which he'd reply, *one man's trash, is another man's treasure, dear.*

"So, you wanna tell me what it is that got your face looking like... that?"

"I... I got lost."

The woman laughed dryly.

"Lost? In here? There are only eighty rooms in the place. Twenty per floor. How'd you manage to get yourself lost, hon?"

Olivia didn't like to feel stupid. "I don't know. Got turned around, I guess."

The woman folded her hands on the desktop and smirked. Olivia wanted to take her head and stick it in the tub of scalding hot water back in her room until that look was burned right off her face.

"Well," the woman said, sighing, as though Olivia had interrupted her, "you're here now. So... what can I do for you?"

"There are no towels in my room, and I'd like to take a bath. Can I get some fresh... ish towels, please?"

"Fresh... ish? What is it you're implying, hon? That the place isn't clean? Does it not meet your usual standards, then? Sorry we're not a five-star chateau in the Swiss Alps. We're a small mom-and-pop hotel that's been in business for fifty-three years and counting. We've got over seven thousand reviews on *Kelp!* Do you think we'd have managed all that if our guests left here with a case of flesh-eating bacteria? After all, we're all—"

Olivia joined in the refrain.

"—friends here."

"Precisely," the woman said. "Now, what is it you were wanting, again?"

Olivia took a deep breath, and said, "Towels, please. Towels."

"Ah, right. So you can take a bath."

The woman did not budge. Olivia wasn't even sure if the woman was still breathing. She merely stood there, frozen like one of those pies in the freezer section of the grocery store. It reminded her of old Flo at The Greasy Spoon. But this didn't feel like Toby messing with her mind, and this woman was not Flo.

Olivia's eyes traced a path down the woman's faded blue sport coat until they landed on her nametag: *Joanne.* The "e" was barely visible.

"Something wrong, hon?"

Olivia shook her head.

"I was... expecting someone else."

Joanne huffed, acknowledging her slight.

"Let me go and see about those towels. If you'll excuse me a moment."

Olivia nodded, not sure why she was suddenly unable to use her words.

Joanne mumbled something that sounded like "puta" as she disappeared into the back room, but Olivia couldn't be sure. All she could do was eye the back room, as though expecting Sasquatch to come sauntering out with the towels.

Something didn't feel right about any of this. She hadn't wanted to stop at the 'otel. It creeped her out—even from the outside. The place had what her Aunt Ciss called "bad energy." From the inside, it was easy to see why. Olivia wouldn't have been surprised to learn that the place had been the sight of multiple murders. It had that kind of feel to it. Restless. It felt restless, like the place itself was unsettled. The 'otel suddenly reminded her of a book she'd seen on the shelf at the library— *Them Rattling Bones*. That's what it was. Olivia felt like the 'otel's bones were rattling.

Joanne muttered indiscernibly in the back. It sounded like she was tearing the place apart looking for towels. Olivia shuddered to think what condition the towels would be in. She was about to call out to her, asking if she needed any help, when she heard footsteps behind her. Light at first but growing heavier as they moved closer.

The smell hit her first. Dreadful and stomach-churning like a roast that'd been sitting on the counter for a month, spoiled and covered in wiggling maggots. Olivia found herself frozen in place, much like Joanne had been moments before. She wanted to move, not to turn around and see the unholy thing that was now standing behind her, but to run. Run for her life. Run through the maze of corridors until she found her way out.

But Olivia Christine Lovejoy could not move. She couldn't even blink. If she had anything in her bladder, Olivia was sure she would have pissed herself. Despite all that she'd seen, all that she'd been through already, Olivia had never been so scared in her life.

The thing stood silent behind her, its breath even fouler than its aroma. Olivia fought the urge to throw up all over the counter. Cover the entire desk with her sick. The thing re-mained still, breathing loudly, deliberately. In slowly through the nose, out even slower through its terrible mouth. Olivia didn't have to see it to know it had a terrible mouth. What else could it have? Her mind couldn't even conjure a picture of what this creature might look like, given its noxious smell. It was something beyond her. Something that could not be imagined but had to be seen. And there was no way Olivia was turning around to see it. No way.

It stirred. Olivia felt something move behind her, and it took a moment for her to realize what it was doing. The thing was reaching out to touch her, to rest a terrible hand on her shoulder. Tears swelled in Olivia's eyes, but she would not cry. All her blossoming powers, and all she could do was stand there useless as underwear at a nudist colony. She wanted to wish the thing away. Send it away with her mind. But her mind was out to lunch, and it left her behind to starve.

Olivia shuddered, moving at last, as the thing's heavy hand

touched her shoulder. It felt cold, without any life in it. And it seemed to Olivia that all of her heat, her life's energy, was being sucked out through the thing's touch. She wondered if it meant to kill her right there, in the lobby of this shithole hotel/motel waiting for towels. A sad ending to a life that held so much promise.

The thing wheezed. The sounds of bones snapping and cracking teased Olivia's ears. The thing gave a long, low moan, and Olivia knew its mouth lay open wide, its putrid tongue sticking out dumbly. Olivia couldn't stop the tears from rolling down her cheeks as she knew what came next. The thing was going to speak.

In a voice that sounded like it spoke through a mouthful of dirt, speaking to her from six feet under, in a grave, and yet from beyond the grave, the thing whispered, "She's coming home."

A Tale of Two Joannes

Joanne Garriga stood in the supply closet. The towels lay neatly stacked on the shelf at eye level, but she made no motion to grab at them. On the outside, she looked like an employee zoning out at work, but on the inside, Joanne Garriga was having conversations, many conversations, all at once. She had checked out, as they say in the hotel/motel biz.

You can do it now. It'll be so easy, one voice said, beguilingly. Had she been offered an apple by the thing behind the voice, Joanne knew she too would've taken a bite in the Garden.

Why not just get it over with? You're just going to kill her later anyway, another, less beguiling voice, urged.

She's defenseless. Alone. Do it. Kill her now, a third voice chimed in.

Yessss. Kill her... now, a fourth voice said.

"I can," Joanne said, her voice sounding disconnected and distant. "Just take the knife out of the drawer and stick it in her heart."

Yessss. Do it, the voices said in unison, sounding like a sinister symphony.

"Or... I can cut her throat open and watch her bleed out like a pig."

A big, fat smelly pig.

"But then I'd have to clean it up. Why make more work for myself? Although..."

Yesss... now you see. Now you see!

"It's not like I'm going to be sticking around this shithole. I could kill her and go. None of those other fools will even know. I'll be long gone by the time they find her body. Gone, like the wind. Poof!"

It'll be just like a magic trick.

"Yes," Joanne agreed. "Abracadabra!"

Joanne grabbed a small stack of towels and returned to the counter. The stupid girl was still waiting for her, eyeing the empty counter like a puppy waiting to be fed. A helpless, innocent little puppy. So easy to kill.

"Here you go," Joanne said, placing the towels on the counter.

"Thanks. I really appreciate it," Olivia said, giving the short stack a quick once-over. "I'm sorry but you wouldn't happen to have a washcloth back there, would you?"

Joanne pursed her lips and bit her tongue. Her right hand reached for the drawer that hid the knife. Long, sharp, shiny steel like that could slice right through that bitch without breaking a sweat.

"Of course," Joanne said, through gritted teeth. Her eyes bore into Olivia, imagining how good it would feel to stab her in the stomach and gut the puta bitch like a fish. Watch her guts spill out all over the floor as her mouth gasped for air and she flopped around. Joanne decided she would stand over the bitch and watch as the puta's lights slowly went out. And she'd do it all with a smile. A great, big, fat, shit-eating smile. *Service... with a smile.* "Just give me a moment."

"Of course," Olivia said.

Joanne's hand moved away from the drawer handle, and she headed back to the supply closet, mumbling all kinds of curses in Spanish, and some in English, under her breath. She didn't think the bitch heard her, but a part of her wished she had, just to see the look on her stupid face.

Again, she eyed the stacks of cleanish linens until her eyes found the lone washcloth on the shelf. She grabbed it, pressed it to her mouth, and howled into it. Screaming for all she was worth. She screamed until her face shone red and was covered in a thin layer of perspiration. When she finally felt like she had gotten it all out, she took the washcloth away from her face, folded it neatly, professionally, and returned to the counter wearing a smile.

"Are you alright?" Olivia asked, giving Joanne a wide-eyed look.

"I'm fine, dear. Never better," Joanne said flatly, placing the washcloth on the counter. "Your washcloth."

"Thank you."

Olivia moved the washcloth to the top of the linen pile and gathered it up in her hands. Her eyes found Joanne's once again, and she stared into a set of cold, vacant, black eyes. Joanne felt the heat of the bitch's gaze and somehow smiled even brighter, bigger. Her lips parted, and Joanne bared her teeth. She felt like her face was going to stretch to inhuman proportions as though it were made of molding putty or bubble gum. But her face held, and so did the awful, unnerving smile.

"Are you sure you're okay? You look..." Olivia began, clearly struggling to find the right word to describe the horrible expression on the woman's damp, crimson face.

"How do I look, dear?" Joanne asked, the smile never leaving her face.

"I don't know... sick? Maybe. You don't seem... yourself."

Just kill her already. Enough of the small talk. Do it! Grab the knife and do it.

Joanne's hand reached for the drawer. She wrapped her fingers around the handle and pulled slowly. The drawer squeaked if you pulled on it too fast, so Joanne took her time, savoring the thought of the moment that was now only seconds away. The bitch would bleed. She would watch her bleed.

"It's just a little... hot in here," Joanne said, unconvincingly. She didn't even believe the words she was saying. The place was colder than her kindergarten teacher, whom the parents had nicknamed "the Ice Queen." She wore three layers, a heavy wool sweater at the very top.

The drawer sat fully open. Joanne's eyes went to the knife, only for a moment, but they went there. She couldn't stop them. She felt like a kid on Christmas morning, stealing a look at the presents under the tree before running up to Mom and Dad's bedroom to wake them up, shouting about how Santa Claus had come in the night.

I got a present for you, puta. Oh, and you're going to like it, too. And I'm going to like giving it to you. Yes, puta. Here it comes.

Joanne's eyes went back to Olivia as her hand wrapped around the knife handle. She squeezed it until her knuckles turned white. Her hand withdrew from the drawer, inching back like a turtle popping its head out of its shell. She pulled the knife out carefully, making sure it didn't collide with anything on the way out. Any noise would ruin the surprise, and Joanne didn't want to do that. She wanted to see the look of complete and utter shock on the bitch's face when the knife came into view, just before it cut her down.

The blade cleared the drawer with ease. Joanne had been careful in its extraction, so very careful, an expert predator on the hunt. The moment was now. The kill shot. Or, in this case, stab, slice, or cut. It was time to kill the puta.

Her fingers wrapped even tighter around the handle of the blade. She took a deep breath and readied herself for the strike. Impossibly, her smile widened, exposing more of her teeth, which somehow now appeared razor sharp. The ends came to sharp, tearing points.

As the muscles in her arms tensed to raise the knife, a solitary voice rose above the legion of other voices in her head. It drowned them out, and they fell silent, falling into line like submissive dogs on the playground.

Don't you fucking dare. That's not the plan. Put it away or I'll come out to play, the voice commanded, and Joanne obeyed. Slowly she slid the knife back into the drawer and tapped the drawer shut without making a sound. Joanne Garriga was no fool. She knew what the foul thing meant by "come out to play," and she did not want to play with that awful thing hiding inside of her. There were other, more terrible things to fear out there. But this thing... this unhinged monster living inside of her like a parasite scared her the most. She knew that once it got out, there'd be no putting it back in its cage. And worse, there'd be no controlling it. This was the kind of thing that took orders from no one. An unpredictable predator. The deadliest kind.

Smart girl. Good girl. Do you want a cookie? the voice teased, and then it was gone.

For now.

Joanne watched as Olivia disappeared down the corridor. The bitch looked back over her shoulder one time, probably making sure the sweaty woman with the fiery face didn't just burst into flames. She smiled at Joanne, and then disappeared. Joanne wondered if the stupid bitch would get lost again on her way back to her room. She hoped that she did.

"Puta," Joanne said, grinning fiendishly. It was the thing inside her smiling through her. She knew that now. But she couldn't deny that she liked it. She liked it a lot.

All Joanne could do now was wait for further instructions. Where to go next. What to do next. There were so many pieces in play, some she knew about, and others she remained in the dark about. The bitches in her head still didn't trust her. Joanne knew this. They were always talking behind her back. Talking about her, as though she couldn't hear every word, every whisper. It was rude, and Joanne Garriga didn't like rude. That was what made her job in the Vegas casino so challenging—all the rude customers making jokes about ICE and green cards, drunkenly screaming in her face to go back to her country, trying to hike up her skirt. She would've killed them all if she hadn't needed the job. It was part of her blending in. Appear normal. Do what normal people do. Wake up, go to work, eat, maybe sleep, and repeat the next day. An endless cycle that ultimately proved fruitless since few could afford to live anymore.

The world was for the rich, and Joanne Garriga was not rich. But in the end, she would be a part of something bigger, something money couldn't buy. How many of those rich fucks living off the backs of people like her could say they saved the world? None. That's how many. They were destroying the world, the rich. Consuming. Taking, without giving. Using. Exploiting. And too many were asleep at the wheel, blind to the truth that their very lives were nothing more than a means for the rich to make money. The Dream was long dead and buried, and there were few left to mourn her. The days of getting rich on hard work, seeking a better life, and buying that house with a garden and a big, old tree in the front yard were over. The best anyone could do now was make it through the day and try to live to see another. An endless cycle. Round and round, running in place, never getting anywhere, while the carrot of a better life dangled in front of your face.

Yes, Joanne Garriga was sick of it all. Next time things would be better. Things would be different. Señor Toby had promised a better world. A just world. A world where the Dream was still alive and not just well but thriving. The world could be a place where change was possible. Things like poverty, famine, homelessness... could all disappear with one little word.

Croatoan.

Joanne still didn't understand how it worked, not really. She understood life was nothing more and she was a mere player. Everyone, everywhere was. Their lives weren't real. Their jobs. Their families... not real.

Family...

They were all just actors playing a role, pawns on a giant chess board, being moved about by unseen hands for their amusement. A few woke up and saw the world for what it was. But, by and large, people were asleep at the wheel, letting their cars crash on the highways of life over and over again until someone won the game. Then, it would start all over again. Maybe she'd still be Joanne Garriga, wife of Jose Garriga, if it pleased the Game Master, but maybe she'd be Maritza Martinez, a high-powered lawyer in Los Angeles. Or maybe she'd play the role of Luce Hernandez, an Olympic gymnast. The possibilities, the combinations were endless.

Joanne had no idea how many lives she'd lived. Maybe a hundred, maybe a thousand... maybe more. Every now and then snippets of past lives, past games, came through in dreams. Flashes of lives she'd lived in another time, in another place.

Family...

With each new remembrance, Joanne felt a strange longing for a life she didn't even remember living, for people she couldn't remember loving. But still, she missed it, and she missed them. Somehow, Joanne had started to see through the veil, and that she kept to herself. She didn't want Señor Toby or the Miller bitches to know she was starting to see. Really see. Soon she'd be able to see it all—whatever it was that lay beyond the veil.

Family...

She'd remember.

Family...

She'd see her part in the play that was rapidly approaching its climax. It wouldn't be long now. Señor Toby, Alex, Imogen, and Olivia would send those Miller bitches back to Hel, win the game, and reset the board. Joanne would start a whole new life, and she'd been promised a better life. That was her carrot. A better life in a better world. A world where no one called her a wetback or asked about her immigration status. A world where empathy and compassion were strengths, and violence, indifference, and want were weaknesses.

It could be, and Joanne could be a part of it. They were so close now. Only a few hundred more miles until they all convened in Valhalla. The Miller bitches and the Dreamers. And her. When it was all over, she'd be a hero. Her life, this seemingly insignificant one, would matter. She would finally matter. Joanne Garriga would, at last, be seen.

As she sat at the broken desk in the manager's office of the 'otel, ignoring the smell of the rotting corpse of the previous manager in the corner, Joanne pictured her next life. Maybe she'd be a college professor, show everyone she wasn't a stupid Mexican. Or maybe she'd be a serial killer that preyed exclusively on racist white men, the kind of men that insulted her with one hand and tried to fuck her with the other. So many delicious possibilities.

But the one constant was that Joanne Garriga wanted to be a mother—

family...

—in her next life.

Joanne's back went rigid. She sat upright as though Sister Mary Helena was walking the classroom aisles, yardstick in hand, cracking anyone in the back who slouched. Joanne had taken her share of whacks, but now her posture was so perfect she knew even the long dead nun would be proud.

A thought bubbled to the surface of her brain. Not so much a thought, but a memory. No, that wasn't right either. It was a... feeling. There was something there. Something blurry. Something she couldn't see clearly, but it was there. Something she was missing. Something... lost. But what was it?

Joanne squinted and concentrated on the thought that threatened to return to the pit of her mind. It had almost faded when she grabbed a hold of it with both hands and reeled it in. She studied it, turning it over and over in her mind. Once it fully revealed itself, Joanne Garriga gasped. How could she have forgotten?

How long have you known the Millers?

Oh, my gosh, for years. Our kids grew up together.

Our kids grew up together...

Our kids...

Something switched in Joanne Garriga just then. A small flame ignited, but it was spreading quickly. Soon it would be an all-consuming inferno of anger. The more she sat with the newly discovered truth, the less inclined she felt to save the world. No, now Joanne Garriga wanted nothing more than to see the whole thing burn. Let the Miller bitches have it. Let them swallow the whole thing and be done with it all.

"I had kids," Joanne whispered, but no one heard the words. She wiped at her eyes, but the tears continued to fall, wetting her face. "We had kids."

For the first time since the race to the finish line began, Joanne thought of Jose. A game... it had all been a game, and nothing more. The Irish *puta* in Boston. Their life on St. Augustine Place. Their kids...

She knew it was a game, but somehow now that she'd been robbed of her kids, Joanne felt like a sore loser. She had something and it had been taken away from her. No, it had been stolen. But how? How had she forgotten her kids? The game hadn't reset, so how?

Joanne clenched her hands into fists, then released them. She did this on repeat until her nails had dug holes in her palms and they bled. Blood dripped onto the dirty floor, slowly painting it red. No one cheated Joanne Garriga. She didn't like cheaters, even more than she hated rude people. Jose had cheated and look what she allowed to happen to him.

A game. It's all a game.

Joanne finally understood what it meant to be a pawn, and she didn't like it one bit. Someone was going to pay for this.

Someone was going to answer for taking her kids away from her. Everything was different now. Joanne Garriga was on her own. Joanne Garriga was a free agent. All bets were off. She'd fucking kill them all if it came to it.

Yes, she would kill them all. She'd win the game herself, and then everything would be different.

Vaya con dios, assholes. Vaya... con... dios.

Stays in the 'otel

The towels weren't as white as Harding's hair, and they weren't as "May Fresh" as Olivia was accustomed to, but they'd do. They would have to, since she wasn't about to dry herself with half a roll of shit paper. She set the towels on the toilet seat, and slipped into the tub, her body sliding beneath the warm water.

Her mind kept replaying what the voice had whispered in her ear—*she's coming home.* When she'd turned around, there was, of course, no one there. The reek of its breath and the foul smell of death lingered in the place where it stood. Olivia assumed it was another one of Aunt Sandra's tricks, or one of her minions sent to mess with her. She wondered if anyone else had received such a visitation, but she was hesitant to ask the others in their fellowship.

The mood had shifted, gotten colder. The long hours spent in the car now felt tedious. The jovial road trip atmosphere gone. Whether the reality of their situation, their mission, had finally sunk in, or something else was rotten in the state of... insert city, state here. Olivia had no clue where they were, or where they were going—other than "to Valhalla!"

The last time she'd gone to their secret mind place, Imogen had said the same thing. She had no idea where their final destination lay, but she was distant. Not the warm, funny sister Olivia had grown used to. It put her on the defensive, made her lock down her own super brain—something she hated doing. She didn't like keeping secrets from Imogen. Since they'd found each other, Imogen and she had shared everything. Their stories, their dreams, their fantasies. No subject was off-limits. They'd even discussed Toby and Alex, wondering what they were up to when they whispered in the car, or had entire conversations, lengthy ones, without ever uttering a word out loud. No, Olivia didn't care for secrets. And she wondered how many they were all keeping, herself included.

She wouldn't tell anyone about her phantom encounter. Olivia didn't want to add to their worries. Saving the world was a heavy enough burden without the added bonus of ghosts and goblins and stinky shades.

Still, the nosey part of her wanted to know if any of the others were seeing... *experiencing* unusual things. Very unusual things. The kind of things that might drive someone to the brink of madness, but Olivia had a strange feeling. Something told her these visions or experiences weren't... bad. They weren't pleasant, but they weren't what most people would call "evil." They were messages from another side. But from whom? That was the million-dollar question. Just so long as they weren't from that Josh Groban guy. Anyone but him.

Against her better judgment, Olivia started to doze. Her eyelids grew heavier and heavier, until they felt like a pair of cement shoes. As they fluttered to a close, she thought about Imogen and the growing divide between them. She told herself that the next time they went to their special place to talk, she'd lay her cards on the table and call. See if Imogen had anything to match what she was putting down. There had to be a way to go back to how they were before things started to get really weird, before the world outside grew darker and darker, and there was less and less of it left.

Her eyes finally cemented shut, and she gripped the side of the tub with one sleepy hand. It wasn't much of a grip, but Olivia reasoned it was enough to keep her from drowning. She listened to the steady *drip, drop, drip, drop* of the water from the tap as it splashed into the tub full of steadily cooling water. The rhythm soothed and lulled her to sleep like a children's lullaby, the kind her mother... not her *real* mother... used to sing to her when she was a little kid. Back when she was still afraid of the dark and all the things that went bump and boo in the night. She didn't know then that there were plenty of things slithering behind the darkness to be afraid of. The kind of things that couldn't be staved off by a simple children's melody. Olivia reasoned there were some things out there it was right to be afraid of, and those things had no fear of anyone. Miller or not.

In her head, there was music. Sweet, luscious music. The music of the gods. It entranced her. Ensnared her. She couldn't have stopped listening if she had the power to do so, and, truth be told, she wouldn't have even if she could turn it off.

The music surrounded her, filling every dirty square inch of the bathroom. It hung heavy like a San Francisco fog. Eating up the bathroom until there was nothing but Olivia, the tub full of now cold water, and the music.

She tried to open her eyes, but they wouldn't budge, as though the lids themselves said *no way, girl. You do not want to see what's out there. Mmm-mm. Trust us. You do not want to see.* This, of course, only made Olivia want to open her eyes even more. She was like Pandora, sitting at her desk, amused by an unassuming box. But surely there was nothing in that bathroom as toxic as the contents of Pandora's little box.

At least, that was what Olivia kept telling herself. As every trace of warmth was suddenly sucked out of the bathroom as though in one giant inhalation of air, Olivia wondered how many more times she'd have to tell herself *there's nothing to be afraid of... it's just my imagination...* until she believed it.

Olivia was no longer herself. She felt like that frightened toddler all over again, cowering under her blankie, terrified of the dark. She could now only imagine what horrors lurked outside of the darkness behind her eyes. It didn't sound like Sandra, but it could've been. She was a master of disguise, having fooled even Toby once or twice since the journey to Valhalla had begun. From the sound of the heavy breathing, Olivia felt convinced it wasn't Sandra in the bathroom, but some other horror. A new horror. Something she hadn't seen before. A part of her wanted to open her eyes and face the thing head on, even in her vulnerable, naked state. There was no reason her powers wouldn't work just because she was stark naked, sitting in a bath. But her eyes had a mind of their own, remaining sealed up tight, as though they were screaming *girl, trust me, you don't wanna see what the fuck is out there.*

The water chilled. The surface iced over slowly, crackling as the ice surrounded Olivia, entombing her. She went to scream, but her mouth was now sealed as well. The only sound she could make through her shivers was a grunt and a groan as she tried in vain to shimmy her body enough to crack the ice. But she quickly found that she couldn't so much as wiggle her little pinky toe. She was sure her lips had turned blue, as inside she felt her blood turning to ice. Her head stopped shivering as the end came. Suddenly she knew, without a doubt, that was how it happened. This was how she died.

The music around her grew louder and louder until the sound shook the tub. She felt the vibration through the ice, but it wasn't strong enough to so much as splinter that oversized ice cube. The thing outside the tub inched closer. Somehow, its sounds—the sticky, slimy, slithering noises it made as it moved across the bathroom floor, along with its labored breathing—rang in her ears louder than that infernal and unholy music.

The cacophony tickled her ears like a loose thread on a sweater, but she couldn't do a thing to scratch that itch. It was unbearable. Tortuous. She tried again to move one hand and then the other, but it was futile. Trapped like a rodent on a glue trap. There was no escape, only death. She knew death was coming when she felt the thing's putrid, hot breath on her face. As loathsome as it was, Olivia had to admit the small burst of heat felt good on her iced skin. But she knew it wasn't nearly hot enough to melt the giant cube that encased her or warm her enough to keep her from freezing to death.

Then something touched her face. She knew something was rubbing at her cheek, almost tenderly, like a lover, even though her face had gone numb moments before. Even though her eyes were sealed shut and she saw only black, a shadow passed over her face. It was so much darker than the black behind her eyes that she saw it move. A giant malformed claw with long fingernails, some of which were broken and cracked at the tips.

Olivia shivered. She didn't know she had it in her, didn't know she could physically still shiver. But she did, and she felt it ripple through her body like a jolt of electricity. Olivia had never felt anything like it. All those nights spent hiding under her pink blankie adorned with castles and princesses, she never felt her body respond to her fear so violently, so physically. Her instincts were screaming, shouting at the top of their voice, telling her to run. But they were clearly unaware of her current predicament—frozen like a pint of Jen and Perry's ice cream. All she could do was sit there and let the thing touch her exposed face. Olivia was sure she'd be throwing up if her stomach hadn't iced over.

"So pret-t-t-t-ty," the thing whispered in a clicking voice. It sounded like a noise one of those awful insects make, the ones that come out of slumber every seven years. The voice was more a chitter than a voice. "You're going to t-t-taste so g-g-good going down."

Olivia shook her head, the movement barely perceptible. Inside, her voice screamed *no*, but her mouth remained sealed. The thing's lustful, heavy breath again slapped her face. Somehow it smelt even more foul this time, as though it swallowed a mouthful of raw sewage between breaths.

"You're m-m-mine, you see," the thing said, licking its lips. Olivia didn't have to see it to know the thing licked its lips. She felt it. Heard the awful sound of its tongue sliding across what she pictured to be decayed, crusty lips. "S-s-she told me so. I can h-h-have you when you fall into Hel. N-n-now... you're m-m-marked. None other c-c-can t-t-touch you. You're... m-m-mine."

The thing laughed; the way a spider might laugh at the fly ensnared in its web. The fly could resist, could fight back all it wanted to. Thrash about. Flap its wings furiously. But the spider knew, and maybe even the fly did too, that the fly was a goner.

The thing moved in closer. Its clawed hand rubbed her cheek. Then it dragged a broken nail across her forehead, making a sound like an icepick chipping at a block of solid ice. The thing's horrid face was nearly on hers. They were nearly touching. Its breath felt hot. The thing chittered wordlessly and then licked at its lips before moving in to place a kiss on Olivia's frozen lips. The thing's claw wrapped around Olivia's neck, but it did not squeeze. It only lingered there, as though saying it could squeeze if it wanted to.

"M-m-mine," the thing said. "She is coming."

The thing from the lobby had said the same thing.

"She is coming home," the thing chittered.

Olivia went to scream, only this time, the sound did come out. It was loud enough to break the ice. The thing laughed as the block of ice cracked and freed her body from its tomb. The water in the tub heated to a boil. The music cut off. Olivia's eyes flew open. She was alone. There was nothing and no one in the bathroom, only the neat stack of cleanish towels piled on top of the closed toilet lid.

She looked down at her body submerged in the water. Her skin was bright red like a fresh strawberry, ripe for the eating.

You're going to t-t-taste so g-g-good going down.

Olivia jumped out of the tub and grabbed a towel from the stack, immediately drying herself off. She wrapped the towel around her trembling body as she stared into the tub, no longer full of scalding hot water but of blood. It rose slowly until it spilled over the brim and rolled across the floor to her feet.

The music returned. The melody in her ears only for a moment, but it had been there. Olivia heard it clearly. She felt like she was waking from a dream where she killed someone only to discover her hands covered in blood as she wiped the crust from her sleepy eyes. This hadn't been a dream. The thing had been there, and something had been in the lobby. She was sure of it. And Olivia also knew with absolute certainty that these visitations were not the work of Sandra Miller. They came on behalf of someone... something else entirely. A new player in the game, one who had not as of yet revealed themselves. But it was only a matter of time now. As the foul things had said—she was coming.

She was coming home.

Wonder Twin Powers

Toby Miller didn't look well. He sat on the bed's edge, pale and sweaty, looking as though he might fall over any second. Alex Miller watched over him like the doting sister she was, looking at him with concern. She placed a hand on his forehead, letting it rest against his skin for a full minute before she withdrew, wiping the sweat onto her pant leg.

"You're on fire, Toby," she said gravely. "It's happening more often."

"I know," Toby said in a barely audible voice, but Alex heard every word. "I... feel sick."

"I can't stop it anymore. The closer we get to... home... the more it's going to happen. I can't hold her back anymore."

"I know," Toby said, falling back onto the bed.

"You have to feed, Toby."

Toby sighed.

"I don't want to."

Alex sat on the bed beside her brother. She stroked his head, running her small fingers through his tousled, damp hair.

"You have to," Alex said. "You're dying."

"I know. I know..." Toby closed his eyes, peering deep into the darkness. "We're so close, Alex. So close. We can win this time. Finally. We can win."

"If you want to win, Toby, then you have to…"

"Feed," Toby said, groaning. "God, we're so close."

"We've never gotten this close before."

"There was that one time. We almost had it. But then she came in at the last second and…"

"Yeah," Alex said, finishing the thought. Neither wanted to relive that particular defeat, when the game was played in a world where JFK was not assassinated, there was no Vietnam War, and a man spray-painted orange didn't seize control of the country and turn neighbor against neighbor. "We're even closer this time. I can feel it. We're going to win. She'll never see us coming. Not this time. We just have to make it home. Play the game one more time."

"Home." Toby sighed. "I don't know if I can make it, Alex. I can feel my body shutting down. I'm so tired. I just want to sleep."

"If you go to sleep, Toby, she wins."

"I know. But I'm just so tired, Alex. I don't want to do this anymore."

"Then feed. Feed so we can go home and win this game once and for all."

Toby tried to sit up, but he fell back onto the rickety mattress. He needed Alex's help to lift his torso off the bed.

"Is it… her, Alex? Can you see?"

Alex shook her head.

"I can't see. It's blocked. It could be… him."

"Charon?"

Alex nodded.

"Yeah. You know… for what you did. For bringing me back."

"I don't think it's him, Alex. If he wanted me, he would've taken me by now. This is something else."

"He'll take you, you know. If we lose."

"I know."

"You shouldn't have brought me back, Toby. You could have won this without me."

Toby rested his head on his sister's small shoulder. It fit perfectly.

"I didn't want to."

"It's time to end this, Toby. Feed. Then, we set off at dawn. We'll be home by nightfall. And then..."

"Then we win this and watch it all go boom."

"Yes. But we have to do it soon. She's awake."

Toby sighed a long sigh.

"I know. How much time do we have?"

"I'm not sure. It might be tight, but if we get there first..."

Toby raised his head and looked deep into his sister's dark eyes.

"Okay. Let's do it," Toby said.

"You'll feed?"

"Yes."

Alex smiled.

"Good. Lie back," she said, easing Toby onto his back. "Which will it be this time?"

Toby closed his eyes, concentrating with all the energy he had left in his body, which wasn't much. He was running on fumes.

"Olivia. She's the easier one. She's so trusting. She just lets me in. The other... suspects something. She keeps her guard up and she's strong. Really strong. If she really knew how to harness her power, she might even be stronger than you."

"I know. So let's not let her harness that power."

"Okay," Toby said, drifting off to sleep. "Okay..."

"Feed now, little brother. Suck the energy you need."

But Toby Miller didn't hear anything Alex had said. He was somewhere else. He was walking the streets of Dreamland, looking for Olivia Christine Lovejoy. It was time for Toby to become the Dream Lover, maybe for the last time. Become the Dream Lover and suck as much of Olivia's energy as he could before she woke up. Suck the life right out her, as he had been doing since the beginning.

Alex Miller watched her brother sleep. She lay beside him and took his heavy hand in hers. It felt cold but was slowly warmed as he fed.

"That's it, baby brother. Feed."

Alex Miller closed her eyes, but she did not sleep. She could not sleep, not since she felt her presence. Somehow, unexpectedly, she had woken up. Alex didn't know how or why, but it couldn't be good. They could still do it, win the game, but it was more complicated now.

It was more complicated now that their mother was coming home.

You Can't Pick Your Friends—

Imogen Rockwell couldn't shake the feeling of dread. It attached itself to her like a leech. It consumed her every waking thought, and when she managed a wink of sleep, it invaded her dreams too. She didn't like dreaming anymore. Not since all of this began. Every dream stirred feelings of guilt, like if only she had known about her abilities sooner... she could have saved Oliver and Janet. And Ally as well, but at least she was still around. Sort of. Imogen wasn't sure if Ally was a ghost, a vision, or just some sort of resurrected phantom she'd conjured to keep herself company on the journey, which had as of late grown lonely and long.

Everyone seemed to be growing apart the closer they got to Valhalla, wherever the fuck that was. Last she overheard it was somewhere in the Bronx? Who knew. Who knew there was a Viking paradise in the middle of New York City. But, as Imogen knew from her world mythology class, Valhalla was reserved for those Vikings who died gloriously in battle. This nugget did little to reassure Imogen that they were not walking into certain death. Her only glimmer of hope was that there were four of them and only one of Sandra Miller. Imogen had to believe with four against one their odds were good. Maybe even better than good.

But then there was *her.* The mysterious one she'd been warned about. The one who was now awake. Another player? And if so, whose side was she on? Imogen wouldn't even venture a guess. Only time would tell, and the mysterious woke woman would reveal herself. And then, and only then, would all their fates be sealed.

This only added to her dread. Absolute, total dread. If she wasn't a born fighter, the feeling would've been paralyzing. She wouldn't have been able to get out of bed, or get into the car, for those long, seemingly endless stretches. There had to be something she could do, an action she could take to turn her glimmer of hope into a raging inferno.

She wanted to talk to Harding, tell him that she felt like this was a fool's errand. But even he seemed distracted of late. The other night she'd caught him mumbling "Margaret" to himself until his voice went hoarse. And not long after, when they returned to the road, Imogen could've sworn he'd said, "Go away! Not now" as they drove on through the night. His eyes had been fixed on the road, just ahead of their SUV. But Imogen saw that there was nothing there. Nothing except the growing darkness. A darkness that was devouring what was left of their world. According to Harding, they were getting closer to the end, closer to the Bronx, but Imogen saw nothing on the road. Not a signpost or a streetlamp, and she couldn't remember the last time she'd seen another vehicle. It was like they were the last five people left in the world. Well, five plus Sandra Miller and the uninvited, unannounced guest.

No, she couldn't talk to Harding, nor did Imogen feel like she could talk to Olivia about the dread she'd been feeling since her last talk with Ally. The miles behind them being erased. Toby not telling them everything. There was something more he and Alex were keeping from them. Something secret. Imogen was determined to find out.

That night, or what was left of it, Imogen Rockwell decided to take matters into her own hands and do something she'd never even considered before.

Imogen Rockwell was going to break into Toby Miller's mind and see for herself what was hiding there.

But You Can Pick Their Locks

Imogen had only snuck behind Toby's walls once, and it had been an accident. Harding had pulled the SUV to the side of the road when he lost visibility in a sudden, brutal downpour. They'd used the opportunity to get some sleep, and that's when it happened. Imogen found herself wandering the halls of Toby Miller's mind.

The experience hadn't been what she expected. It was different from the special place she went with Olivia. She should have expected Toby's mind would have its own design, but she didn't think it would be so... complicated.

Toby's mind was mapped like a small city. A small, confusing city with winding streets that lead nowhere or ended abruptly. The buildings were all shuttered. They looked as though a tornado had blown through. Somehow, they were still standing, but Imogen wondered if a good, strong wind might just take them down one by one.

The buildings had no numbers, and the streets had no names. The deeper she went, Imogen felt like it was a design unfinished. A model lacking details, as though the architect was still tweaking the design. But Imogen knew deep down that it was designed to be confusing. Toby wanted any interlopers to get lost, frustrated, and ultimately give up. He kept his secrets well hidden, and Imogen suspected well-guarded. But somewhere, in that maze of city streets, Toby Miller had his secrets stashed.

Imogen sat on the edge of the bed and lay back. She placed her arms at her sides and opened her legs slightly, just enough so they weren't touching. Then, she closed her eyes and willed her body to relax. In her mind, Imogen pictured a warm, sunny day on the boardwalk at Point Pleasant on the Jersey Shore. The smell of the hot dogs, pretzels, cotton candy, and sausage and pepper hero sandwiches teased her nostrils, making her mouth water. She breathed in a hearty lungful of the saltwater air, turning her face up to feel the sun warming her skin. Imogen missed it all—the food, the breeze off the ocean, but most off all, Imogen missed the sun. She couldn't remember the last time she saw it hanging in the sky. As her body slipped even deeper into relaxation, Imogen wondered if she would ever see it again.

The boardwalk was deserted. She walked its long wooden planks, focusing her energy on filling in the details. Slowly she added the sounds of the rides, chiming and chirping their electronic lures. Then, she added the distant sound of cars driving up and down the streets beyond the boardwalk, likely looking for a coveted parking space. Finding a spot on such a beautiful day felt like winning the lottery. Finally, Imogen added the sound of chatter and karaoke coming from inside the oceanside restaurants, and the musical fanfare from the games in the arcade—her favorite place. She used to spend hours playing *Rampage* with Oliver, her father. What she wouldn't give for two more hours with Oliver in the arcade.

The ghost town felt alive, even though there wasn't another soul in sight.

Imogen sauntered into the arcade, her face lit by the glow coming off the dozens of games flashing their welcome screens and high scores. But she was on a mission. She walked past them all, heading down a long row of neatly lined-up pinball machines, toward the games in the corner just outside the bathrooms. That was the spot where she stood side by side with Oliver playing *Rampage* while Janet, her mom, walked the boardwalk sampling every variety of snack food from end to end. Usually by the time Janet's stomach said it had had enough, Imogen and Oliver were done rampaging.

She stood in front of the game's cabinet, staring at the screen, which was decorated with smudges and tiny bits of food, hot dog mostly, from the looks of it. Imogen always waited for the high score screen to pop up. She loved seeing their score still sitting at the top of the list. The day they broke the record had been a good day. Janet couldn't understand why Oliver and Imogen made such a fuss, but she was as supportive as she could be.

The score screen lit up, and Imogen's heart swelled. She wiped at her eyes, then fished a shiny new arcade token out of her pocket and fed it to the hungry machine. The screen went black and instead of the game, a door of sorts opened. It was more like a portal, but Imogen could open and close it like a door. And right then, it was open wide, inviting her in.

She saw Toby in her mind. Conjuring his likeness out of the black. As his face became clearer, the wrinkles and bags under his eyes filling in, Imogen focused her thoughts on his mind. And then, after a second when everything around her went still and quiet, a bright light flashed. It was blindly bright, but Imogen kept her hands on the game's cabinet, not wanting to sever her connection. When the light faded, Imogen saw the familiar streets of Toby Miller's mind, only this time, it was alive with details.

Street signs had names. The buildings stood tall, intact. Cars sped up and down the narrow streets. And there were all kinds of people. Businesspeople racing down the street or hailing bright yellow taxi cabs. Bored commuters standing at the bus stop. Street vendors hawking falafels, hot dogs, bagels, and salty peanuts and pretzels.

The other thing Imogen noticed was the streets no longer appeared random, haphazard. It looked more like a familiar grid, like Manhattan—save for the Village, which was about as random as random could get.

As she wandered the streets, looking for a place to begin, Imogen noticed that the street signs had peculiar names. There were no "Elm Streets" or "Main Streets," and there was certainly no world famous "42nd Street." Instead, the names were more like labels on files. "Era 7312, variation A–C2." "Era 919, variation M–S4." It didn't make sense to her, but Imogen knew there had to be a system to it. Toby was meticulous, so Imogen knew somehow these files were in order. The only thing she didn't know was where they began. The eras weren't in any numeric order. They jumped wildly, from 87 to 4911. Each street, or file, was made up of tree lined streets with brownstones and town houses. The doors were numbered sequentially, starting with 1.

Imogen made her way down the first street, or what she presumed was the beginning since it was the first one with a sign—Era 22, variation A–9. She walked up the steps to several brownstones and tried the front doors, but they were locked. Imogen tried to peer into a window or two, but she could make out nothing inside. And from what she could tell, nothing stirred in any of the houses she observed. Despite all the activity, the place was starting to feel like an abandoned theme park in the middle of the desert. With clowns. It creeped her out just a little.

She tried several other streets at random, walking up to front doors and peering into windows. But every door she tried was locked, and every window had its blinds drawn neat and tight. Imogen wondered if it was all a ruse, that maybe this wasn't Toby's actual mind but a decoy of some kind. A trap for uninvited guests. There was no other explanation she could think of for the lack of... anything substantial. No memories, no thoughts. Just row after row of empty boxes, like someone cleaned out the files before an audit.

But Imogen wasn't ready to give up just yet. She decided to walk straight down the nameless main street all the way until she reached its inevitable end, however far in the distance it lay. She figured it had to end somewhere. And, eventually, it did. There Imogen found a wall of black in front of her and a lone brownstone on a street called "Era 9742, variation T-1."

"This has to be it," Imogen said softly, not wanting to stir the sleeping lion. She felt like she had lingered too long already and wondered why she'd been able to remain so long without triggering any alarms. Like Alex, Imogen assumed Toby's mind was bricked up even when he was asleep. She reasoned at that very moment he must have been occupied doing something else. But what? She had no way of knowing.

Imogen approached the unassuming brownstone cautiously, minding each step. The way things were going in the world, or what was left of it, she worried the building might come to life and swallow her up. The two things she'd learned on this quest were that anything was possible and always expect the unexpected.

She climbed the three porch steps, taking each with careful deliberation, waiting for something to happen. Some trap to spring. Some awful thing to be released from its cage.

But she didn't expect *nothing* to happen. She breathed a little easier but did not let down her guard. This was Toby she was dealing with. Her Dream Lover. The one who created worlds within a world with the sole purpose of finding her and Olivia. She could only imagine the breadth of his power, especially when he was plugged into Alex.

As Imogen approached the front door, she noticed for the first time that the lights were on inside. There was no noise. No hushed voices. No shuffling of feet. The house was asleep. At least that was how it felt to Imogen. Asleep and unguarded, she thought to herself.

She reached for the doorknob and gave a small, surprised gasp when it turned, then clicked, and the front door creaked open. A rush of cold air hit her face as she pushed the door fully open and stepped inside Toby's mind.

Oh, Mother!

There was nothing but the great abyss.

She was the thing that stared back if you were brave enough, or foolish enough, to stare into it. They say she was older than time itself, there at the beginning of all things. No one really knows how she came to be, only that she was the oldest creature in the universe. Yes, even older than Him.

Her power was boundless. Nothing was beyond her. Anything and everything she desired, she birthed into existence. Breathed life into darkness. She lit the dark with stars so that others might find their way. She made the sun so that she might bask in its heat. She made the Earth, and all the planets in the known universe and beyond, because it amused her to do so. Pretty baubles to keep her entertained. But they weren't enough. Quickly she lost interest. Quickly she needed something more... amusing.

And then, she birthed them. Her children. A spawn of demons from the very pit of Hel where she reigned, not by decree but by choice. It was her children that would now keep her entertained. She watched as they wreaked havoc and destruction, brought plague and pestilence, killed everything they touched. Yes, her children amused her.

But how quickly children grow bored. You can give them

a million shiny playthings, and still, they want more. There is never enough to placate them. And when they are bored, children will be children. Acting out and acting up. She despised her children when they misbehaved, when they were disobedient.

So, finally, she created man. Man and woman. The ultimate playthings for her children. Living dolls. What could be more fun than playing with something that plays back? She thought this would finally keep her children in line. Keep them entertained. Keep them obedient.

But she was wrong.

Still, they wanted more. They needed more. How quickly they found man a bore. It wasn't long before the living dolls were misused and then neglected, almost forgotten entirely. Until she had an idea. An idea that she hoped would finally keep her children amused. It was a game. A game they could play over and over and over again, resetting it at any moment they saw fit. Create a world, live in it for a thousand years, and then BOOM! Tear it all down and start anew. And their dolls would inhabit these worlds. Always. Their roles would change. Their identities would change. And the dolls would not remember who they were or what they were. They would have no idea that their lives were nothing more than amusement for a foul race of demons whose mother had grown absent as of late.

No, the dolls would not remember the events of one world to the next. Every once in a while, a fragment might float to the top of one's memory. This would be a dream. They would never know that they had once been Cleopatra, or JFK, or, worst of all, Josh Groban in another time, and in another place. They were merely players in a play, acting out their roles so that the game could be played.

And her children were happy. They liked the game. Living among the dolls. Pretending to be one of them. Killing them one by one. There were times the dolls killed them first. And that was okay because it only meant they were "out" until the game reset. A mere doll didn't possess the power to kill them. Any of them. Only she could do that. Mother. Only Mother would dole out such a punishment. And she had. Oh, had she. Their number had been too great to count in the beginning, but now... they were merely legion. Many, but able to be counted. And tracked.

Mother kept track of her children, much like Mary kept track of her lambs. But like Mary, sometimes Mother lost one or two for a time, and she didn't see what they were getting up to. And a time came when Mother decided it was time for a rest, a long sleep to recharge. She trusted her children would follow the rules, because every game has rules. They would follow the rules and not misbehave.

But Mother had been foolish. Now that she was awake, she knew that. Children were born to misbehave. Children were born to disappoint their mothers. Turn your back on them, and they will do the darnedest things the very first chance they get.

They had been bad. They had disobeyed her. Broken the rules. They had grown too accustomed to her absence. And it was time, past it really, to remind them who it was that was in charge. Who it was that had the power to end it all.

And that was exactly what she intended to do. End the game and end it all. Teach her children a lesson they would never forget. The punishment for their insolence would be severe. They knew the consequences for breaking the rules, and still... they did so anyway.

So now, a price needed to be paid. Some would be spared. Not all of them had been disobedient. Flaunted their disobedience in her face. No, some would live to see another day. Perhaps there would be a new game. Once she was restored, she too would need something to keep herself amused. Boredom is a bitch. She would ponder this. Consider carefully if her children deserved a new game.

It was a long journey ahead, and she had time to mull it over.

For now, she concerned herself only with making her way out of Hel and heading up to where her children were. Heading home. It was time. She'd been asleep too long. Her bones were tired. Her body ached. She longed for the taste of fresh blood. All those years asleep beneath the earth had left her hungry. So very hungry. And everything tasted better at home.

There was, after all, no place like home.

Yes, Lilith, the Queen of Hel, was going home.

Sleeping Beauties

"More c-c-offee, d-d-dear?" Flo asked, holding up a steaming hot pot of freshly brewed Joe.

"I'm good, thanks, Flo," Imogen said, taking a small sip of her coffee. It had cooled a little, but that was fine with her. Flo's coffee, while undeniably the best she'd ever tasted, sometimes burned her tongue, as though it had been brewed in hell's kitchen—the actual hell, and not the old home of the Irish mob in Manhattan.

"Waiting on your friend?"

Imogen nodded.

"How's about some pie? While you wait," Flo asked, her eyes opening wide behind her oversized spectacles. "I can warm it up for you. Put a little whipped cream on top, just how you like it."

Imogen's stomach grumbled and groaned. It'd been some time since she'd eaten anything that resembled actual cooked food. They'd mostly been eating protein bars, nuts, canned meats, and anything else they happened to come upon in their travels. The pickings were slimmer than your chance of getting a date with a rock star, but beggars can't be picky eaters. And even though this wasn't real, Imogen's tastebuds somehow managed to savor every imaginary morsel Flo served up in The

Greasy Spoon.

It was their special place. Hers and Olivia's. It was where they went when they needed to talk without the ears of the others listening in. Imogen couldn't recall how they decided their special place would be The Greasy Spoon, but she enjoyed it every time they visited. Sometimes, Imogen slipped in without telling Olivia. She just liked to sit in the corner booth and watch the show. The Village People showed up twice. Even Elvis made an appearance. The hot one. Hollywood Elvis. The Greasy Spoon fast became Imogen's haven, a place to get away from the outside world and find a moment's peace from the horrors that awaited them. It was the only place she could just... be.

"Hey! You still with me, d-d-dear? How's about that pie?"

Imogen hadn't even realized that she'd gone away for a moment until Flo called her back. She knew she was tired, dog tired, but she didn't realize how easily she could fall into a waking sleep. That could prove dangerous down the road. She'd have to be more careful.

"Sure, Flo. I'd love some pie," Imogen said with a smile.

Flo tapped the end of the table with her swollen hand and fingernails that once had been painted with glittery, silver nail polish but now were chipped and worn down.

"Coming right up, d-d-dear."

Flo disappeared into the kitchen as the bell above the door clanged. Olivia had joined the party. She sidled up to the booth and slid in opposite Imogen.

"Hey," she said weakly.

"Hey," Imogen replied, eyeing Olivia. "You okay?"

"Yeah. I'm just... tired. I guess I'm not really sleeping."

Imogen took a long sip of coffee.

"I know what you mean. The 'otel? Do not recommend. Zero stars."

Imogen looked down and there was a fresh cup of coffee on the table in front of Olivia.

"Here," she said, sliding the mug closer to Olivia. "Drink up. It'll wake you right up. It's—"

"Ow! Fuck," Olivia yelped, setting down the mug and fanning her burnt tongue with her hand.

"It's hot," Imogen finished. "It's extra hot today."

"Yeah, thanks for the warning!"

Imogen shrugged.

"I tried to tell you."

"Yeah, yeah," Olivia said, cradling the mug in her hands and lowering her head to blow into it to cool down the scalding java juice within. "Where is Flo anyway?"

"In the back—"

"Getting pie," they both said, then laughed.

Imogen realized how good it felt to laugh. If it weren't for the whole end of the world thing, they could be two sisters, sitting in a Jersey diner on a rainy night, eating pie and drinking coffee instead of studying for finals. But outside the diner it was the end of the world, and the closer they got to Valhalla, the less either of them felt like laughing.

"Two orders of apple pie. The best in the county," Flo said, sliding two plates of warm apple pie topped with a mountain of fluffy white whipped cream onto the table. "You know what they say?"

Imogen and Olivia looked at each other, then looked at Flo, saying, "Pie makes everything better."

"That's r-r-right, girls. Pie makes everything better. Go on now. Eat up. The floor show starts at 8. Sharp."

"Who's playing?" Olivia asked, digging into her pie with a fork. She shoveled it into her mouth, closing her eyes as the taste flooded her mouth. "God, that's good."

"I told you. Best in the county," Flo said, puffing out her ample chest like a proud peacock. "And we got the original Broadway cast of *Hair* performing selections from the show. Ain't that exciting?"

"*Hair*? Again?" Imogen asked, disappointed.

"Yeah," Olivia agreed. "Let me know when you get the OBC of *Evita*."

"That young Mandy Patinkin... mmmhm. He was fine," Imogen said, fanning her face dramatically.

Flo brushed the girls off and sauntered back to the counter, chest still puffy.

"She can be so... temperamental sometimes." Olivia laughed, stuffing another forkful of pie into her mouth. "Christ, I wish this was real."

Imogen took up her fork and dug into the pie. Her mouth opened wide and accepted the large bite of pie with ease. Her eyes fluttered and a yummy sound came from somewhere in the back of her throat.

"I know what you mean. I wonder, though. Is this my pie, or yours? I mean, like... which of us made it?" Imogen asked through a mouthful of pie.

"Huh. I don't know. Maybe we both did?"

"Yeah, or maybe... yours is yours and mine is mine. You know?"

"Could be," Olivia said, washing down the pie with a chug of coffee, which had since cooled down enough to drink safely. "So, what's up? Why did you want to meet here?"

"Can't I just want to spend some quality time with my

sister?" Imogen asked, feigning innocence. She batted her eyes for effect and pouted her lips.

"I'm happy to see you too," Olivia said, blowing Imogen a kiss. "But really. What's up? I'm tired. I want to go to bed, even though I'm kind of worried about sleeping on that thing."

"I think someone may have died on mine," Imogen said.

"Are you serious?"

"Yeah. I think if I stripped off the bedding, there'd be a bloody outline on the mattress, kind of like the shroud in Turin. You know? The towel that's supposed to have the imprint of the face of Christ?"

"It's a fake. I saw it on TV. Carbon dating."

Imogen rolled her eyes.

"I know it's a fake. I was just giving you an example."

"Okay, fine," Olivia huffed, downing the rest of the coffee. "Flo? Can I get a—"

"C-c-coming right up, d-d-dear!"

"Have you..." Imogen began but stopped to consider her next words.

Olivia leaned closer to the table.

"Have I... what?"

Imogen leaned toward Olivia. They were close now, barely a foot between their heads.

"Have you seen anything... odd here?"

"NO!" Olivia said at once, practically shouting at Imogen. "Nope. Nothing weird here. At. All."

Imogen leaned back as Flo appeared at the end of the table, clutching a fresh pot of Joe. She refilled Olivia's cup first and then topped off Imogen's mug. She smiled, and then she was gone. Back at the counter, wiping at it with a wet rag.

"Really? You've seen nothing out of the ordinary here?"

"Well, unless you count a cockroach the size of a watermelon, wearing a sombrero, strumming a guitar, and singing 'La Cucaracha'... then no. It's just a divey motel, Imo."

"Okay," Imogen said, licking at her lips. "Okay. Well, I've seen some... stuff."

"What kind of... stuff? Sex stuff?"

Imogen rolled her eyes so hard she thought they might never come back.

"You're stupid."

Olivia grinned behind her coffee cup.

"Love you too, bitch."

"I saw... Aunt Sandra."

Olivia nearly slammed the mug through the table. Flo glanced over, eyed the sisters, and then went back to wiping down the counter.

"What? Here? She was here?" Olivia asked in a panic.

"No, she was in Sausalito," Imogen said, exasperated. "Yes, here. In the 'otel."

"What did she want? Wait, why didn't she kill you?"

"She showed me something, but I don't know if it was real. I mean... I don't think it was real. I think she's just trying to mess with my head."

"What was it? What did she show you?"

Imogen stared at Olivia. She wanted to tell her what she'd seen, but she also wanted to wait. Sit back and observe. There was no reason to get Olivia on the defensive around Toby and Alex, especially if what she'd seen was real. Imogen didn't want Toby getting a look at her hand. She had to keep a poker face while she tried to figure things out.

"It's not important. It isn't! But... it got me thinking."

"About what?"

"Well," Imogen began, sitting back in the booth, getting comfortable. "About this game for one. We're all playing, right? Like... all of us? And we're not supposed to know about it."

"Right..."

"Well, who made the rules, Livs? Who started the game?"

"Toby?"

"I don't think so. Alex was around before Toby, so it'd have to be someone older than Alex."

Olivia's eyes lit up like the eyes of the mechanical bull at Bustin' Broncos whenever you fed it fifty cents.

"Aunt Sandra! She's old enough. I mean, she looks old enough."

"I'm thinking... even older."

The words hung between them, heavy and palpable. Imogen could tell something was working itself out inside Olivia's head. She didn't know what it was, but it was there. It was definitely there, bubbling just beneath the surface. Slowly coming to a boil.

"Oh my god!" Olivia suddenly shouted. "It's her, isn't it?"

Imogen raised an eyebrow.

"Her... who, Livs?"

Olivia sighed, realizing she'd been caught.

"Okay, fine. So I've seen some... stuff in the 'otel. More like heard some stuff. But this creepy voice said something to me in the lobby, and I can't get it out of my head."

"What did it say?"

"'She's coming home.' It's her, isn't it? It has to be."

"Mother," Imogen said softly.

"Mother?"

Imogen nodded.

"I think she's the one that started all of this."

"You mean Agnes? You think that sweet thing did all of this?"

Imogen shook her head.

"No, not Agnes," she started, then leaned in as close to Olivia as she could get without jumping over to Olivia's side of the table. "Our real mother."

Olivia leaned in to meet Imogen.

"And who is that... exactly?"

"I don't know, but I think we're going to find out soon. Really soon."

"In Valhalla?"

Imogen nodded. "In Valhalla."

Olivia huffed. "Where is this place anyway? I feel like the more we drive, the less we're getting anywhere. We're like a hamster running on a wheel. Running, running, running, but never moving an inch further than where we were when we started."

"I don't know. Harding said something about the Bronx."

"The Bronx? The Bronx? Like... New York City? You're joking."

"No. That's what he said."

"Unreal. Of course, it had to be in New York City. Couldn't be in like Hawaii or someplace warm and tropical. It just had to be in rat-infested New York Fucking City. Ugh."

"Livs?"

"Yes, Imo?"

"Do you think there are others... like us... out there?"

"Other Millers, you mean?"

Imogen nodded.

"Yeah. Other Millers. Ones we haven't met or even heard of

yet."

"I don't know. I suppose. But why wouldn't Toby say anything if there were?"

"I think," Imogen began, then took a breath. "I think Toby's keeping a lot to himself. Alex too. I think we should be careful around them."

"What are they hiding, Imo?"

"I don't know, exactly. I just think we should be careful is all. I think there's more to all of this, a lot more, then they're letting on. I think..."

"Yes, Imo?"

Imogen sighed.

"I think we're walking into a trap."

"A trap? Really?"

"Yes, Livs. I think when we get there, it's not going to be what we think it is."

"I don't know, Imo. It's Toby, right? The Dream Lover? Why would he lie to us? Why would he go through all of that trouble to find us if he didn't want to stop Sandra and save the world?"

"Livs, do you ever wonder why there's nothing behind us?"

"What do you mean?"

"The darkness. It follows us. Everywhere we go, everywhere we stop... it disappears into the black, like it was erased from existence. Almost like it was never even there."

"Yeah, but that's Sandra, right? She's devouring the world. She's in Valhalla. That's why we're going there."

Imogen's face told no story.

"Right? Imo?"

"If that's true, if Sandra is in front of us... why is the darkness behind us... with us... around us? It's like another passenger in that damned SUV."

"Oh, god, no. We can't fit anyone else in that car. It's tight enough as it is, and Alex farts in her sleep. It's awful."

Imogen cracked a smile, reluctantly.

"Yeah, they smell like corn dogs that've been dipped in sour milk."

Olivia scrunched her nose and winced.

"I'm serious, Livs. I think we should be careful around Toby. Well, Toby and Alex."

"The Bobbsey Twins," Olivia said.

"The Bobbsey Twins."

The sisters leaned back as far as the booth would allow. They took a hit of java and stared at each other silently for a long time as the clock ticked closer to 8.

"Do you want to stick around and see the show," Imogen asked.

"Nah, not really. Not unless you do?"

Imogen shook her head. "Nah, not really. You going to go to sleep, Livs?"

"I'm going to try. I feel like I could sleep for a month."

"Yeah," Imogen said, studying every inch of her sister's face. "What did you see, Livs?"

"Nothing. I... I don't want to talk about it."

"Okay," Imogen said, throwing her head back onto the booth, staring at the grease-stained ceiling.

"What did YOU see, Imo?"

Imogen thought about telling Olivia what she'd seen in Toby's mind, but instead, she said—

"Nothing."

They sat in silence as the cast of *Hair* wandered in through the door, and they sat long enough to hear the first chorus of "Aquarius." Later, alone in her room, Imogen realized what it was she would have to lose to win the game. The great sacrifice she would have to make to save their dying world.

And she wondered if, when the time came, she would be able to let her sister die.

Secrets and Lies

There was nothing of note on the first floor, only the usual suspects—a dining room with a long wooden table, set for twelve; an old-fashioned lime green kitchen; a living room, also decked out like it was the 1950s, complete with a massive, boxy TV set that had the smallest screen Imogen had ever seen. The picture was black and white and fuzzy. Every now and again it glitched, and the scene restarted from the beginning. It was a movie, an old one from the look of it. Although given the quality of the image on the screen, Imogen figured everything appeared old on that set.

"Don't you trust me?" the guy with the bushy mustache on the TV asked the dame in the fancy fur coat.

The woman laughed, then took a long drag of her cigarette. It was on one of those long black holders. She blew the smoke into the guy's face.

"Trust you? Why, Billy, I hardly know you!"

Imogen turned down the volume on the TV. She didn't want any distractions as she climbed the stairs to investigate the upstairs.

The stairs creaked. Every one of them. No matter where Imogen placed her feet, a creak followed. By the third step, she stopped wincing and carried on. Even though it seemed quiet upstairs, that didn't necessarily mean there wasn't something hiding in the shadows. There was always something hiding in the shadows. Always.

She reached the landing without incident. No alarms or booby traps had been triggered, so far, anyway. And what Imogen now faced was a long, narrow hallway with six doors on each side. She went systematically down the row, trying the one on the left, and then the one on the right, finding each door locked. When she placed her ear to the door, no sounds came from the other side. And looking through the keyholes, Imogen saw only darkness.

Except for the last room on the right. Behind that door, there was light. And something appeared to be stirring.

Imogen snuck up to the door as quietly as she was able, minimizing every creak and groan the floor gave, and then dropped to her knees to look through the keyhole. Quickly her hands went to her mouth to stifle a scream. There, inside the room, was Toby Miller's secret.

Olivia lay prone on a bed, arms and legs spread open wide. Her eyes were closed, but her mouth lay open as though it'd been frozen in a terrifying scream. Only the whites of her eyes showed as the lids fluttered at great speed. Occasionally her fingers twitched, and a hand jumped off the bed, but otherwise, Olivia lay as still as a corpse.

And there, beside her, sucking the life, the blood right out of her through an open slash in Olivia's neck was Toby Miller. But... it wasn't the Toby Miller Imogen had come to know. It wasn't the version of him she'd come to love. What lay before her eyes was a nightmarish vision of Toby, barely recognizable. His skin was dark green, adorned with boils that leaked a thick, glowing fluid onto the bed. With every suck Toby took from

Olivia, more fluid leaked out of his body. His eyes glowed yellow, then red, as they rolled around in their sockets. Row after row of sharp, pointy teeth poked out of his mouth as it stretched impossibly wide to bite down deeper into Olivia's soft, supple flesh. His teeth tore through her skin as though it were nothing more than tissue paper. Biting down until something snapped in Olivia's neck. The sound reminded Imogen of Thanksgiving and breaking the wishbone with Oliver.

And there, above the horrific scene, was a voice. Alex's voice, saying over and over again—*feed*.

Imogen thought she'd been quiet. She hadn't so much as taken a breath since watching the terrible tableau through the keyhole. But she must have made some sound because for an instant, no more, Toby's flaming eyes flew right to the keyhole. Imogen backed off slowly, retreating into the hallway until she could no longer see inside the bedroom.

She expected the door to fly open, and Toby to drag her inside the room and feast on her flesh as well, but he did not. In fact, nothing happened. Now, the only sound Imogen Rockwell could hear was the slow sucking sound of Toby Miller draining the life out of Olivia Lovejoy. It was the most horrible sound Imogen had ever heard.

And then, it was over. She was back at the arcade, standing in front of *Rampage*. Blood seeped through her fingers as her grip on the game's cabinet tightened until it could tighten no more. Her body trembled as a freezing sweat soaked through her clothes.

Imogen wanted to move. She wanted to run out onto the boardwalk, find a trash bin, and vomit right into it. Let everything come spilling out of her in pastel-colored chunks.

But she remained frozen in place by the nightmarish vision still burned into her mind.

"Oh my god," Imogen said softly, barely audible over the din of the games.

"Guess again," a voice suddenly came from behind her.

She knew that voice. She recognized the smell of cigarettes and mothballs. As the fur from Sandra's coat teased Imogen's neck, Imogen felt her skin erupt into an armor of gooseflesh. As the thing behind her reached around and placed its hands over hers, Imogen stopped breathing. She was caught.

Caught by Sandra Miller.

"Come now, dear," the thing that was Sandra Miller whispered into Imogen's ear. "You didn't think you could do that... break into that boy's mind... without a little help from your dear old Aunt Sandra, did you? You're not that strong."

Imogen knew the beast was right. It all made sense now. She never could have slipped so easily inside without a little outside help. And in this case, it came from the very thing they were trying to defeat.

"Did you get an eyeful?"

Imogen nodded her head almost imperceptibly. It was the only part of her that she could move. The rest of her felt solid, almost hardened, like she was one of those department store mannequins, frozen forever in a showy pose.

"Did you like what you saw?"

Imogen shook her head, again there was barely any movement, just enough to signal her response to the beast.

"Do you know why he does it?"

Finally, Imogen found some of her voice. "No."

"Because he has to. He's dying."

Imogen's forehead wrinkled as she tried to puzzle out the

equation.

"Dying?"

"He," Sandra began, inching closer to Imogen's ear. For a moment, Imogen thought the thing might just take a bite out of her ear like that famous boxer did in the ring. Instead, Sandra continued. "Doesn't belong here."

"Doesn't belong here?"

Imogen felt the wisps of Sandra's stringy hair graze her neck as the beast shook its head.

"No. He's not a real Miller."

"But... he... and Alex. They... they..."

The thing groaned, as though encouraging Imogen to think harder on the problem, to go deeper. Unravel the mystery of the Bobbsey Twins once and for all. Discover who they were, and even more importantly, what they were.

"They... what?" Sandra prompted.

Imogen fumbled for her words as her thoughts jumbled and her mind went blank. She'd lost the plot. All she could do was repeat herself, hoping to stumble into the third act of her personal melodrama.

"They... they... did all this. They have powers."

"We all do, dear. The gift comes with the territory."

"I don't understand," Imogen said, feeling a headache coming on. A massive one. When she returned to that shithole motel, the first thing she was going to do was get caffeinated. Well, maybe that would be the second thing she did.

"You're a smart girl, Imogen. Use that Ivy-League brain of yours. Reason it out. What's the one thing we all have in common?"

Imogen pondered the question for a moment before saying, "We're Millers. We're family."

Sandra made a buzzing sound, as though Imogen had just blown the million-dollar question on a game show.

"Wrong. Now try again. Think."

And think Imogen did. She pictured each of them in her mind, everyone but Harding, since he wasn't a Miller. Toby. Alex. Olivia. Sandra. Herself. Toby. Alex. Olivia. Sandra. Herself. Wait... there was Grandma Cassie, too. And her real mother, Agnes. Toby. Alex. Olivia. Sandra. Grandma Cassie. Agnes. Herself. Toby... Alex... Oliv—

Finally, Imogen landed on it.

"Smart girl. I knew you'd get it, eventually. Pinocchio is not a real boy. And this is... a girls-only kind of club. No boys allowed."

Imogen remembered the story of how Toby came to be. He was created... by Alex. Did that make him not real? Not really a Miller? Would the same hold true for her and Olivia, since the Bobbsey Twins conjured them out of the ether?

"No, you're different. You're special. You... belong here. I think Mother will agree. We'll find out soon enough. She's awake, and she's coming home. And then... well... let's just say... this will not end well for some of you. Tell me, Imogen. Are you willing to lose something you hold dear to save this world you seem to care about so much? What price are you willing to pay to win the game?"

Imogen had no answer. She'd already lost everything, or so she thought at first. Then she realized she had only one more thing left to lose.

"I'm not the big bad wolf, Imogen. I'm not the monster you think I am," Sandra purred.

"Aren't you, though?"

The thing laughed.

"My dear, we're all monsters underneath. That's who we are. Like mother, like daughter. You'll see... before the end."

The end...

Imogen recoiled as Sandra leaned in even closer. The thing's putrid stench turned Imogen's stomach upside down.

"Why do you want to do this? Why do you want to end the world?"

The thing laughed again.

"Oh, my dear. You have me all wrong. Did he tell you that? I don't want to end this shitty little world. No, I want to save it. Despite its obvious... flaws... I like it here."

"Wait... what?" Imogen asked, the words Sandra had spoken failing to compute. "That's... that's not possible."

"Isn't it? Think about it," Sandra began, backing away from Imogen. Her hands retreated and soon her body followed. "Just think about it. I'll see you in Valhalla. I can't wait for you to meet mother. She's going to love you."

"But... I've seen it. I've seen the veil. Beyond it. I know what's coming," Imogen protested.

Sandra laughed.

"Oh, my dear. You have no idea what's coming. You forgot to consider one very simple thing."

"Oh yeah? And what's that?"

"The meaning of the word 'veil'."

Imogen thought about it, and at first all she could conjure up was the image of a wedding veil. But then, her smarts kicked in and it came rushing to her—

veil: a thing that serves to conceal, cover, or disguise.

"It's all... a lie, isn't it, Sandra? Sandra?"

Imogen spun around, but Sandra was gone. A million questions raced through her mind, but she found no answers.

She walked the boardwalk from end to end one more time before leaving her special place and returning to the real world, or whatever the fuck it was.

As she lay there on what was the most uncomfortable bed she'd ever lain on, Imogen couldn't escape the nagging feeling that somehow the beast was right. They weren't on a mission to save the world, but to end it. And if they won the game, however Toby and Alex intended to do that, then everything, everywhere, would fall into the darkness of inexistence. The only real question she had now was if she could do anything to stop it.

Or was the game already lost?

Too Late for Goodbyes

Harding coughed into a washcloth, watching his blood slowly seep into the fabric. His chest felt heavy, clogged. There was a scratch in the back of his throat, and he knew his temperature was rising. His skin felt hot to the touch, slick with a thin coat of perspiration. As he stared at his reflection in the mirror, with great hesitation after recent events, he wondered how long he had before the virus did its thing. Would he get the gang to Valhalla before the end came? Or would he expire in some fleabag motel off a desolate road in the middle of nowhere?

"Fuck," Harding said to his reflection. "You're not looking good, old man."

He couldn't believe how, in just one night, he'd turned a ghostly shade of white beyond his hair. Harding remembered something his grandmother used to say, and it seemed fitting. "He looks like walking death." And, indeed, Harding looked like death on two wobbly legs. There'd be no hiding this from the others. He knew this. They'd take one look at his face and know something wasn't right with him. And then there'd be the coughing fits. There were only so many chesty coughs Harding could swallow, not to mention the blood. But then, Harding had another thought, and his heart sank to the bottom of the well.

"Shit... what if I pass this on? What if they get it? It will have been for nothing. All of this. The world will end because of me."

Harding wrestled with these thoughts as the sun fought its way through the 'otel's busted-out blinds. Morning had come. They'd be hitting the road soon. He had little time to decide. As that old classic rock song went—should he stay, or should he go?

He had no idea. He didn't want to be the reason the whole thing ended on a roadside with all of them gasping their last breaths in the SUV, but he didn't want to disappoint them either. Leave them stranded on the yellow brick road. They needed him. This was his job, his role in all of this. He had little else to offer the group. He had no powers beyond that of his power of observation. Harding was an ace detective. His instincts had kept them out of trouble and alive on more than one occasion on the journey to Oz. It killed him to think he wouldn't be there, standing beside his companions as the journey reached its end. But the alternative seemed far worse to him. The quest failing because of him.

To be or not to be, Harding mused.

Another coughing fit seized him, and then the answer seemed obvious to him. He stared at his blood-soaked fingers, wiping them on the comforter. There were so many thoughts running through his head, but there was one that rose above the others.

He slid over to the nightstand and picked up the phone, dialing the number from memory. He listened as it rang on the other end, a lump gathering in his throat. *Ring. Ring. Ring.*

"Come on... pick up. Pick up. Pick—"

"Hello," a throaty, croaky voice said on the other end, as

though they'd be woken up from a long winter's hibernation.

"Hey," Harding said, his voice crackling with restrained emotion. "Margaret... it's me."

Margaret cleared her throat of crud.

"Joe? Is that you? What time—"

"Yeah, it's me. I don't know. It's early."

A rustling came through the line as Joe pictured Margaret rolling over in bed—their bed—to look at the clock on the bedside table.

"Jesus Christ, Joe. It's six o'clock in the morning."

"I know. I'm sorry," Harding said, nearly letting the dam of emotion break, but he held it together.

"Are you okay? You sound... funny."

"Yeah, I'm fine, Meg."

Something clicked on the other end, and Harding knew she'd just clicked on the antique lamp that she'd found at a yard sale in Yonkers. It had been quite the find. She'd bought it for five dollars, but it turned out the thing was worth well over two-fifty. It was an ugly lamp, Harding thought. But she loved it, and that was more important to him.

"You don't sound 'fine' Joe. What's going on?"

A cough tickled at the back of his throat. He felt it rolling up from his chest like a tumbleweed on fire. The burning sensation hurt like a motherfucker, and Harding struggled to stifle the cough. Finally, the pain got to be too intense to bear, and Harding covered the receiver as he coughed into his hand, painting it red with his blood. He looked down at his hand, remembering how he used to love finger painting back in Miss Wolfe's preschool class. He wasn't very good at it, but it was his favorite activity—aside from snack and nap time.

"Was that a cough, Joe? Are you sick? Tell me you're not

sick!"

Harding debated what he'd say next.

"Joe? Joe? Are you still there?"

Harding cleared his throat with a small cough.

"Yeah, Meg. I'm still here."

"That's it, isn't it? You're sick. You got it."

Harding sighed into the phone.

"Yeah. I think maybe I do."

"Fuck, Joe. Fuck."

"I know, Meg. I know. But it'll be okay."

Margaret laughed dryly on the other end of the line.

"Okay? How can you say that, Joe? This is not going to be..."

Her voice trailed off as she fought off a wave of tears. Harding heard the sniffle loud and clear.

"You're going to be okay, Meg."

"I'm not worried about me, Joe. You're not going to be okay. You're..."

"Yeah," Harding began. "I know."

"Where are you?"

"I'm not sure. A few hours from New York City, I think. The roads are pretty bad. It's hard to tell north from south."

"It's crazy out there, Joe. Are you being careful?"

"I am."

Margaret sniffled again, more pronounced this time.

"Promise me."

"Meg—"

"Promise me, Joe. And don't give me any of your double-speak bullshit."

Harding sighed in defeat.

"I'm being careful, Meg. I promise."

"Good," she said with a sigh of relief. "Good."

"Yeah," Harding said, his words and his thoughts drying out.

"What are you going to do, Joe?"

"That's the million-dollar question, isn't it?" Harding stopped, mulling over the options in his head. "I don't know, Meg. I just don't fucking know."

"Why did you call me, Joe?"

The answer wasn't as easy as the question. Like their relationship, it was complicated.

"I just wanted to hear your voice."

"To say goodbye? Is that it, Joe?"

"No. Well, maybe just a little."

The sniffles on the other end quickly turned to full-on sobs. "Christ, Joe."

"I know. It's okay, Meg. I'm okay," Harding said, lying through his teeth. "Listen to me. Just listen to me for a second, okay?"

The crying slowed as Margaret sucked snot up her nose.

"Okay. I'm listening, Joe."

"Look. Things may get real bad out there. Soon."

"Worse than they are now?"

"Yeah, Meg. A lot worse."

The world may come to a fucking end. Poof! Gone, just like that. I'm trying to tell you that you're going to fucking die and there's no use hiding under a blanket or running to a fallout shelter. If the twins fail, nothing in heaven or on earth will save you.

"Be careful, Meg. Stay inside. Don't go outside. No matter what you hear. No matter what you see. Stay inside, you hear?"

"But how will I know—"

"You'll know, Meg. Trust me. You'll know."

"There's something you're not telling me, isn't there?"

"Yeah, Meg. I'm doing it for your own good. Because, even after everything, I still love you. And I forgive you for dragging me to see *Oliver*."

Margaret laughed through her tears on the other end of the line.

"I love you too, Joe. This isn't how I pictured the story ending."

Tell me about it.

"I know. Not everyone gets a happy ending."

Margaret sobbed into the phone.

"Oh, Joe."

Harding listened to his ex-wife cry into the phone for several minutes. No words were needed. Through the miles, through the copper wires, they connected without bitter feelings and angry words. Harding wondered why it'd been so easy to speak the truth when faced with his own mortality. Why, when he knew the end was just around the corner, was the one person he wanted to talk to the one who got away? Life and death can be pretty funny sometimes. Death makes honest men of us all.

"Bye, Meg," Harding said finally. He was crying now, too, and he made no effort to conceal it. There was no point now.

"Oh, goodbye, Joe."

Harding listened as his ex-wife broke down into a loud, heart-wrenching, mournful aria of tears. It was operatic in scale. He wondered, as he sat on the bed coughing, how things had gotten so bad. How had everything managed to just slip through his fingers? And why now, as he prepared to take his final bow, did he see things with such clarity?

"Isn't life a bitch?" Harding laughed between coughing fits. "I should've gotten the shot."

On the Road... Again

Imogen knocked on Olivia's door and waited until she heard the shuffling of Olivia's feet on the floor before exhaling. After their jaunt to The Greasy Spoon, Imogen found herself more worried about Olivia than ever before. Not to mention the horrific vision she'd witnessed in Toby's mind. She still couldn't be sure if it had been real or just another trick by Sandra. Misdirection. Something to throw her off, get her off balance. Splinter the group from within.

But it *felt* real to Imogen. And when Toby gazed at the keyhole, Imogen thought he had seen her. She was almost sure that he had. Or, at the very least, he'd seen *someone*. Maybe he'd thought it was Aunt Sandra paying his mind a visit. Surely Toby would never suspect Imogen had broken into his secret place.

"Good morning, starshine," Imogen sang.

"It's too early for *Hair*, Imo," Olivia said, pulling the door fully open.

Imogen stepped into the room. She noticed the bed was unmade, with the blanket gathered in a messy pile in the center, which was a good sign.

"Did you get any sleep, Livs?"

"A little, I guess. I kept waking up. I'll sleep in the car."

Imogen thought back to all the times Olivia slept in the car. She wondered if it was because Toby had drained her the night before. The other thought that came to her was that Olivia seemed to need more and more sleep to recharge. At first, they were quick cat naps. But now, she slept most of the day in the car. Imogen wondered how much juice Olivia had in her. And what would happen when the tank was empty?

"You're sleeping a lot, don't you think?"

Olivia shrugged it off.

"I'm just tired, I guess. All this traveling. It takes a lot out of you," Olivia said, gathering her stuff. "Aren't you tired of being in that damned car all day?"

"Yeah, I guess. But I don't know how you can fall asleep so easily. It's not very comfortable. Those seats are... ooofff. My back is so sore."

"I don't know. I just do. It's not like we've been staying at The Spritz or The Five Seasons, either. We left comfort back in the parking lot of The Greasy Spoon."

"Yeah, and good coffee, too."

Olivia closed her eyes and groaned.

"What I wouldn't give for a real cup of coffee right now. How hard is it to make a decent cup of Joe? You worked at the Coffee Cavern. What's the secret?"

"Honestly? It's the water. Most places double or triple their water. We filtered it four times. Really brings out the flavor of the beans. Shitty water makes shitty coffee. It won't matter how rich the beans are."

Olivia opened her eyes. Her body relaxed, crumbling in defeat.

"I guess we're just fucked, huh? What are the odds this place filters its water?"

Imogen put a finger to her mouth and struck a thinker's pose.

"Zero chance. Wouldn't be surprised if they just pump it in from the sewer line. I definitely would not drink it. If I wasn't getting a little ripe—"

"A little?"

Imogen huffed.

"A little! If I wasn't getting a little ripe, I wouldn't have taken a shower. But I figured I owed it to the rest of you to get a shower, however brief."

Olivia laughed. "Those were the smallest bars of soap I've ever seen."

"Right? Christ, I dropped it washing my legs, and I thought it was going to get swallowed up by the drain. Caught it just in time."

"Thank god for small favors," Olivia mused.

"Fun-ny. Are you ready to get the hell out of here?"

"Are you kidding? I was ready as soon as we got here."

Imogen laughed.

"Same. Come on. Let's go."

Olivia moved to the door, and Imogen thought she saw her sister stumble, as though she'd lost her balance and then regained it at the last second. But Olivia didn't react to it. She just kept on walking through the door, pulling it shut behind her.

As they walked down the corridor, Imogen noticed Olivia turn back and look at the door to her room, eyeing it suspiciously as though she expected someone—or something—else to come walking through it. And then Imogen saw her sister's face ease into a pleasant resting face when nothing happened. Imogen wondered what Olivia had seen in her room, and if it was somehow following them.

* * *

When nothing came barreling through the door, Olivia breathed a sigh of relief. She tried not to react but was sure her face had betrayed her.

Again.

She wasn't the best at hiding things or keeping secrets. Back in school, her friends used to tease her, saying—*she doth protest too much.* Yes, Olivia Christine Lovejoy wasn't a very good liar. But she had gotten better since they pulled out of The Greasy Spoon. She had to. Sometimes she didn't know if she was going crazy or if the shit she was seeing was real. So many things. Shadows watching her everywhere they went. Eyes staring out of the darkness. Hands reaching out of the black that followed their car everywhere they went. Somewhere between Nevada and here, Olivia saw the ground open up, a fountain of flames shoot up to the sky, and a sinister clawed hand reach out of the fire. It felt so real.

And then there were the dreams. Gone was her Dream Lover, replaced by night terrors that she was being feasted on by unseen mouths. She woke feeling like she'd been in an old-fashioned Hammer gothic horror film. But she found no bite marks anywhere on her body. She kept telling herself *it was only a dream.*

Still... she wondered if it was.

In the lobby, the desk was unmanned. A small sign stood propped up haphazardly: "Back in 20 minutes. Drop keys in box. Have a blessed day."

Olivia was relieved she didn't have to see that woman again, if she was even still on duty. Something about her creeped Olivia out. She was... off. Off in the same way Jeff Dahmer or John Wayne Gacy were, how you could just look at their picture and wonder how anyone had been surprised by their misdeeds. They practically had "serial killer" carved into their foreheads. Bad mojo. That's what it was. And that woman at the desk last night had it in spades. She wore it comfortably and proudly, like an ugly Christmas sweater. Olivia couldn't put her finger on it, and she was glad she didn't have to. When they pulled out of the 'otel, she would leave this place and that odd woman behind.

She only hoped that she'd never lay eyes on her again.

* * *

Toby knocked on Harding's door.

"Detective?"

Nothing stirred on the other side of the door.

Toby knocked again.

"Detective? It's time to go. Are you in there?"

When no reply came, Toby put his ear to the door and listened. At first, there was no sound. No obnoxiously loud air conditioning unit breathing its last breaths. No rhythmic *drip, drop* from a leaky faucet. No toilet groaning as its basin refilled and emptied on its own.

Nothing.

But then, there was... something. It took a moment for Toby

to realize it was a stifled cough. Stifled unsuccessfully.

"Detective," Toby said, stopping to pound on the door. "Let me in."

On the other side of the door, Harding coughed again, this time making no effort to hide it.

"I know you're in there. Let me in."

"I think it's better if you stay out, Toby. It's for your own good."

"You got it, don't you, Detective?"

Something squeaked and groaned behind the door, and then Toby heard footsteps. He pictured Harding getting off the bed and walking to the door. When the coughing sounded louder, Toby knew Harding was directly in front of him on the other side of the door.

"Yeah, Toby. I got it. I got it bad."

Toby sighed. "I'm sorry, Detective."

"No, I'm sorry, Toby," Harding said between coughs. "I wanted to go all the way with you. Til Valhalla."

"Til Valhalla," Toby repeated softly. "You'll get there, Detective. This isn't the end."

A series of heavy, chesty coughs knocked the wind out of Harding. The door shook as something heavy fell into it. Toby knew it was Harding teetering on his feet like a top.

"Yeah, Toby. Yeah," Harding said without any conviction. "Tell the others... tell the others... I'm sorry."

"I will, Detective," Toby said, putting his hand to the door. "Take care of yourself, Detective."

"Will do, Toby."

As Toby walked to the end of the hallway, he turned back to Harding's room and listened to the awful coughing fit that came on.

* * *

"Where's Harding?" Imogen asked.

"He's not coming," Toby said, opening the rear passenger doors for Imogen and Olivia. "Come on, get in. We have to go."

"Wait, I'm not leaving Harding... HERE." Imogen pushed past Toby.

"Yeah, there's no way I'm leaving the detective here. This place is..." Olivia added.

"It was his choice, Imogen," Alex said, stepping in front of Toby.

"I don't believe you."

"Don't you trust me, Imogen?" Toby asked, doe-eyed.

Imogen instantly debated how to answer. "I want to hear it from Harding."

"He's got it," Alex said flatly.

Toby stepped forward, putting his hand on Imogen's shoulder. "The virus. He's got it. Bad."

"No," Imogen said, pushing forward, toward the 'otel and Harding. "No. He was fine yesterday."

"Imo," Olivia cried.

Imogen broke free of the pack. She ran toward the 'otel with everything she had inside of her. She might have given Olivia a run for her money in Olivia's old track days. Imogen had reached the doors of the 'otel when Toby yelled, "IMOGEN!"

She froze in place. It wasn't a simple utterance of her name, but a command. And Imogen knew it. She looked through the glass, peering into the empty lobby of the 'otel, which somehow looked even sadder than it had only moments ago.

The "Back in 20..." sign had fallen to the ground and the lobby was dark. The place suddenly felt not just empty but abandoned.

Imogen pictured Harding alone in his room, coughing on the floor of the bathroom, lying on his side so he didn't choke on his own blood. So much of her wanted to bust through the doors and go to him, but she knew there was nothing she could do for him. There was nothing anyone could do for him now. From the first cough, he was as good as dead.

She slammed her fist on the door, rattling the thing to its hinges. Imogen turned back to the group, what remained of them now that they were a man down.

"This isn't right. This is so... fucked," she said, her voice dripping with emotion.

Toby moved closer to Imogen but still kept his distance.

"We can stay, hold his hand, and wipe the blood from his mouth until he's gone."

"Fuck you," Imogen said under her breath.

"But then it's over. All over. Sandra wins and everything, everywhere ends like that," Toby said, snapping his fingers. "Harding knew the risks. We all did. It's his choice to stay behind, Imogen. It's the right thing to do. We have to go."

Imogen looked to Olivia for backup and noticed for the first time that her sister was crying. Olivia wiped at her eyes, but the tears kept leaking out of the corners of her eyes.

"Livs?"

Olivia averted her eyes.

"We have to go, Imo. It sucks, but..."

Imogen looked at the group, not with trust and admiration, but with disappointment that bordered on disgust. Most of that was directed at Toby, with a fair amount spilling onto Alex.

The Bobbsey Twins.

She stormed away from the 'otel, pushing her way past Toby and Olivia.

"Fuck you all. I wouldn't leave any of you behind," Imogen said, each word forced out of her violently, as though they burned her tongue leaving her mouth. "I wouldn't."

Imogen jumped into the SUV without looking back. Toby turned to Olivia, whose face was soaked with salty, guilty tears.

"Come on, Olivia. Get in," Toby said, motioning to the backseat.

Olivia said nothing as she climbed into the SUV. Toby closed the door behind her, then looked at Alex. They stared at each other a long, quiet moment. Whatever it was that passed between them did so without words.

"I'll drive," Toby said.

"Obviously," Alex replied sarcastically.

"Right," Toby laughed, "I keep forgetting you're too young to drive."

"Come on. We're running out of time," Alex said. "She's getting closer."

The Bobbsey Twins climbed into the SUV. None of the group said anything as the engine turned over, screaming back to life, and Toby shifted the car into drive. Imogen kept her gaze out the window, avoiding making eye contact with any of her companions.

As the SUV drove out of the desolate parking lot, Imogen turned back to take one last look. There, in the encroaching darkness, standing in the empty lot, Imogen swore she spotted Harding, watching them leave.

In the moment before he was lost to the darkness, Imogen whispered, "Til Valhalla, Harding. Til Valhalla."

As the darkness chased the SUV, Imogen felt Olivia's eyes on her, but she did not turn her head to look at her sister. Imogen kept her eyes locked on the vanishing world beyond the window.

* * *

Before the darkness ate him alive, Detective Joseph P. Harding was greeted by a familiar voice, one he almost expected to hear.

"Well, hello, Detective," Sandra Miller said with some amusement. "Fancy meeting you here."

"It is you," Harding said, tossing a Tums into his mouth and looking at the darkness as it bore down on him. "All of this... it's you. It's always been you."

"Oh, Joe. I'm here for you. I've always been here for you. I've loved you in another life, and I've killed you in a dozen more. But I assure you, this is not how our story ends," the thing said, reaching its tentacles out of the darkness and wrapping them around Harding in a tight embrace.

Harding screamed as the beast opened its mouth wider and wider until it was stretched to its limit. The thing's teeth were slick with thick, oozing saliva. Its long tongue poked out of its mouth, teasing Harding's head, flicking in and out almost seductively.

"Just imagine all the things I can do with my mouth, Joe," the beast said, tearing into Harding with its teeth, cutting him right down to his bones. "Look. No gag reflex."

Sandra Miller swallowed Detective Joseph P. Harding in one gulp, and although it seemed a cruel act, it was a kindness. A mercy killing. For in another time, in another game, the beast loved Harding so.

And in the end, Harding was correct—that bitch *was* the death of him.

Thanks for the Ride, Lady

They rode on in silence.

They were no longer the same group from when the journey began. The road had tested them, sometimes showing the cracks in the foundation. Nameless doubt hung in the air between them, each holding their cards close to their chest.

Imogen eyed Toby from the backseat as Olivia slept beside her. Her eyes occasionally caught his in the rearview mirror. She was looking for cracks. Something small that might tell her what she saw hadn't been a dream or a lie conjured by Sandra Miller. But she came up empty time and time again. The mask clung to his face tighter than ever, and he wore his best poker face.

"How're you feeling, Toby?" Imogen asked, finally breaking the silence and putting an end to the standoff in the SUV.

"Never better. And you?"

Alex turned around to look directly at Imogen. Imogen saw this out of the corner of her eye as she kept her gaze locked on Toby in the mirror.

"Never better," Imogen said, repeating the words without an ounce of feeling. "Never better, Toby."

"Good," Toby said as Alex slithered back into her seat.

"Yeah, good."

Imogen turned to Olivia, who by now had a small trail of drool running down her chin. She snored loudly as Imogen wiped away the drool with her sleeve.

Silence returned to the SUV as they pushed on, mile after mile, all the while the darkness hot on their tailpipe. Every now and then, Imogen stole a look at it through the SUV's trunk window. Sometimes it was just a moving cloud of black. But other times, Imogen thought she saw shadows moving in the darkness. Shapes. Figures. Things that were... alive. Alive and not human. Once, Imogen swore an impossibly long arm reached out of the darkness and nearly latched onto the back of the SUV. Toby accelerated just as the hand inched closer.

The SUV sped off into the unknown road ahead of them, the darkness falling behind them for the moment, but still fast on their trail and catching up. It was then that the most unexpected of things occurred. A figure appeared on the road ahead. A girl standing alone on the roadside. She held her hand up in a fist and her thumb popped up in classic hitchhiker fashion.

"Is that... a girl?" Toby asked.

"It can't be," Alex replied. "What's she doing out here?"

Imogen leaned over and looked out the passenger window, careful not to stir her sleeping sister. Out, in the middle of nowhere, there indeed stood a lone figure. A hitchhiker.

Beware the hitcher.

"We should stop," Imogen said. "Look at it out there. There's...nothing."

"I don't think so, Imogen. I have... a bad feeling about this," Toby said, side-eyeing Alex.

Imogen saw the look that passed between Toby and Alex. She was almost positive that they were talking in their minds.

Imogen wondered what they were saying.

"But we can't leave her out there," Imogen pleaded. "I mean, can we? That's be as good as murder!"

"Can't we?" Alex responded. "I didn't hear you pleading for Harding's life."

"That was different," Imogen said, shooting venom at Alex with her words. "Pull over, Toby. Or I'll pull us over. I mean it."

"Fine," Alex sighed. "Do it, Toby."

"Are you sure," Toby asked Alex. His eyes never left the lone figure through the glass.

"I'm going to pull over," Toby said, slowing the SUV and steering it off the road.

"But whatever happens, it's on you," Toby said as the SUV slowed to a stop. "Last chance."

Imogen ran through every imaginary scenario in her mind. All but one she never could have imagined.

"Pull over. We can't let the darkness take her," Imogen mumbled, but her message got through.

Alex rolled down her window as the girl approached the SUV. There was no hesitation in her stride, as though she'd been expecting them.

"Get in. Get off the road. It's not safe. We'll take you to the next rest stop," Toby called to the girl, whom Imogen thought looked to be her own age, maybe even slightly younger. "Get in the back."

The girl nodded in understanding and headed to the passenger door.

"Give her room, Imogen," Alex chided.

Imogen put her arms around Olivia and pulled her to the center of the seat. Olivia groaned in her sleeping state, but did not wake. Imogen kept an arm around Olivia protectively. Olivia's head bobbled until it landed on Imogen's shoulder.

The stranger slid into the SUV and pulled the door shut behind her. Toby eyed her in the mirror for a second before shifting the car into drive and steering it back onto the road. Imogen turned to the stranger, trying to see her face, but the girl's hoodie and Olivia's bobbling head concealed most of the girl's features.

"Hey, I'm Imogen."

"Hey," the girl said quietly, almost reverently. "I'm Amanda."

Beware the hitcher.

The First Interlude: It Takes a Village, People

Florence Johnson was pregnant. There was no doubt about it. The two lines on the test she'd picked up at McCrory's Pharmacy told her so. Pregnant? She didn't know something like this could happen. Well, she knew, but she didn't know. Florence was no virgin, but she wasn't an "easy woman" either. Not like Brenda Williams. That bitch was a certified ho, and she had the antibiotics to prove it.

No, Florence had been careful. She could count on one hand the men she'd taken to bed over the last few months. They were "regulars." She kept a small stable of fuck buddies when her battery-operated friends didn't cut it. There was an agreement between them—no attachments. What they had was sex and nothing more. And there'd be nothing more. Ever. That was the deal. The guys readily agreed. They always did. So predictable. An attractive enough woman appears and says, hey, wanna fuck? No strings attached? It was like winning the Powerball.

But sometimes things got messy. Complicated. Boys could be so... well, they could be boys. They said one thing, did another. Swore up and down they accepted the terms of the agreement, then a week later, they wanted to steal you off to

Cancun for a quickie wedding. Or they got jealous and started prying into things that were none of their damned business. Boys. Right?

Florence had to cut three of her recent studs loose. She hadn't cared so much about Brad and Daniel. Brad was a quick draw, if you know what I mean. And Daniel annoyingly made small talk during sex. One minute he'd be pounding her into next week, and the next he'd start talking about taxes and healthcare. If he hadn't had a golden tongue, Florence would've ghosted him weeks ago.

Trevor. The concrete guy. Hot in or out of his clothes. Big hands. And an ass that would make JHo jealous. Prime A beef. Florence had been sorry to see Trevor go, but he broke their agreement. He'd gotten clingy. Texting.

Hey babe. How's your day going?

Good morning, beautiful!

Sweet dreams.

It didn't take long for that Grade-A Filet Mignon to turn into bargain-brand frozen hamburger patties. She had to change her number. Trevor kept getting those app phone numbers and texting away as though Florence hadn't just blocked his old number the night before. Hot, but maybe not so gifted upstairs.

There'd been a scene when he showed up at the diner. He brought flowers, which maybe in another time would've been sweet. But then, it was desperate and pathetic. Florence had said some terrible things, lies, to cut Trevor down to size. She hated doing it, but it was the only way to repel the persistent gnat. If that didn't work, Florence resigned herself to getting one of those bug zappers and ridding herself of poor Trevor once and for all. Luckily for the both of them, he got the message and became nothing but a fond, distant memory.

Florence stared at the test. Her eyes found the opened box sitting at the top of the trash can. It boasted "99.9% accuracy."

"Just great," Florence groaned, tossing the test into the trash to join its cardboard coffin. "Just fucking great."

She went into the bedroom and slipped into her uniform. There was a moment Florence thought about calling out, but she needed the money, now more than ever. Whether or not she kept it, the kid was going to cost her. Plenty. And these days, money was in short supply. Thank you, student loans. Another useless degree. Her father warned her about getting another degree, that it would end up costing more than it was worth. Florence would rather eat Hamburger Buddy for a month straight than admit her old man had been right. All that schooling, and she ended up waitressing at a hole-in-the-wall diner in midtown. Not exactly the glamorous life Florence had imagined for herself.

As she rifled through the unfolded mountain of clean clothes that overtook the chair in the corner of her bedroom, looking for her apron, Florence ran through the list of play dates she'd had over the last month or so. There hadn't been many. Either the guys were unavailable—code for their girlfriends were around—or she was too tired to put any energy into sex. And there was nothing worse than lifeless, uninspired fucking. No sex at all was better than a routine wham, bam, thank you ma'am encounter.

Off the top of her head, Florence came up with only three encounters, and two of them had been with one of her steadier dates, Matt. He was reliable. Almost predictable. If she texted, he usually came. Literally. Matt was super careful. He was a germaphobe, so he always insisted on protection. Florence wouldn't have been surprised if he secretly double wrapped it, just to be sure.

And then there was Damien. She'd put the condom on herself. Magnum. Florence had thrown it in the garbage when they were done, and it was full. The likelihood that one lone swimmer got through the latex and did the doggy paddy all the way to her eggs was one in a million. Not impossible, but unlikely.

So, unless this was an immaculate conception, Florence didn't know how—

Wait.

There was that guy. He came around the diner at closing.

What was his name?

Shoot. I don't remember. Didn't I ever get his name?

Dammit. I can't remember.

He was... in grad school? What was he going for?

It's all a blank.

I can't even remember what he looked like. Isn't that strange?

Just... those eyes. He had the most piercing blue eyes I've ever seen.

Wait... were they blue? Or...

He was gone in the morning. No note. No number. Hell, no thank you for a good time.

It was like... an assignment.

I don't know. That's crazy. It's crazy. It'll come to me.

As she threw her wrinkled apron into her bag, Florence pored over her memory of that night, trying to remember if they'd used protection. She almost always did. Justin was the only exception to that rule. He'd been snipped, so there was no worry there. And she knew Justin was cleaner than the bathroom at Buckingham Palace.

It'll come to me. It will.

Florence told herself this repeatedly as she walked the fifteen blocks from her apartment to the diner. But she found the more she thought about it, the less she could recall the escapade.

By the time she walked through the door to the diner, Florence had all but forgotten him entirely. There were only thoughts about the thing growing inside her belly, clinging to life, eager to be born.

II

VALHALLA

Sunday Drivers

The darkness followed.

Always on their heels, but far enough away to almost be out of view. While Olivia slept, Imogen undid her seat belt and watched in equal parts awe and horror as the world she knew, and sometimes loved, disappeared into the dark's hungry mouth. Occasionally, the darkness gathered, taking form. Always the same form. Sandra Miller. Her glowing red eyes stared out of the darkness, tracking her prey with hungry eyes.

Alex said little. Sometimes her head would turn to Toby, and she'd smile. Imogen was sure they were having a private conversation, as the Bobbsey Twins often did. Since pulling out of The Greasy Spoon, Toby and Alex said few words aloud, at least in front of the group. And when they did speak, it was always logistical—meet back here in fifteen minutes, refill the gas tank, don't talk to strangers. Shit like that.

Imogen always found that last one funny. *Don't talk to strangers.* As if there was anyone out and about to talk to. The only people they *ever* encountered were workers—gas station attendants, cashiers, motel receptionists. But another living soul? A family traveling on the same road, running from the darkness? Some lone survivalist in fatigues stocking up on supplies for their underground bunker? Medical personnel en route to the nearest facility to relieve tired, overworked nurses, doctors, and custodial staff?

No one. There was no one. The road hosted none but their SUV.

No one... except for Amanda.

Beware the hitcher.

"Why didn't you listen to me?" Ally asked, poking her head up from the third-row backseat, where Olivia lay sprawled out, fast asleep.

Imogen turned her head slightly, just enough for her eyes to catch Ally's. She didn't want to draw unnecessary attention. The last thing she wanted Toby or Alex to think was that she was talking to ghosts or imaginary friends. This was her secret, and she'd keep it to the end. They had more than their fair share of secrets. Imogen reasoned she could keep one or two herself without feeling guilty.

She pretended to check on Olivia, but opened her eyes wide as though saying, *what the fuckkkkkk, Ally? Can't talk now.*

"Everything okay back there?" Toby called back from the driver's seat. He watched Imogen in the rearview mirror, observing every movement as though waiting for a slip-up.

Imogen turned her head back to center and wiped her expression clear.

"Yeah. Just checking on Livs."

"How is she?" Toby asked, his eyes fixed on Imogen and not the desolate road ahead. "She still sleeping?"

Imogen nodded.

"Yeah. Sleeping Beauty is still fast asleep. She's sleeping an awful lot, don't you think, Toby?"

Toby's eyes returned to the road, and Imogen noticed.

"I guess she needs her beauty sleep."

Alex peered around the passenger seat. She kept most of her face concealed behind the backside of the seat so only some of her hair and eye stuck out.

"Maybe it's too much for her," Alex said. "She's not as strong as you."

Imogen squinted her eyes, trying to see deeper into the dark cloud that hung over the front seats. With no light streaming in from the outside, it was like Toby and Alex lay under thick, heavy blankets that made them almost invisible.

"Darkness likes the dark, Imo," Ally whispered into Imogen's ear.

Just then, Imogen realized Amanda had turned and was staring right at her. She was humming a melody Imogen knew all too well, having committed every note to memory long ago.

"How does it feel to be damned?" Amanda asked quietly, grinning. Imogen thought the girl looked almost feral. Wild. Untamed. Unpredictable. "No one can save your soul now, don't you know. Tell me, how does it feel to be damned?"

Imogen knew the words all too well. The lyrics to "The Devil's Requiem" from *Black Mass*, the album by Dakotah Fucking Dark. They went with the melody Amanda had been humming.

For the first time since they'd picked up the lone hitchhiker, Imogen saw Amanda's face clearly. She didn't need any light to confirm her suspicions. She knew this girl, kind of. Amanda Grimmes had a reputation. A bad reputation. She took "bad girl" to a whole new level.

"Tommy Tuttone fingered her in the backseat of his car," Ally said. "Can you believe that shit? We went to the movies. What the hell did we see? Shit, I can't remember. That 'Sugar Tits' guy was in it. The asshole who beat his wife. You know the one I'm talking about. He looks like a homeless person. Crazy eyes. Anyway. Tommy and I messed around a little, but I wasn't feeling it. He was a sloppy kisser. Asshole dropped me off and picked up Amanda. Fingered her cooter in his car while they were parked at some playground. Gives new meaning to the word 'playground', heh."

"You like Dakotah Dark, Amanda?" Imogen asked.

Amanda nodded. "He's the best."

"Yeah, he's pretty cool."

"Ever play *Black Mass* backwards?"

Imogen shook her head, suddenly recalling the last time she'd listened to Dakotah Dark. It'd been the night her parents were killed during the game. That... thing... that was death that had crept up behind her. Imogen still smelt its putrid scent in her nose. But then... wait. A thought formed in Imogen's head, but as quickly as it'd come on, it went away as Amanda distracted her.

"Hey! Are you listening to me?"

"What? Yeah. Sorry," Imogen said, taking in the girl's crazed expression. She thought Amanda looked like a rubber band, stretched to its limit and about to snap. "No. I never played his records backwards. One time..."

Amanda leaned forward, practically salivating like a rabid St. Bernard. "Yeah? One time?"

Imogen shrugged. "Nothing. I chickened out, I guess."

"Buck, buck, buck," Amanda shouted suddenly, doing her best imitation of a chicken. She sat back in her seat and rubbed her hands together anxiously. "Do you want to know what I heard when I played *Black Mass* backwards?"

"Don't, Imo," Ally said imploringly. "It's some fucked-up shit. You don't need Dakotah Dark in your head. Hell, you'd be better off with that Josh Groan-bad guy your mom loved so much. At least your intense hatred of him will fuel you. You let Dakotah Dark in? You end up like her."

Imogen looked Amanda over.

"Crazy bitch," Ally said. "Usually I like crazy bitches, but that one? Uh, uh. She'll shove a la crosse racquet up your ass, dry, and not even bother to give your clit a little rub a dub dub."

Imogen thought, but did not say *that's awfully specific, Ally.*

"You know I'm right, Imo," Ally said, as though she had read Imogen's mind.

"You know what, Amanda? Some things are just better left a mystery. I don't want to know. Maybe when this is all over, I'll grab a copy of *Midnight Offerings*, toss it on the turntable, and spin it backwards."

Amanda laughed. "After this? What makes you think there will be anything after this?"

"I don't know what's going to happen, but I have to believe things can and *will* get better. This isn't the end. Far from it."

"Mhmm," Amanda mumbled, turning her head away from Imogen to look out the window.

Imogen saw Amanda pat her side, where it looked like there was something poking out under her oversized hoodie. When they'd first picked her up, Imogen had wondered why Amanda had been wearing such a big hoodie. She didn't want to be hard on the girl, thinking she probably grabbed whatever she could before running. Maybe the hoodie had belonged to an older brother. Hell, maybe it belonged to Tommy Tuttone.

"Hey, Imo! Do you think his fingers still smell like her cooter?" Ally laughed.

Imogen fought back the urge to crack up. Still, a small crack escaped her throat as she swallowed her laughter. Toby gave her a suspicious look in the rearview mirror. His eyes lingered on her for a long moment. Imogen sat frozen. She cleared her mind and molded her face into the portrait of an innocent woman.

Toby's eyes returned to the road.

"He suspects, Imo. Watch your back. He knows something's up. But, most of all..."

Amanda began humming softly. The devil's music. Darkness calls to darkness.

"Beware the hitcher, Imo."

In between hums, Amanda laughed and whispered to herself, as though answering questions only she could hear. Imogen couldn't make out any of the answers, though. Later, she'd wish she had.

Beware the hitcher, Imo.

And with that, Ally was gone. Imogen sat back, relaxing into the seat. Relaxing as much as she allowed herself to. She wanted to sleep, but she knew she had to keep one eye on Toby and the other on Amanda. So, she forced her eyes to stay open, but her mind went back to the last round of the game she'd played. The one that killed her parents. And Ally.

The game where something foul, something undead, something that wore death like a skin, stood behind her and had said *I think Daddy lost his head.* The thing had been there only a moment, smiling at her with its fetid mouth and decaying teeth. But when it was gone, someone else stood in its place. Someone she knew she'd seen before. *Twice* before.

And she'd seen her again recently—behind the desk at the 'otel.

It was that crazy Mexican bitch that had grabbed her. Imogen heard the woman's almost gleeful cry of "gotcha!" in her head as she wondered when they'd be seeing that *puta* again. If, and when, they did... Imogen planned on whacking *her* on the head with the heaviest thing she could find and asking the bitch how she liked it as Imogen beat the woman's head into kibbles and bits and bits and...

Gotcha, bitch.

Hush

The thing was talking in Amanda's head. It was always there, but it didn't always say anything. Sometimes it just listened. Eavesdropped. Tried to get inside intel on what the little gang of dreamers were planning. It wanted to stay one step ahead, even though it had more tricks up its sleeve than Harry Blackstone, the late magician extraordinaire and later a peddler of cheap tricks, whoopie cushions, and fake dog shit. It was an honest living, albeit a far less glamorous one.

The monster had been with her in the 'otel. They hadn't seen her, but Amanda was there, lurking in the shadows and winding hallways. Darkness likes darkness. She'd been there when that stupid Mexican bitch almost gave it all away. How could she have been so stupid? To show her face like that...

Fucking idiot.

Amanda despised Joanne Garriga and it had nothing to do with Joanne being Mexican. Amanda hated Joanne because Joanne was careless. Messy. Her mind always seemed distracted, like she was betting on greyhounds at the horse track. She wanted to chalk it up to Joanne just being a stupid bitch, but Amanda thought there was more to it. A lot more.

Where are you? the thing asked.

"Not far from New York City."

How far? Exactly.

"I don't know. The last sign I saw—"

What did it say?

"New York City. 102 miles."

The thing shuddered with excitement and anticipation. Amanda heard the thing's body shimmy and shake as though it were wearing a grass hula skirt and a lei.

So close now. I can taste you.

"There's something else…"

What? A problem?

"I don't know. Maybe. It might be. I'm not sure."

Well, don't just sit there with your thumb up your ass, Amanda. Spit it out!

"I think… she recognizes me."

Who?

"Imogen. She keeps staring at me. The dumb bitch doesn't think I see her looking at me, but I do. I see her out of the corner of my hoodie. It's like she's trying to remember where she knows me from. I think… she might have remembered."

Are you sure?

"Pretty sure, I guess. Not certain… not like I'd bet my life on it… maybe Joanne's, but… yeah… I think she knows who I am."

The thing sighed a long, frustrated sigh.

And it was going so well, too. It doesn't matter. It changes nothing. Stick to the plan. It doesn't matter if she remembers you from the mall or the malt shoppe. It's not like you killed her cat or something.

Amanda laughed.

You didn't, did you?

"Didn't… what?"

Kill her fucking cat!

"NO! We barely even met. It was just one time, and I didn't think she even noticed me! It was her friend that was giving me the evil eye. I thought the bitch was gonna pull a gun on me and shoot me in the parking lot. All over that idiot. He didn't even know what to do with his fingers. Ugh. I was just bored."

You know, Amanda. Sometimes I wonder what I saw in you back at The Willows.

Amanda giggled. "Pussy Willows."

The thing sighed. *Do not disappoint me, Amanda. I tore the head off the last person that disappointed me, and really, if I'm being honest, she just annoyed me. A little.*

"I won't disappoint you."

You better not. If you do, you'll never hear that music again.

"Oh no, please! I won't disappoint you!"

Do you want to hear that music now, dear? The devil's music?

"Oh, yes! Please! Please!"

Alright. Sit back. Close your eyes.

"Okay. Okay. Okay..."

Are they closed?

The thing asked this, even though it knew Amanda's eyes were shut tighter than a hipster's skinny jeans.

Good girl. Now let me just reach down into—

BOOM!

BANG!

CRUNCH!

CRASH!

Amanda?! WHAT THE FUCK WAS THAT?!

Amanda opened her eyes and looked around the car, taking in the look of shock on everyone's face. Her eyes moved to the rear window, and then Amanda sighed.

Amanda?

"It's your fucking girl, Joanne."

You Shall Not Pass

"Toby! Watch it," Imogen screamed. "On your left! LEFT! She's coming around on—"

"I see! I see," Toby shouted, without taking his eyes off the road ahead. He gave the side mirror a quick glance, then his eyes moved back to the windshield. He hit the accelerator hard and floored it. The SUV lurched forward with a jerk, then rapidly gained speed.

Outside, the chasing vehicle, a shit box if there ever was a shit box, kept pace.

"What was that?" Olivia screamed, sitting up in the far backseat. "What did we hit?"

"How the fuck is that little piece of shit car going so fast?" Imogen asked, watching Joanne's shit box of a car match their speed. "How? That thing looks about as well put together as that idiot's Cyber Trukkk. Held together with glue, spit, and a prayer. But at least those ugly fuckers blew up on their own if you, you know... actually drove them."

"What the fuck is going on, Imo?" Olivia shouted at Imogen.

"Someone is trying to run us off the road," Imogen said, watching the shit box cruise up beside them.

Olivia's head turned just in time to—

BOOM! CRASH! CRUNCH!

The shit box plowed into the side of the SUV.

"Jesus Christ! That felt like a fucking tank hit us," Olivia hollered.

Olivia crawled across the seat and pressed her face to the glass, ready to retreat if the shit box launched another assault.

Toby clutched the steering wheel tightly, keeping their vehicle on the road. His foot hammered the accelerator, and the SUV sped off, momentarily getting ahead of Joanne's little shit box.

"Hang on," Toby shouted. "Buckle up!"

"We're buckled," everyone but Amanda shouted in near unison.

Amanda had her eyes shifting between Olivia and Imogen. They moved so rapidly it looked as though she was watching a tennis match. She watched and then waited. Stalking like a good predator.

"Toby, floor it," Alex pressed.

"Not yet," Toby replied calmly.

"Wait a second!" Olivia shouted over the roar of the car's engine. "I know her! I FUCKING KNOW HER!"

"What?" Toby asked, glimpsing Olivia in the rearview mirror.

"I do! That's the weird fucking lady from the 'otel! The front desk lady!"

Toby turned his head but saw the shit box gaining. He turned back to the road.

"Are you sure?" he called back to Olivia.

"Yes," Olivia said, taking another look, just to be certain.

"I know her, too," Imogen added. "She's the bitch that grabbed me."

"Dallas..." Amanda said in a hush. No one heard her over the excitement of the chase.

"That's her! What the fuck was her name? Jolene? Jo... JOANNE! Joanne!"

"... we have a problem," Amanda finished.

You Got a Friend in Jesus

Joanne jerked the steering wheel to the right.

CRUNNCCHHHHH!

"Jesus loves me," she sang, without losing a beat. "This the BI—"

She hit the gas, and her shit box attacked the oversized SUV.

"—BLE TELLS ME SO!"

She threw her head back and laughed wildly.

"Oh, Señor Toby! The look on your—"

Joanne rammed the back of the SUV with the front of her shit box. A headlight shattered and dangled lifelessly for a moment, before it jumped ship and was lost in the darkness.

"—FACE!"

Joanne crowed, hitting the steering wheel with her palms until they were red.

"Little ones, to him BE—"

The shit box took another bite out of the SUV's ample ass. The SUV's license plate came undone and flailed.

"—LONG!"

Another fit of belly aching laughter overtook Joanne. Tears streamed down her face. Her head bobbed as though following the rhythm of a song only she could hear.

"Uh huh," Joanne sang out terribly. "You know, you

KNOW—"

The shit box crept up on the SUV's right side. She hit the gas. The shit box moved forward with growing reluctance. Then, she hit the brake, falling behind the SUV. The SUV shot off faster than little Donnie Drump, Jr.

Joanne's leaden foot slammed onto the accelerator. The shit box moaned and groaned. The engine howled as though Joanne were astride a horse of the apocalypse, which, in a way... she was.

The shit box caught up with the SUV.

Joanne steered it up beside the SUV's right side. Her hand slapped the wheel.

A–1... 2... 3... 4!

"You know, you know... you got a friend in JESUS!"

With that, she turned the wheel hard to the left and crashed into the front passenger door.

"Uh uh... a friend, a friend, a friend... in Jesus!"

Joanne allowed Toby to pass the shit box.

"You shallllll not passssssssss," Joanne howled, laughing.

What the FUCK do you think you're doing?

Joanne's hands slipped from the wheel. The shit box swerved out of her control.

"Hark, who goes there?" Joanne asked, regaining control of the car. "Jesu Christo?"

Jesus? Are you fucking—

Joanne fumbled with the radio dials, even though they were laid to rest around the time the whole shit box should've made a last ride to the junkyard. When nothing happened, she realized the voice was not on the outside, but on the inside... of her head.

Knock, knock.

"Who's... who's there?"

If you don't pull this fucking car over, right now, I'm going to beat your stupid Mexican ass with a stack of Bibles!

Fuck, Joanne thought.

It was one of the Miller bitches.

But then, just before she could turn off the radio in her head, another voice came knocking on her mind's secret back door—the only back door action Joanne Garriga had ever seen in her life.

"What the fuck are you doing, Joanne?" Señor Toby yelled.

"Uh huh... I've got, I've got, I've got a friend... a friend, oh yeah, in Jesus."

Joanne turned off the radio in her head and the voices were gone.

Some of them.

There were always more.

They were legion.

And, like it or not, Joanne still had a passenger inside of her.

A passenger who, at the very moment, was quite unhappy with her. One might even say the passenger was enraged with Joanne. If she could, the passenger would shove a large print Bible up Joanne's dried-out fishing hole, and thumb through its many pages.

But Joanne paid her no mind.

After all, Joanne Garriga had a friend in Jesus.

You Sank My Battleship

"Holy shit, Livs," Imogen shouted, staring out her window. "I think you're right!"

CRRUNNNCHHHHH!

The shit box assaulted the SUV's backside.

"Christ, I feel like we're the Titanic," Olivia began.

And then, at the same time, she and Imogen said, "That shit box is an iceberg!"

"All hands on dick," Amanda shouted, sounding like a military drill sergeant.

"What?" Imogen asked incredulously, rounding on Amanda.

Amanda covered her face with her hands and laughed into them.

"Ha, ha, ha! DICK! I meant 'deck'."

Imogen shook her head, thinking about Tommy Tuttone and his "StarKissed Tuna" fingers.

BOOM!

CRRAAACKKKK!

"I just want to know... what the fuck is that shit box made of? Solid fucking gold?"

"Ooh, S–S–Solid Gold! I loved that program," Amanda said, gyrating her body as though she was dancing on a tacky disco-inspired dancefloor.

CRRRRUNNNCCCHHH!

This assault came at the right passenger door. It rocked the SUV, sending a shockwave through its steel bones. Even with their seat belts on, everyone was shaken around a bit like a martini. Amanda didn't seem to mind it.

"Wheeeeeeeeee! Again, daddy! Again," she begged her imaginary daddy.

Olivia looked at Amanda. "This bitch is crazier than—"

BOOM!

THUD!

The shit box took a bite out of the rear bumper. It was a mortal wound for the bumper.

"CRAZIER THAN A MORMON SCIENTOLOGIST ON RUM-SPRINGA!"

Imogen turned around to look at Olivia.

"What does that even—"

CRASSHHHHH!

"MEAN?!"

"It means the bitch is crazy," Alex finally said.

"Well, craz-eee. That's just how it goooooo-ezzzzzz," Amanda sang out of tune and out of rhythm.

THUD!

CRRUNNNCCCHHHH!

"Fucccckkkk! That one hurt," Olivia moaned.

"You okay, Livs?"

"Yeah, I think I'll live," Olivia said, rubbing at her elbow.

"But for how long? That's the question? To be, or not to be," Amanda said dreamily.

"Somebody shut her up," Toby called from the driver's seat.

Imogen leaned forward so her mouth was at Toby's ear.

"I'll make you a deal. Lose that crazy bitch out there, and

I'll silence the crazy bitch back here?"

Toby's eye searched the SUV's mirror, looking for the shit box in the darkness. The crazy Mexican lady had turned off the shit box's head lights so now it was as good as invisible.

"Deal," Toby said to Imogen, bracing for another BANG as the shit box appeared out of the black in his side mirror. "HOLD ON!"

BOOM!

"Yeah, stop at a creepy long motel for the night, pick up a hitchhiker in the middle of the apocalypse..." Imogen mumbled, sitting back in her seat.

"Not helpful," Toby tisked.

"Sorry, not sorry," Imogen shot back as Joanne's shit box rammed the back of the SUV again. She grabbed onto the back of Toby's chair to steady herself. "Hey, Amanda."

Amanda, who had been lolling her head in laughter since her dick joke, quieted and looked at Imogen as though she held up a pair of shiny keys.

"What's your favorite Dakotah Dark song, huh?"

Hail Mary

"Jesus loves me," Joanne sang out at the top of her lungs. "This I know!"

The SUV was on the defensive. Toby dodged and weaved on the road, faking Joanne out. He was the better driver, which surprised Joanne, since she'd been driving a car before the little shit was even born.

Or had she?

Did she really know how old Toby was? On the outside, he might look like a young man, but on the inside? Joanne thought on the inside Toby probably looked like an old, old, pruned-up old man, kind of like George Burns, but even older and wrinklier.

She amused herself by picturing the old man inside of Toby when her eyes caught sight of her hands on the steering wheel. Joanne got one look at the monstrous things that now only vaguely resembled their previous human form and screamed. Her hands flew off the wheel. The car veered to the left. She grabbed the wheel with one malformed hand and guided the shit box back onto the road.

I don't know what you think you're doing, but cut the shit right now, Joanne.

The Miller bitch, Joanne thought. The OTHER Miller bitch.

The passenger riding inside of her body. The one she was strangely more afraid of.

Mary Miller.

Cut. The. Shit.

"Jesus loves me, this I know," Joanne sang out, even louder. It sounded more like a banshee's cry than a song of praise.

You think you drown me out? DO YOU?

"BECAUSE THE BIBLE TELLS ME SO!"

Blah! Blah! Blah! Pull the fucking car over right now. You know what I did to my family? You think I won't do that... WORSE to you, you nosey bitch!

"LITTLE ONES TO HIM BELONG!"

Remember your good buddy, Bob?

Joanne stopped singing.

Of course, she remembered Bob Buchanan, mail carrier and wanna-be best-selling true crime writer—with a potential podcast tie-in.

Do you know what I did to Bob? Busybody Bob?

Joanne knew exactly what Mary had done to her partner in true crime, Bob.

I sliced that nosey, limp-dicked pedo like a Christmas ham.

Joanne saw the leaked crime scene photos—*Inside the "house of horrors!" Cannibalism! Incest! Roleplay!*

A small tear rolled down Joanne Garriga's cheek. She went to wipe at it with her hand but was quickly reminded that her hand was no longer her own, but the foul thing's hand. She screamed and flailed her hand in the air, as though the motion could flick the foul thing's rotting skin away.

The car veered wildly as she let go of the steering wheel.

Don't think for a second you're going to crash this piece of shit foreign jalopy and kill us! I'll fucking DRAGGGGGG your busted-up ass home. You can't kill me, you stupid bitch. I'm already dead.

Joanne screamed.

Ugh, again with the screaming.

Joanne screamed louder. Shook and flailed her hand more intensely.

"UH, UH, UH! I'VE GOT A FRIEND IN JESUS!"

Put your fucking hands on the wheel!

"IN JESUS!"

PUT YOUR FUCKING HANDS ON THE WHEEL, YOU BUSYBODY, CUNT!

"A FRIEND! A FRIEND! A FRIEND IN—"

LISTEN, BITCH! I'M DONE FUCKING PLAYING WITH YOU!

Joanne Garriga's hands turned on her. Without thought, without hesitation, they seized Joanne by the throat and SQUEEZED.

HARD.

The shit box started and stopped, swerving in figure eights as her foot alternated between the accelerator and the brake. She used her elbows to steer the shit box, or at least keep it on the road.

She gasped. There was no air.

The brakes SCREECHED.

The shit box almost spun out, but somehow Joanne kept it on the road.

Her vision was getting hazy. It was hard enough to see shit in the absolute darkness, but now everything had an annoying halo around it. She wanted to curse her own fucking eyes for betraying her, too. It was like she'd gotten shampoo suds in both eyes, and not that "no tear" shit. The real deal. Shampoo that'll burn your fucking eyes out. No amount of rinsing can get that shit out. You walk around seeing halos for days.

"GAAAHHHHHHHH," Joanne choked, trying to pull her own hands off her throat. But they weren't budging. She laughed—or laughed as much as she could—as her own hands wrapped tighter around her neck. "A FRIEND... IN... JEEEEEE-SUS!"

AHHHHHHHH! YOU INSUFFERABLE, MISERABLE BITCH!

Joanne Garriga laughed. She slammed her foot on the gas and watched as the shit box headed off the road—heading straight for a concrete containment wall.

GODDAMMIT, JOANNE! REALLY?

"I GOT A FRIEND IN—"

Um... WTAF?

"Um," Olivia said, pointing to the shit box car speeding off the road, on a direct course for the containment wall. "What the actual fuck is she doing?"

Imogen threw her hands up.

"I got nothing."

Amanda, no longer distracted by Imogen, who was now distracted herself, burst out laughing, as though someone had just cut a fart in the middle of finals.

"She's got a friend, got a friend, got a friend... in Jesus," she sang, catching her breath between laughs.

"If she crashes..." Toby began.

"WHEN she crashes," Alex corrected.

Amanda laughed harder.

"Can't you guys... like... MAKE her crash? WTAF?"

The SUV went silent, as though the Monsignor of St. Peter's Prep had walked in on the Guinness Book of Records' largest recorded circle jerk. Toby, Alex, Olivia, and Imogen all felt like they'd been caught with their dicks out.

"Could we?" Olivia asked Imogen. "I mean, should we? But also, could we?"

"I don't—" Imogen started, but Alex sliced the thought down.

"No. It's against the rules."

Imogen raised an eyebrow.

"But haven't we—"

"NO," Toby said more definitively. "We just can't, Imogen."

"Okay. Alright," Imogen said, backing down.

Olivia mumbled under her breath to Imogen, "I still don't understand *why* we can't."

"Tisk, tisk, tisk," Amanda taunted. "Lame. So lame."

Imogen fought the overwhelming desire to unbuckle her belt, dive across the seat, and choke the life out of the crazy bitch.

Amanda smirked, as though she knew exactly what Imogen had been thinking.

"I got a friend, I got a friend..." she sang like a broken record, reducing the volume with every repeat.

Olivia huffed.

"I really hate—"

"Yeah, I do, too," Imogen agreed. "Again, great idea— picking up a hitcher in the middle of the apocalypse."

Toby slammed on the brakes, jerked the wheel to the left.

Imogen felt like she was in that old *Star Trek* TV show as everyone's body tilted to the right as though they'd just been struck on the right side of the SUV by a photon torpedo.

"What the hell," Toby grunted, righting the SUV on the road, "is she doing?"

Toby or Alex, really any of the Millers in the SUV, *could've* just taken out Joanne Garriga with nothing more than a simple flex of their super-charged brains. Fuck with Joanne's reality a little. Open a window and send her to another place, in another time... like they'd done before. Toby usually didn't like to do shit like that, but, man, he just had to admit that it was just so much fun messing with her.

She was like a science project on pressure. How much pressure did it take to make Joanne Garriga explode and lose her shit? It appeared they might have an answer as Joanne's car swerved on and off the road, once again on a direct course toward the containment wall.

But he knew he couldn't let her crash and burn. Not this time. He needed her alive. Joanne still had a role to play, an important one. He knew he might just have to intervene like the hand of god and turn that crazy bitch's car around before she ruined everything.

Toby wasn't going to let that busybody bitch take away their victory, not when they were so close: "New York City: 38 Miles."

Joanne! Don't make me turn this car around!

With Friends Like That

Mary Miller was more than just about to lose her shit. She was pretty sure she lost it half a mile ago. From the beginning, she didn't want to do this—ride in Joanne Garriga's body. Live in her skin. She hated that busybody bitch. She always did.

Mary hated how Joanne walked around with her stubby nose in the air, like everyone else smelled like dog shit to her. The bitch thought SHE was actually better than everyone else. Mary thought the thought itself was laughable. Had Mary Miller been a different person, a little less psychopathic, she might've had sympathy or empathy for poor old Joanne.

But Mary Miller was not that kind of person. In life, she was crazier than crazy. She wasn't a mere passenger on the crazy train. She was its fucking conductor. And the best part of it all was that Mary Miller KNEW she was bat-shit crazy. She LOVED that she was bat-shit crazy.

When it came down to it, Mary Miller was a "Miller" in name only. Before she was "Mary Miller," she'd been "Mary Bukowski." And before that, "Mary Shelley"—no relation. She was just a mere player, strutting her stuff on the stage. And all the world was nothing but one great, big old stage. And as far as players went, Mary Miller was a constant favorite. She never disappointed.

If the game were a reality TV show, Mary would've easily been what's known as a "fan favorite." Everyone's favorite brand of crazy with a side of sociopath and a touch of narcissism. She'd earned a special place in Sandra Miller's cold, black heart. The thing all but adopted Mary, making her an "honorary" Miller. Assigned her the best roles in the best games.

And Mary NEVER disappointed.

But the Miller name alone didn't bestow any special powers on Mary. She was extraordinarily ordinary as players go. You slap a shit patty on a hot dog bun, add onions and sauerkraut, mustard and cheese, and call it penne a la vodka, but that didn't make it true. What's in a name, after all, eh?

Mary Miller may not have been able to bend shit, move shit, teleport shit, or open doors to other worlds, but she wasn't powerless. Her power resided in her madness, in her warped view of the world. Or, worlds. In its simplest terms, Mary had no fucks to give and took no shit.

So, when she screamed —

PUT YOUR FUCKING HANDS ON THE WHEEL OR I'M GOING TO CHOP THEM OFF!

—she meant it.

And Joanne Garriga knew Mary meant every word.

"Gaaahhhhh," Joanne gurgled. "Stop... choking me... and I will, you crazy bitch!"

Mary was not sold on Joanne's delivery. It smelled like five pounds of horseshit in a doggie poop bag.

"Let... me go, or... we're gonna crash," Joanne said.

And, on that one small thing, Mary agreed Joanne had a very valid point. If she didn't stop choking her former neighbor, something she envisioned doing a million times, the shit box was going to crash and likely kill the both of them in one fiery, bloody instant.

On three!

"Uh, uh..."

One!

"I've got a, I've got a..."

Two!

"A friend in Jesus!"

Three!

Mary gave Joanne her hands back, and they went right to the wheel. Joanne turned the wheel to the left and hit the gas, the shit box only narrowly avoiding a head-on collision with the containment wall.

As the shit box limped back onto the road, its one working front headlight slicing a hole through the darkness like the eye of a cyclops, seeking the SUV, Joanne hummed away with a shit-eating grin on her face.

Meanwhile, Mary had only one thought running through what was left of her psychotic, fractured brain—

Stupid, stupid bitch. I'll get you. If it's the last thing I ever do...

Knight Takes Pawn

The SUV's headlights hit the green roadside sign, making it shimmer and glow in the surrounding darkness. "28 miles to New York City."

"We're almost there," Toby said, checking the mirrors for the shit box. It wasn't long before he eyed the car's lone, flickering headlight. "I need to lose her. This might get bumpy."

"Get bumpy?" Olivia questioned.

Imogen laughed. "It's been pretty fucking bumpy, Toby."

"Yeah, well… just hold on. I'm going to try to lose her," Toby said.

He steered the SUV to the center lines and rode it. The road was smoother, less potholes and craters along the double yellows. He lifted his foot off the gas pedal and let the car decelerate but not slow to a stop. The idea was to let Joanne catch up, not make a final assault on the SUV with her jalopy. From there, it would take some slick driving to lose her once and for all.

But Toby knew it wouldn't be forever. There were other ways home. Back roads into Valhalla. And he'd told Joanne all about them—just in case. This was just in case. Appearances needed to be kept up. He felt cracks in the cement holding their group together, and they were growing deeper with every mile they got closer to home. Although he wasn't sure what the twins knew, or what they suspected, the fact that they'd grown less… pliable in recent days meant they were starting to ask questions.

And there was something else. Imogen. She was always looking at him out of the corner of her eye, like she was waiting for him to fuck up. Say or do something that would trigger a "gotcha!" moment. But Toby knew better than that. This wasn't his first game. He was an expert role player, and he wouldn't be taken out by a novice, not when they were so close. So close to winning it all. Finally… winning. The sweet taste of victory filled his mouth, but Alex had warned him not to get ahead of himself. There was still much work to do. Sacrifices needed to be made. Sandra needed to be taken out.

And Mother…

Well, they just needed to win the game before Mother came home.

That was the plan.

So close.

So close now.

Feed on Olivia one more time. Drain her power entirely. Suck the energy out just before entering Valhalla. Then, there'd be nothing Sandra could do to stop him from winning the game—especially with Imogen on their side. It'd be so easy to blame Sandra for Olivia's death. And she'd believe it, too, because they'd all seen the terrible things Aunt Sandra could—

A Good Day to—

—do.

Suddenly, the black sky was ablaze with light. The sky itself was on fire, burning out of control. A steady, heavy rain of ash fell to the ground. The windshield was quickly covered in it. Toby couldn't see an inch in front of them. He clicked on the wipers, but they only smeared the ash into the glass, obscuring his vision even more.

"Shit," he mumbled.

Toby pulled an arm on the steering console and a steady stream of blue fluid sprayed all over the windshield. He clicked the wipers on "super." They swung up, then returned home faster than a Republican buys a drink for an "almost legal" girl at a party.

He found the road, but it wasn't clear. And that was the idea.

"Ashes to ashes," Amanda muttered to herself. "We... all... fall... down."

The darkness glowed as a massive bolt of lightning shot out of the fire and struck the road ahead of them. The asphalt exploded into the air in thousands of fiery bits like diarrhea after eating a gas station burrito.

The road broke in two as a crevice formed out of the flaming asphalt and quickly spread up and down the center of the roadway, splitting the road as though it were a piece of notepaper. Thick clouds of smoke rose out of the crack as an orange-yellowy light flickered somewhere not far below the surface. Flames.

Above, thunder BOOMED as more crackles of lightning shot out of the fiery sky. The bolts struck the road and the roadside, occasionally landing a blow on the road itself. But Toby dodged them. The SUV's tires screamed and screeched as they peeled and hauled ass on the burning asphalt. Small puffs of gray smoke lay in their wake.

Toby hit the wiper fluid again. It did little, but it was just enough to clear a porthole in the blanket of ash that settled on the windshield. He checked the rearview for Joanne's lone headlight, but the glass was covered in ash. He'd forgotten to turn on the rear wiper. He rotated a nob on the wiper arm and the rear wiper slowly came to life.

With a little blue fluid, Toby could just make out the shimmer and flicker of Joanne's headlight trailing behind them in her shit box. He couldn't be sure, given the piss-poor visibility through the window, but it looked as though the roof of the shit box was on fire and one of the front tires had blown out. Sparks flew off the asphalt with every rotation as Joanne kept the pedal to the metal, literally.

"This is Sandra again, isn't it?" Olivia asked the group, although she already knew the answer. This was a fine example of what old folks refer to as "just making conversation."

"Bingo," Amanda said with a giggle.

"Well, it's not the Easter Bunny," Toby shot back, keeping his gaze locked on the small clearing in the ash, which was the only thing keeping them alive.

"She's going to kill us," Imogen said, straightening her back and tightening her shoulders. They were so high that she could have worn them as earrings.

"No," Alex said, without looking back. "She's just trying to slow us down. Toby…"

"I know!"

"We're so close, Toby! SO CLOSE! Twelve miles, Toby! TWELVE MILES TO HOME!"

"There's no place like home, there's no place like home, there's no place…" Amanda whispered like a broken record.

"Turn her off!"

"Can I throw her out of the car?" Imogen asked, only half-jokingly.

"I don't care. Just shut her up. I can't—"

A deafening, thunderous BOOM rattled the SUV. A small crack appeared in the right corner of the windshield, slowly splintering out like a spider's web.

"—see," Toby hollered.

Imogen moved to unclick her belt as she turned to Amanda.

"Touch me, and I'll feed you all ten of your toes like grapes, bitch. Back off," Amanda growled.

Imogen knew she meant it, too. The image was seared into her mind's eye. She didn't care for grapes, and she liked feet even less than she liked grapes—her feet, with their grabby, crab-like toes, especially.

She threw herself back into her seat and sighed.

"You're lucky I can't just…" Imogen made a POOF gesture with her hands. "Because I SOOOOO want to right now…"

SKANK!

"… but I need to save it."

"Ooohhh," Amanda mocked. "Better stock up on all that juice. You're gonna need it."

"Just... sit there and shut the fuck up," Imogen said, without looking at the hitcher.

Out of the corner of her eye, Imogen watched Amanda lock her lips with an imaginary key and toss it out the closed window.

The raging inferno in the sky continued to burn out of control. For the first time in a long time, light shone down as if the sun had come home and was saying, *Hello, world! Did you miss me?* But instead of a warm, golden hue, the world was painted crimson. Red, like blood.

The clouds and the smoke gathered, taking shape. Morphing from nothing into a solid, lifelike form that appeared to breathe. Slowly, a face appeared. Then, long, reaching arms and tentacles slithered out of the smoke as more and more ash rained down.

Finally, as the loudest BOOM of thunder rang out and the brightest crackle of lightning struck the road, a pair of flaming eyes opened in the sky.

Everyone in the SUV knew at once what it was up there, looking down on them and reaching out. A long tentacle slapped the side of the road, sending debris, fire, and ash a mile high.

I don't think she wants to finger pop you, Imo, Ally said in Imogen's head.

Amanda rolled down her window and stuck her head out.

Even as the earth burned outside, thunder cracked and boomed, and lightning struck, Amanda's words flew back into the SUV along with a spray of ash that came down like confetti.

"SHE... SEES... YOU!"

Damned You

"Tell me," Amanda said, pulling a large silver, shimmering knife out from under the oversized hoodie. "How does it feel to be damned?"

She raised her hand over her head, cocking it back to arm the knife. In less than an instant, her eyes met each one of theirs, and then she moved quickly. So quickly that she was nothing but a blur. No one and nothing could have slowed her down on her mission. Not even with all their combined gifts, their awesome power... not even with all of that could they keep Amanda from bringing the blade down, slicing through the tenderest flesh, cutting and piercing down to the bone. All the way down, until none of the blade was visible.

The only thing anyone could see was the knife's wooden handle and a steady pool of blood running down onto the snow-white upholstery.

Send Your Regrets

You can't stop this, Imo, Ally said in Imogen's mind. *I'm so sorry.*

The Second Interlude: Daddy Issues

By the lunch rush, Florence Johnson forgot all about the bun cooking in her oven. Mostly forgot about it, anyway. Every time a mother came in toting a kid or two under an arm, or in a stroller, reality came crashing back down on her.

The mysterious one-night stand that didn't even buy her breakfast in the morning. The overall fogginess about that night. Other than the fact that he'd been a customer in the diner and that she'd gone to bed with him, presumably, everything else was a blank, as though the security tape of her misdeeds had been wiped.

There were those eyes, though. *The windows of the soul.* She kept recalling those eyes. They were nothing short of unforgettable, a work of art. Florence thought they should have been captured on canvas and hung at a museum somewhere in Paris or London. Those stranger's eyes were... magnificent.

Piercing.

Deep.

Brimming with life, with emotion.

Green.

They were green. How could she have forgotten? They shone in the light like emeralds. The shine was so intense that at one point Florence thought they glowed, and that they might even glow in the dark. But as far as she recalled, they did not. Her memory of their in-the-dark shenanigans was still hazy.

But like she said that morning... "It'll come to me."

It would.

It *had* to.

She couldn't even imagine deciding to keep it—the baby was, for now, an "it" until she decided on their future—without talking to the guy who owned the penis that'd gone and impregnated her. And yes, that was exactly what he had done. HE impregnated HER. It didn't matter if she knew his name or not, or if she was wearing a short skirt that night, or even if she was the one who did the seducing—she didn't think she'd done the seducing—it takes two to tango, but only one dick shooting baby batter to make a baby.

So, if anyone was to take the "blame" for a single gal who worked as a waitress downtown while she figured her life out finding herself with a little cinnamon bun baking in her belly, it was Mr. No Name.

But... Florence had to admit she'd been moving slower than a minivan in the fast lane when it came to "figuring her life out." The diner gig was originally only meant to be a couple of months, six at the most. And now Florence was going on her third year, and she wasn't a mile closer to getting her shit together, meeting Mohamed at the top of the mountain to sing "Kumbaya," or making a single plan outside of washing her uniform and coming in for her next shift.

That was it. The whole of her life, and there was, she knew, a great big hole in it where something bigger was supposed to have gone. Florence thought she must've slept in the day they were handing out "greater purposes." She wondered how long she could go on being "happy" with her life, squeaking by financially, having random trysts with men who had lives, more exciting lives, outside of her bedroom. Although Florence had to admit, SHE probably was the excitement for more than one of her steady stable of studs. It was something, but still not a greater purpose. She was not called to be what a pearl-clutching Southern Baptist might call a "loose woman."

At the end of the day, Florence knew there was nothing loose about her. That shit was almost as tight as it was back in high school when she let Freddie Logan stick it in under the bleachers between Phys Ed and Chemistry. The break between classes was only three minutes, and Freddie needed less than one to finish.

Thankfully, it got better the more she did it, and the older she got. Sex got better, but her life kind of stalled going up the hill. Her tank ran out of gas and her engine wouldn't turn over. The thought of walking back down the hill to get a fresh can of gas, filling up her tank, and resuming her ascent to the top of the hill never crossed her mind. She just left her car on the roadside and went to the first place she saw—the diner. This diner.

And the rest, as they say, is history. Or, HER story.

But now, everything was different.

Or it could be.

Was she really thinking about working ten-hour shifts on her feet with a big old watermelon belly? Birthing a baby with medical insurance that wasn't worth the paper it was printed on and would just as soon let her die, bleeding in the streets from a gun shot wound before throwing her a Band-Aid as she bled out on Gold Street.

How would she pay... for any of it? Having "it," raising "it," feeding "it," clothing "it," daycare, babysitters, pediatricians, dentists, eye doctors, preschool, high school, college, graduate school, med school...

How the fuck does ANYONE pay for all that?

Florence rubbed at her no longer empty parking lot, knowing it was too soon to feel a kick or a punch, but wondered if "it" could feel her touch. Probably not, since it was still just a cluster of cells, coming together to grow and bake, and over time somehow go from being something that looked like cottage cheese in a petri dish to coming out—oh, she forgot about that part... the coming out of her—to coming out of her a fully formed human baby. Science was, at its core, truly magical. Mother Nature had more up her skirt than Harry Blackstone had up his sleeve.

She took her break in the alley behind the diner. It was clean, mostly, and rat-free, mostly. And it was quiet. Somehow, being surrounded by those two walls just drowned out all the other noise. The honking horns. The loud conversations. Telephones ringing. For just a few minutes at a time, Florence could forget the city, forget the diner, and forget herself. There, in the alleyway, Florence was free to dream.

And that's just what she planned on doing.

Taking the first train to La-La Land and dreaming the best daydream her tired, over-worked brain could throw at her.

And maybe, just maybe, she'd remember something else about the baby's daddy. Maybe a name would come to her, or something more, like what he did for a living, where he was from... something like that.

Or maybe, more likely, she'd be frustrated and stuck with nothing more than the stranger's piercing green eyes, staring down at her, out of the darkness.

—Die

"Nine miles to New York City."

Imogen screamed.

Amanda howled and shrieked with maniacal laughter. Her cheeks were painted red from her bloodied fingers. Toby slammed on the brakes. The tires SCREECHED as the SUV skidded off the road, narrowly missing a lightning strike. Their bodies lurched forward, testing the limit of the safety belts.

"Toby?"

Alex stared into Toby's wide, frightened eyes, and waited for her brother to answer, to say some words of comfort, as Olivia bled out in the rear seat.

"No, no, NO," Imogen screamed.

She unlocked her seat belt and was over the seat in a flash, sitting beside Olivia as she gasped and clutched at the knife sticking out of her chest. Blood spilled out of the corner of her mouth. Large drops of crimson painted her face, having sprayed outwards and upward after the mortal blow had been delivered.

"Fuck, no, no, no," Imogen cried.

She fumbled with Olivia's seat belt, unable to press the latch in to unlock the belt. Finally, after several tries, in a fit of fury and strength, Imogen tore the belt apart, easing Olivia out of it and lowering her onto her back gently.

"Livs? Livs? Can you hear me?"

Olivia nodded her head weakly. Blood spat out of her mouth when she tried to speak, the words drowning in a pool of thick blood. Imogen's face was covered with Olivia's blood, but she didn't wipe at it. In that moment, she hardly felt it.

"Toby," Alex said softly. "How're we going to win now, Toby?"

"I don't know, Alex. I... don't know," Toby said, his voice trailing off, signaling defeat.

"YOU FUCKING CAN'T," Amanda yelled, covering her mouth with her blood-soaked hands. She laughed into them and kicked her legs about wildly as though she were seizing. "It's over, Tobes. YOU. LOST."

Amanda roared with a crazed, intense laugh. It didn't belong to her. The laughter belonged to the beast.

"Oh no, Toby! NO," Alex cried.

Imogen surveyed the SUV, feeling Toby's eyes burning holes into her skin as Alex looked to her brother, pleading for him to offer words of hope, words of comfort. And then there was Amanda, whose eyes had gone blacker than the night outside and whose face wore a mask of red—Olivia's blood.

Imogen wanted to throw up. It was all about the game. The fucking game. They didn't care about her. They didn't care about Olivia. Alex was crying and whining like a baby because they thought they'd lost the game, which, admittedly, would suck because that would mean the end of the world.

She could tell from Toby's vacant stare that he was thinking along the same lines as Alex. Again, it was all about the game. Maybe he was strategizing. Coming up with a new plan. A way to bounce back and snatch a victory out of Sandra's monstrous, malformed hands. Or maybe he, too, was quietly deflating at the inescapable realization that all was lost. Losing again, when they'd gotten so close.

Imogen saw much, but the one thing she did not see was a single tear being shed FOR Olivia, for her sister, whose life was rapidly slipping away. No one mourned for the life that was, or the future being taken away from her as she coughed and choked on her own blood. And Imogen was sure that in the end, none but her would even remember Olivia's name.

Olivia Christine Lovejoy.

Her mind filled with rage. The energy coursed through her, igniting and charging every cell in her body. Imogen Rockwell was awake now. Wide awake. She'd been good and played by the rules, conserved her energy, didn't use her abilities for frivolous entertainment. She'd respected her gifts, and she'd respected the rules.

But now, Imogen Rockwell had no fucks left to give, and she was making her own rules.

"Hold on, Livs," Imogen said, taking Olivia's wet, limp hand in her own. They were now connected literally by blood. "Hold on."

In that instant, two things happened at the same time. One seen, and one unseen.

First, the door closest to Amanda blew right off and away, as though it had been torn off from the outside or pushed with so much force from the inside that it broke off. Either way, Amanda shrieked. She looked at the missing door, and then at Imogen, whose eyes were glowing red.

And second, Imogen and Olivia went to their special place.

A Table for Two

"I'm dead, aren't I?" Olivia asked, taking a sip of her coffee.

Imogen wiped at her eyes and shook her head.

"No."

"But I'm dying, right? It's only a matter of time, and given how much blood…"

Olivia saw the color drain out of Imogen's face and let the thought end there.

"Well," she said, "I don't think I have a lot of time left. Do you?"

Imogen shook her head.

"Then… why are we here?" Olivia asked, holding up her empty mug of coffee. "Hey, Flo! Can I get a—"

"Sure, d-d-dear," Flo said, appearing at the table's edge with a fresh, full pot of coffee. She refilled Olivia's mug and then looked at Imogen. "And you, dear?

"No, Flo. I'm alright, thanks," Imogen said, eyeing the full cup on the table in front of her.

"Alright then, d-d-dear. You let me know if you change your mind," Flo said. A second later, she was behind the counter, wiping it down with a wet rag.

"Huh, Imogen always has a second cup of coffee at home," Olivia joked, riffing on *Airplane!*—that famous movie from the early eighties they both loved so much.

"Well, then maybe you'd like to tell me why you brought us here if it isn't for the coffee," Olivia said, taking a long sip. "Damn, that's a fine cup o' coffee."

Imogen stared blankly at Olivia, who despite knocking on heaven's door back in the real world, seemed in good spirits.

"Because I thought this was a better ending. I thought it might—"

"Hurt less," Olivia said, picking up the sentence where Imogen had left off, unable to say the final words.

Imogen nodded her head.

"Yes."

"Here. Have some p-p-pie, d-d-dear," Flo said, sliding two pieces of hot apple pie with a mountain of whipped cream on top across the table. The little plates stopped perfectly in front of Imogen and Olivia. "On the house, of course."

"Thanks, Flo," Olivia said.

"Don't mention it," Flo said, nodding her head. Her coiffed hair remained perfectly in place. "And you know what that they say? Pie—"

"—makes everything better," Olivia said, joining in with Flo for the punchline.

"Eat up, girls. You're gonna need your strength."

Flo winked, and then she once again stood behind the counter, dabbing some invisible spot on the counter with her rag.

"Out, out, damned spot," Flo mumbled under her breath.

Olivia dug right into the pie. She frowned at Imogen, who sat pouting on her side of the booth.

"Seriously? You're not going to take a bite?"

Imogen pushed the plate away.

"You know," Olivia said, swallowing a mouthful of Flo's apple pie, the best in the county. "If this is my last meal? I'm okay with that."

"I don't know how you can be like that," Imogen said gruffly. "At a time like this."

"Well," Olivia said, stopping to wipe at her lips with a paper napkin, "why don't you tell me what we're really doing here?"

"I need... I need to keep you here... for a while," Imogen said.

"For how long, Imo?"

"I don't know, exactly," Imogen said, finally unable to resist Flo's coffee any longer. She emptied the mug into her mouth in one gulp. "Until it's over, I guess."

"Why are we doing this?"

"You know why, Livs."

Olivia cleared bits of pie from her teeth using the tip of her tongue.

"Yeah... yeah, I guess I do," Olivia said.

She reached across the table and held out her hand to Imogen, who took it in her own.

"You've been the best sister I could've ever asked for, Imo," Olivia said. She wrapped her fingers around Imogen's hand and squeezed. "I mean that. The best."

"No, Livs," Imogen cried, placing her free hand on top of Olivia's and resting it there gently. "You were."

Olivia smiled, small at first, but it quickly exploded until her whole face beamed.

"Damned right I was."

Tears rolled down Imogen's face as she stared into her sister's eyes. Her long, lost sister, whom she'd known for all of fifteen minutes of her life. It'd been longer, of course, but it felt like no time at all. Not enough time. It seemed so unfair for it to end this way, so Imogen would stash a part of Olivia in the diner, keep a drop of her energy alive, tucked safely away from Toby and Alex. Here, in this place, Olivia felt no pain. Not even as death took her in its embrace on the other side. Here, in their special place, Olivia would live on. Her power would live on, charging until it was fully restored. Replacing all that Toby had stolen from her.

Toby and Alex may not have been able to win the game without Olivia, but Imogen knew she could win WITH Olivia. With her power.

"This isn't goodbye, Livs."

"I know, Imo."

"I will find you again. I promise."

The sisters squeezed each other's hands tenderly as their eyes filled with tears. And while this should have felt like an "all is lost moment" for the twins, it didn't. It was a "goodbye for now" moment, and they both felt it.

"I WILL find you again."

A Sort of Homecoming

Imogen threw Amanda out of the SUV and onto the fiery, broken road. She did this not with her hands, which were stained red with her sister's blood, but with an easy, simple flex of her wonderful Ivy-League brain. Amanda flew out, seat belt still attached, and landed hard on her ass. The tie string of her hoodie caught fire, and she frantically swatted at it to put the fire out.

"Imogen, don't," Toby cried, opening the driver's door.

Before he could move or step out, the door slammed shut and locked.

Imogen.

Imogen had stormed out of the car and was now standing in the middle of the fiery road.

"Don't, Imogen! Don't," he shouted again, but Imogen raised a hand and everything around her fell still. For a moment, even the ash seemed to stop falling, and the thunder ceased its booming.

"Shut up, Toby," Imogen said, without looking back.

Her eyes were fixed on Amanda, who was still on her ass, hoodie smoking but no longer on fire, and she was backing up like a crab, using her arms and legs.

Imogen took a deep breath and her eyes pulsed and shone

brighter.

"I got this," she said, stepping toward Amanda. "I got this...
"

"Don't touch me, bitch," Amanda screamed. Bits of broken gravel and rocks cut into her hands as she backpedaled to no avail.

There was no escape for Amanda. The open road was engulfed in flames, torn in two by a giant fissure, which shat out flames of its own. Hel was punching its way into this world. Hel was rising from the bowels of the earth. Mother was getting closer.

Imogen felt her. Mother. She'd never known her, but now she felt her presence. She was everywhere. The thing in the sky... that was Sandra. But this thing coming out of the ground? The things crawling their way out of the pit? That was Mother. That was Lilith.

Alex pounded her little fist on the window, shouting at Imogen, "Don't waste your energy!"

But Imogen silenced her, too.

They'd been strong, Toby and Alex.

But right then, right there, standing on the edge of Hel as fire and ash fell from the sky, Imogen just might have been the strongest Miller left in the game. And Imogen knew, somehow, she knew, that Mother would be proud.

"Don't come any closer, bitch! Or I'll... or I'll..."

Amanda searched the ground for a weapon. The best she came up with was a handful of pebbles, which she threw at Imogen's face. They fell back to the ground, none breaking through Imogen's energy field. Amanda found a larger rock. The kind hipsters and granola-crunchers might have in their front yards beside their stupid-ass gnomes. She struggled to pry it off the ground as her hands dripped blood from all the cuts they'd sustained during her reverse crab walk.

But finally, she had the rock, and Amanda stumbled to her feet. She held the rock in her trembling arms. Held it over her head and prepared to shoot her shot just as something snapped in her right arm. A bone. In her forearm. A loud SNAP! Amanda howled. The rock fell to the ground, dead and limp.

Then another SNAP! Followed by a CRACK! This time in her other left forearm.

She looked down at her arms, which hung like gummy worms at the elbow, swinging uselessly from side to side. Amanda went to scream, but something else CRACKED and BROKE inside of her.

"Oh my god, stop it, you bitch! STOPPPPPPPP!"

CRACKKK!

POP!

SNAP!

CRACKKKKK!

SNAP!

POP!

Every bone in Amanda's legs was broken. They tore through the skin and poked out like little toothpicks in those "meat" samples cheap Chinese takeout restaurants hand out in shopping malls. Blood pooled under her feet as bone after broken bone cut through her skin.

Amanda fell to the ground like a broken toy. Every part of her was busted beyond repair. She gasped and cried, spitting out blood with every exhalation. Tears cleaned a path in the blood—both her's and Olivia's—on her face.

Amanda was down, beat, and broken. Death, on its pale horse, was riding to her.

But Imogen wasn't done with her yet.

She held out her hand in front of her, pointing it toward the mangled mass of flesh that had been a teenage girl only moments before. First, she flexed her fingers out. Out and open. Amanda's body jerked and rolled backwards. She yelped like an injured puppy.

Imogen squeezed her fingers into a tight fist. This locked her mind around what was left of Amanda's destroyed body. She squeezed her fist tighter, then tighter, and then tighter still until her nails had dug so far into her palm that they should've come through the other side. Drop after drop of her blood dripped onto the broken road beneath her. Imogen gripped the wreckage of Amanda with her mind, and dragged her across the roadside, from where she had been thrown out of the SUV, dragged her down the road until the flesh had been torn from her face, arms, and legs. The pitiful thing gasped and wheezed, and Imogen moved her hand to the flaming sky. Amanda's near lifeless body followed, rising off the ground until it hovered some twelve feet in the air.

Imogen moved her hand across the road, toward the flaming crevice. Moving it, and Amanda's body, toward the open mouth of Hel. Before she dropped Amanda into the fiery pits, where countless hordes of unknown demons and other monstrosities were crawling to the surface, all likely her kin, she broke Amanda in two at the waist like a doll.

There wasn't much of a crunch, since most of the crazy girl had been broken already, but she gave one final admirable crunch before Death took her. Imogen opened her hand, and the two halves that used to make up Amanda Grimmes fell into Hel where she belonged.

Imogen worried for a moment that even Hel might not take

Amanda, but then a burst of flames from the pit, almost like a well-fed, satisfying belch, shot into the sky and Imogen knew she'd seen the last of that crazy bitch.

As Hel accepted its offering, devouring the bits wholly and completely, somewhere else, somewhere not far from where Imogen, Toby and Alex now stood, the beast sighed.

Oh, you stupid girl. What did you go and do that for?

Well, I'm not going to let myself get... all broken up over it, the thing said, laughing at its own joke. *It's time to come home, Toby. Wait until you see what I've got in store for you.*

You Can Never Go Home Again, Part 1

"Which way is it?" Imogen asked Toby and Alex.

Alex and Toby did not speak, only looked at each other.

"Don't do that," Imogen said, irritated. "Use your words. Talk to ME."

Toby pointed to the broken road ahead. It was lit by a fiery pathway that stretched on for miles into the darkness. The fire led straight to a massive cloud that shot down lightning and burned from somewhere deep within its fluffy mass.

Imogen's head turned, and she studied the dark cloud formation in the sky ahead. Only minutes before, the crazy Mexican bitch had tried to run them off the road.

That crazy Mexican bitch...

Imogen turned to look behind her, looking for any sign of the crazy lady or her shit box of a car. Instead, there were only thick clouds of smoke as fire consumed the road and the long crevice that stretched on and on for miles in the distance. Imogen wondered if it stretched across the country, if anything was left of it. She wondered what unholy things were, at that very second, climbing their way out of the gates of Hel.

"The gates are open, you better pray," Imogen sang softly. Dakotah Dark. "The gates of Hel are open. It's time to play. You can never go home again."

Imogen turned back to where the road led straight on to Valhalla, to where Sandra and the end awaited, and she started walking. She didn't care if Toby and Alex walked along with her or if she went to her death alone. Imogen just wanted this nightmare, this stupid game, to be over. Maybe for it all to be over. What use did she have for a world where she was alone? With Olivia dead, the only one left Imogen could trust was herself. And after what she did to Amanda Grimmes, Imogen wasn't sure how much she trusted her own judgment at the moment. Still, Imogen reassured herself that the bitch had it coming. An eye for an eye, isn't that what the Bible said? Well, Imogen took more than an eye, and she took more than her pound of flesh. And she was satisfied. For the moment.

"We have to talk about... everything, Imogen," Toby started, following her. "Wait!"

"You can either stay here and have your little private jokes and private conversations with Alex, or you can come with me so we can win this thing. Either way, I don't care."

"It's not that simple, Imogen."

Alex stepped up to the plate, saying, "We can't beat her. Not without Olivia. That's why we sought you out in the first place. To win."

"And here I thought it was so we could all have a nice family reunion. Maybe a picnic or barbecue in the park. Eat some hot dogs. Toss a frisbee."

"Imogen—"

"No, don't," Imogen said, holding up her hand. "You found me... US... to save the world. To stop Aunt Sandra from winning. So, are we going to go down quietly? Sit here and wait for that darkness to take us to god knows where? Or are we going to fight?"

"Fight," Alex said, turning to Toby. "We haven't won in a long, long time. It's our turn. Come on, Toby. Let's go home one last time."

You can never go home again.

Alex held out her little hand, and Toby took it in hers.

Imogen walked ahead of them, never looking back, not even a quick glance over her shoulder. Her eyes were fixed dead ahead. Fixed on the monstrous dark cloud calling to her. With every crack of thunder, with every flash of lightning, Imogen heard the thing's voice in her head.

This isn't going to end the way you think it is.

She wondered how many miles it was to New York City, to Valhalla, the famed hall where fallen Viking heroes went after they died in glorious battle. Maybe it was no coincidence that they were walking right into the mythic hall, walking straight to their deaths. Maybe winning meant losing. She'd already given all that she had to the game. All that was left was herself, and Imogen didn't know if she was willing to give that to save a world she no longer cared about. What was the use of saving a world she didn't have a place in?

Imogen Rockwell thought about something else on the walk to Valhalla.

She thought about the game. That stupid game. How did her entire life, everything in her memories, every moment—the good and the bad, come down to just turns in a game? How had none of it been real? She felt real. The memories felt real. All of this... felt real. How the fuck was it all a game?

"Toby," Imogen called over her shoulder, but her eyes never left the looming place where Sandra Miller awaited.

"Yeah, Imogen?" Toby asked. He sounded surprised to hear Imogen's voice. She hadn't so much as said "boo" since they'd started walking. It'd been a long, quiet walk so far.

"If everyone is just a player in a game..."

"Yeah?"

"And we, the Millers, are the ones playing it..."

"Yeah..."

Imogen stopped walking.

This isn't going to end—

"Who made the game? Who made the rules?"

Toby did not respond. He didn't have to.

The ground beneath their feet quaked as the crevice grew larger. Chunks of the road broke up and fell into the crevices open, hungry mouth. Towers of flames erupted from deep within the Hel mouth as it digested the bits of road.

The gates of Hel are open.

And she is coming home...

The Final Interlude: What's the Use of Dreamin'?

Florence Johnson was dead on her feet. She hadn't wanted to work a double, but Billy, her boss, had guilted her into it. He was a silver fox, with a thick, slick mane of gray hair and a silver tongue that could convince the devil to sell HIM his soul. He was good. A smooth talker. And, once again, Florence had been hooked and reeled in.

It was going on 11 p.m., and she'd just turned off the twitchy, neon "OPEN" sign in the window. Everyone had abandoned her, as usual, and left her to clean up and reset the diner for the morning rush alone. The joint used to be twenty-four hours, but then the pandemic hit, and nothing was ever really the same after. Twenty-four hours dropped to eighteen hours when business owners tallied up how much money they were wasting staying open all night. Past 11, the streets were a ghost town of shuttered windows and "CLOSED" signs.

On paper, it was a solid business move. But overnight workers, night owls, and writers who spent all night at the counter drinking coffee had nowhere to go. Truckers had fewer places to stop to get a hot meal at 3:30 in the morning. But, if somebody, somewhere, was saving a dime, it was okay, right? No reason to care about the rest of us. The almighty dollar is king.

Florence scrubbed at the counter. Those high schoolers who'd been in at 8 really did a job on it. They'd sat there for over an hour downing burgers and fries. The fries were covered in so much ketchup that they were barely visible under all that red stuff. And now, the counter was speckled with gobs of dried-up ketchup.

"Little shits," Florence mumbled as she scrubbed at a particularly stubborn blot. "You'd think they'd never used a napkin before."

It'd been a long day, full of low tippers, handsy men, condescending women, and loud, obnoxious children. They came in all shapes, sizes, and ages. The kids in strollers fussed, screaming bloody murder and throwing their Cheery-OhOhs onto the floor.

One little... darling got some of his cereal on the ceiling. Florence was not getting that rickety ladder to clean that shit up. She figured eventually they'd either dry out and fall off, maybe crashing into someone's bowl of chicken noodle soup, or those damned OhOhs would fossilize up there and become part of the décor along with the other bits of grease and food that'd managed the voyage from table to ceiling.

The toddlers had been insufferable. *I want this. I don't want that. Why'd you get me this? I hate that. I'm not hungry. I'm so hungry. Why don't they have—*

Listening to that noise all day, Florence understood why some mothers ate their young in the wild. She had no doubt some mothers just got tired of listening to that shit all day and it fried their last good nerve.

And then there were the tweens and the teens. They were the worst of the worst. Know-it-alls. They knew everrrrryyyyything, about everything—except what the hell they wanted to order. *Do I want... waffles or do I want a gyro?*

How the hell should I know? I only work here, Florence wanted to say as she tapped her pen on her pad, doing her best to keep a smile painted on her impatient face.

But what pissed Florence off the most about the tweens and teens was that they knew better. They knew to clean up after themselves. Pick up that French fry that got away from their plate. Clean up the globs of ketchup, mustard, or mayo that they somehow covered the table or counter with. She wondered if sometimes they didn't just pour the stuff onto the table directly just to fuck with her. Give her more work to do.

And they were the worst tippers. Mommy and Daddy gave them $20 to get something to eat, so they spent fourteen and change, kept the five, and left her the change. Not to mention a pig sty to clean up.

Babies turn into toddlers who turn into tweens who turn into teens who turn into young adults who turn into adults. That was the routine. Even Jesus had been a diaper-shitting toddler once upon a time, although those were part of his "missing years" in the Bible. Florence figured they were left out for a good reason—because even Jesus had been an insufferable twat as a teen.

She wasn't a believer, but thought it made for a good story. A story with a lot of holes and inconsistencies, but a good story none the less. Florence wasn't a great believer in much beyond what she could see, touch, taste, smell, and hear—like ketchup stains on her counter. She believed that was a pain in her already sore ass.

And believed there was a life growing inside of her.

A cluster of cells that'd make up a fetus that'd come out the other side a baby, which would grow into a toddler, and so on. She didn't believe she had a soul or any of that superstitious mumbo jumbo, nor did she think there was anything morally wrong with deciding to terminate the pregnancy. It was unplanned, and she had no idea who the father really was beyond remembering he had the greenest eyes. That wasn't a lot to go on.

Maybe she wasn't ready to be a mother. Maybe she just didn't want to be one. Some women, many women, had no desire to birth or raise a kid until they moved out, hopefully before they turned thirty-five, only for the kid to stop calling or visiting—except for birthdays and Christmas.

It was a life Florence wasn't sold on. Her life might not be perfect, but it was hers. She was free to pick up and go anytime she wanted to. Onto some place new. Some place greener, with more trees and more space. Get away from the city and find a small patch of peace and quiet somewhere nice where she didn't have to be on her feet for eighteen hours and didn't have to spend an hour scrubbing ketchup off the counter.

Somewhere out there had to be a better life.

A different life.

The kind of life she sometimes dreamed about.

Exotic places. Exciting jobs. Friends. Happy hours. Family that didn't judge and chastise her every opportunity they got.

Yes, Florence was convinced there had to be more to it all... than this.

But she also wondered what use there was in dreaming when dreams rarely ever came true for people like her. Knocked-up single waitresses with the losing lottery ticket in their purse.

No, Florence was through with dreaming.

From now on, she'd deal only with the cold, hard reality of

her life and the sometimes-harsh world in which she lived. Dreams were for suckers, and Florence Johnson was no sucker.

But she *was* pregnant. That was her reality now. And time was running out for her to make her choice—to be a mother, or not to be a mother.

An hour later, Florence Johnson walked home in the pouring rain. There wasn't a single taxicab in sight, and as luck would have it, she'd left her umbrella at home by the front door. Rain had not been in the forecast, nor had a baby been in hers.

By the time Florence walked in her front door, she felt confident in her decision.

Only time would tell if she'd made the correct one for once in her life.

You Can Never Go Home Again, Part 2

The miles counted down.

6

5

4

3

2

1

Sandra eased up on her meteorological assault, allowing Toby, Alex, and Imogen to follow the opening gates of Hel straight to their final destination—

Home.

The house of horrors on St. Augustine place, or what was left of it.

Broken and faded police tape caught the wind and flew like a kite. Most of the windows on the first and top floors were broken. One of the front porch steps was split in two. "Monsters" was clumsily spray-painted on the mailbox. Weathered stickers decorated the front door, most of them long faded—

Do not enter

Condemned—were just a few of the words still visible.

"This is it," Imogen said, standing at the end of the driveway. "THIS is Valhalla?"

Toby nodded.

"It's home."

"I don't know," Imogen began. "I was just expecting… more somehow. I mean, did dead Vikings really come all the way to the Bronx to die in a generic split-level that isn't even an open plan?"

Toby laughed and gave Imogen a small wink.

"It's way more impressive… on the inside."

Suddenly, the lights turned on inside. The broken glass on the windows repaired itself. The porch step was made whole again. The stickers vanished from the front door, and the graffiti on the mailbox faded away until only "The Millers" remained. The dead flowers in the garden sprang back to life. The tree in the yard was instantly covered in thick, green foliage.

The Miller House, the house of horrors, had woken up from its long, deep sleep.

The Miller house was alive.

The front door opened slowly. Light from inside spilled onto the front porch. A figure emerged from within—tall, well-dressed, neat hair, and wearing a fancy, fluffy vicuna coat. It stuck a cigarette into a long, black, old-fashioned holder and it seemed to light itself. The tip glowed orange as the thing on the porch took a drag, then exhaled.

"The gates are open, you better pray," Imogen sang softly. "The gates of Hel are open. It's time to play. You can never go home again."

Sandra Miller smiled. "Welcome to Valhalla, Imogen Rock-well."

III

STAYCATION 3.0

The Other Side of the Rainbow

"I can tell you're disappointed." Sandra smirked. "It's long overdue for a remodel. Maybe you can, I don't know, fix her up or spruce her up. Give a little of the modern woman's touch."

Inside the Miller house was transformed. With Imogen, Toby, Alex, and Sandra present, the house revealed its true form—Valhalla. The Great Hall was vast, spirals and archways reaching into the darkness, disappearing from view. Candelabras inadequately cast light up and down the endless empty corridors and passageways. Portraits painted in oil on canvas decorated the walls, hundreds, maybe thousands of them. The faces weren't clear, as though they were being blurred out on a newscast. Nor were the names readable. But Imogen knew they were all Millers. Every last one of them.

"Jesus, how many of... us are there?" she asked as her eyes wandered over the portraits.

"Oh, darling," Sandra said, stepping toward Imogen. "We are legion."

"The Children of Lilith," Toby said, looking up at the portraits.

Sandra laughed.

"The DAUGHTERS of Lilith. You're not a real boy, Pinocchio," Sandra snarled.

Toby's face reddened. His hands flew up, and Alex did the same.

"CROA—" they started.

Sandra clapped her hands together and laughed until she started coughing.

"That won't work in here, Toby," Sandra sneered, leaning down to whisper in Toby's ear. "And you'd know that if you were a real boy."

Toby went to flex his mind, but Sandra was one step ahead of him. She'd noticed his tell—a small wrinkle at the bridge of his nose. It always appeared when he was about to tap into his powers. Without hesitation, in a flash, Sandra threw Toby against one of the hall's far walls. His arms and legs were stretched out forming an "X" on the wall. She had him pinned.

Alex screamed, "Toby!"

She went to run to him, but Sandra held her in place, wrapping her long, invisible fingers around Alex's small frame. Alex fought back, resisting, but it was futile. She was caught like a roach in one of those roach motels.

"This is too easy." Sandra laughed. "Is this all you've got, Alex?"

Alex groaned. Toby hung his head low.

"Don't kill them, please, Aunt Sandra," Imogen said, rushing to Sandra, whose true form had revealed itself. Like a snake shedding its skin, Sandra Miller slowly unveiled the monster that hid beneath the skin suit. Her arms morphed into tentacles. Her feet became the devil's hooves. Slime dripped down the length of her body as she opened her mouth wide, wide enough to swallow an entire world. Rows of sharp teeth glistened in the candlelight.

When at last Sandra Miller's transformation was complete,

Imogen's hands went to her mouth, stifling whatever sound tried to make a run for it. Imogen always knew Sandra was a monster, but KNOWING and SEEING are two very different things. Staring at the beast, her Aunt Sandra, Imogen cried. She didn't know how such a foul, unholy thing could exist. The very sight of her made Imogen sick. It made Imogen question everything she thought she knew; everything she believed about heaven, hell, and the earth itself.

"Oh, my dear," Sandra chortled. Her hooved feet clacked as she moved toward Imogen. "We're ALL monsters on the inside."

Sandra's head whipped to Toby and Alex. She waved a tentacle and in an instant their skin peeled away, revealing not muscle and bone underneath but horrid, nightmarish forms with flaming eyes. Demons from Hel masquerading as people.

Imogen screamed.

"Welcome to the family, dear." Sandra howled with laughter as Imogen's screams echoed through the empty hall. "Sorry your sister couldn't make it. But we all have to make sacrifices in times like this, don't we?"

Rogue

Joanne Garriga eventually made it to St. Augustine Place. She'd sworn after that night, after they finally sold the house and moved away, that she'd never step foot back here again. But that had been before all... this.

Jesu Christo.

In her wildest dreams, Joanne never thought she'd be standing on the edge of the end of the world, carrying what might just turn the tide in the final battle... in the final game... to either save the world or destroy it.

Señor Toby was counting on her.

But so were the Miller bitches.

Someone had lied to her. Maybe they both had. But in the end, did it really matter? She had to choose a side. Throw a match on the world as the Miller bitches poured gasoline on it or do what Señor Toby told her to do. Choose to save the world. She'd seen beyond the veil. She knew what was coming if the Miller bitches won the game, and she knew what was coming if Señor Toby won. She might just get her old life back, or something like it. And her kids. They were what she was doing this for. Now that she could remember them, she wanted them back.

She wanted it all back. Her busybodying. Her spying. Her

snooping.

But, to get it back, she'd have to decide which side she was on. She had to decide once and for all who'd been lying to her. Decide who it was that had taken her kids away. Who it was that changed the game while they were playing it.

Joanne knew they were both probably nothing but filthy liars. And after all she'd been through, the things she'd done to find Imogen and Olivia, she wanted to kill them both. But one side had to win, or else her kids would be lost forever.

She walked up the drive, stepped onto the front porch, and turned the doorknob. A surge of electricity shot through her body as Joanne turned the knob and the door popped open. She shielded her eyes from the blinding light and stepped into the house of horrors for the last time.

Playdate

"Her? Really, Toby? You brought her into this," Sandra said, eyeing Joanne with near disinterest. "That's like bringing a dildo to a Supperwear party. Sure, it might be useful when the party's over, but mostly it's just—"

Sandra tossed Joanne aside. She slid down a long hallway, howling as she traveled the length of the floor.

"— NOT NEEDED," Sandra finished. She turned back to Imogen. "Now, where were WE, dear?"

"You were going to tell me why I don't fucking kill you right here."

Sandra threw her monstrous head back and laughed. It resonated through the hall, sounding more and more terrifying as it made the rounds.

"You can try, dear. But I'll have you skinned, basted and cooked before you can—"

FLEX.

Imogen flexed her mind, and Sandra recoiled. A small trickle of blood oozed from a wound on Sandra's shoulder.

"Ooh, aren't you the real surprise of the evening? A real fighter. I've been at this a long—"

FLEX.

Imogen knocked the wind out of Sandra, sending the beast

tumbling off her hooved feet. Her miscreated body flew back twenty feet until she landed hard on her back.

The thing laughed.

"Oh, I see. You like to play rough." Sandra grinned, getting to her feet. "I can play ROUGH!"

FLEX!

Imogen's head snapped back as though it'd taken a punch. When her head returned to the center, a thin trail of blood ran down her lips from her nose.

"You want to play?" Imogen asked, taking a battle stance, her hands at the ready. Sandra matched Imogen, preparing herself for the next assault. "Let's play."

Joanne's Box

Joanne Garriga watched the monsters battle from the shadows. That Miller bitch, the one that had put the box inside of her all those years ago at the house of horrors, she had a lot of power. She'd seen its power in Vermont when it made her do terrible things. Awful things. She'd seen its true form then. A devil hiding in plain sight.

She recognized it now as the thing was in the air. Crackling wildly like a frayed electrical wire on the side of the road. Sparks danced through the air like little ballerinas, their tutus ablaze with fire.

Sandra had Imogen pinned to the floor. She stood over her, roaring as her mouth opened to gigantic proportions. But then Imogen disappeared and reappeared on the other side of the Great Hall. The beast howled and gave chase, tearing across the shimmering floor. Its red eyes fixed on Imogen.

Imogen stood motionless, spreading her arms, acting like a red cape for the charging bull. As Sandra closed in, Imogen sent a wave of electricity into the beast's head. It flew back, screaming in agony as its body soared through the air, landing at the feet of the still imprisoned Toby and Alex, bit of their human skin still clinging to their terrible true forms underneath as though they were paper dress up dolls not fully dressed.

When the beast stood, there was blood at its awful mouth.

Joanne cowered in the shadows. The big one was strong, but the little one... could it be that she was the stronger of the two? The strongest of them all? It appeared that way. Señor Toby sat pinned to the wall, as useless as a eunuch in a cathouse. Alex, too, was a mere spectator of the game, observing the blood sport taking place on the main floor.

But Joanne still had the box inside of her. She could open it. Unleash Hel. Change the course of the game. She wondered to what end? Who was trying to save the world, and who was trying to end it? Joanne needed to figure that out before she let the crazy out.

She'd need to wait just a little longer, linger in the shadows until she was sure. She hoped in the meantime neither of the Miller bitches killed the other. If anyone was going to get to do some killing, Joanne wanted her slice of that pie. A great big piece with whipped cream and cherries on top.

Confessions

Imogen Rockwell had the thing cornered. She'd made the floor disappear, open, revealing the fiery pits below. The beast clung to a tiny section of floor, holding on with its tentacles for its dear life.

As Imogen stared into the fire below, she had a terrible realization.

"This... isn't Valhalla," she said.

"No, my dear," Sandra grinned through a mouth of bloody teeth, "it's Hel."

"Hel?"

"Welcome home, Imogen Rockwell," Sandra said, holding her grip on what remained of the floor. "He didn't tell you what you were, did he?"

Imogen looked at her hands, running her eyes up the length of her arms. She wondered what it was that hid under her skin.

"Go on. See for yourself," Sandra encouraged, gripping the floor tighter, almost slipping for a moment there as the flames tickled her hooved feet.

"Don't, Imogen. Don't do it," Toby said, speaking for the first time in a long time.

Imogen looked at him and then at Alex.

"It's all been a game to you, hasn't it?"

Sandra laughed.

"Of course it has, my dear. Don't you even know why they brought you here?"

Imogen's eyes remained locked on the skin covering her arms and hands.

"They couldn't win without you. They're not strong enough, you see."

"Not strong enough?"

Imogen thought back to all she'd seen Toby and Alex do over the last few weeks, months. Had it all been an illusion? A deception? A *veil*?

Pay no attention to the man behind the curtain.

And then there'd been Olivia. Imogen had seen Toby sucking the energy from her sister. Was that how he did it? Was that how he stayed "strong"? Sucking the life out of another? Was he nothing more than an energy vampire?

"You saw for yourself, Imogen," Sandra said, reading Imogen's thoughts. "You know what he is, and what he did. Your sister... was food, nothing more."

Imogen scratched at the skin on her arms, gently at first, but then more savagely. Red claw marks appeared first and then blood as her fingernails tore through the soft flesh of her meat skin. Bits of her human skin hung off her body as the monstrous form underneath became visible. Parts of her human skin clung to her body, so the sight was truly horrific. A beast tearing its way through a human meat suit.

"And what about what YOU did, Aunt Sandra?"

Sandra felt her grip slipping. She felt the power; the rage surging in Imogen.

"You mean Olivia?"

"Yes," Imogen raged, tearing more of her flesh away, tearing down until a new layer of skin revealed itself. It was not human skin. It was the same ungodly skin that Sandra wore. The skin of a demon, a foul creature of Hel.

"I had to take her out of the game, you know that. I had to win, and it was the only way. The Bobbsey Twins over there don't have enough juice to power a blender. But you... and her... well, you could've ended it all."

"The game?"

The skin covering Imogen's arms fell to the ground in a bloody pile. Now her true form was revealed. The clawed hands at the end of a pair of long, reptilian-looking black arms.

"Oh no, my dear," Sandra laughed. "Ended this lovely world of ours. You see, that's been their plan all along. Hasn't it, Toby?"

Imogen looked at Toby and Alex, who seemed to shrink further into the wall that held them like flies in a spider web.

"Toby," Imogen roared, "I think you have some explaining to do!"

The ground trembled beneath Imogen's heavy steps. She crossed the distance between her and the Bobbsey Twins lightning fast. A mere thought, a mere FLEX of her mind, and she was there, standing in front of them, wielding the most dangerous and powerful weapon of all—her beautiful Ivy-League brain.

Alex went to talk, but Imogen sealed her mouth up. Sealed it by removing it entirely.

"Hush," Imogen said, closing in on Toby. "I was asking the Dream Lover here."

"Imogen..."

"Go on," Sandra called, clinging to the floor and clinging to her life. "Ask him! Ask him who wants to end the world,

Imogen! Ask him!"

"Tell me, Toby," Imogen said, rounding on him. Her face was nearly touching his. She felt his breath on her face, especially on the areas where she was shedding her human skin. "Is it true? Has this all been a lie?"

Toby said nothing. Imogen heard the rapid rhythm of his heart pounding in her ears.

"TELL ME!"

The Great Hall trembled and quaked. The floor, what remained of it, vibrated so violently that Sandra almost lost her grip and fell into the fiery pits below.

Imogen raised a hand to Toby's face. A look of terror and fear came over him as her hand moved closer. It appeared that Imogen was going to strike him with the back of her hand, but at the last second, she touched his cheek tenderly.

"I believed in you, Toby. I thought you were one of the good guys. I thought we were going to save the world... together. I thought..."

Flashes of memories ran through Imogen's mind all at once, playing in a loop—

Oliver. Snake Hill. Looking at the stars.

Janet. Joking about her wine consumption.

Ally Cat... just being Ally Cat. Freeze, you turkey! BAM! BAM! BAM!

The Gemeo Project. Click the sparkling tree graphic to begin your journey!

Olivia. Seeing her face for the first time. Knowing her before she knew her.

I'll find you again.

Imogen Rockwell didn't like liars.

"I need you to say the words, Toby. Were we ever trying to

save the world?"

Toby's head hung low. It was an answer, but Imogen still wanted to hear the words.

FLEX!

An imaginary hand wrapped around Toby's throat and squeezed HARD.

"WERE WE?"

Toby looked up and sneered defiantly.

"No."

Return to Sender

And there it was.

The truth, at last.

Joanne heard it loud and clear.

They all did.

Now it was time.

It was time to open the box inside of her and let the foul thing out.

It was time to set Mary Miller free.

Wild Thing

"Why, Toby? Why?" Imogen pleaded, shaking.

"So, we can be together," Toby indicated Alex. "Together forever. It's against the rules."

Imogen wanted to scream. She had a thousand feelings rushing to the surface, fueling her rage. The energy was coursing through her.

"But there's something else you should know, Imogen," Toby said, smiling devilishly.

"And what's that, Toby?"

Toby's hand suddenly broke free and wrapped around Imogen's throat.

"I'm not nearly as helpless as I let on," Toby whispered in her ear.

FLEX.

Toby tossed Imogen across the hall like she was one of those ugly Cabbage Patch dolls Janet collected. He released himself from the spider's web, and Alex joined him on the floor. They walked toward Imogen, whose only instinct was to back away.

"Well," Sandra groaned. "Shit."

"Did you really think you could hide her from me?"

FLEX.

An invisible hand struck the side of Imogen's face.

FLEX.

Then another.

Imogen looked up in time to see both Toby AND Alex had their demonic hands outstretched. It was a double assault. Their eyes slowly ignited until they glowed a solid, bright red.

FLEX.

Whatever it was, Imogen deflected it.

"Did you think I didn't know about your little 'special place'?"

FLEX.

Imogen rolled onto her side. The phantom assault missing her.

"Did you think you could hide in MY place? The diner? Stupid, stupid girl."

FLEX!

FLEX!

FLEX!

A giant, unseen pair of hands pounded onto the hallway of the Great Hall, the only solid stretch of flooring left intact there. Imogen had backed herself into it, retreating from Toby and Alex's assaults.

"You let me in. You both did."

FLEX!

That blow landed. Imogen's stomach. It knocked the wind out of her sails. She thought she heard something inside CRACK. Despite her newly revealed form, she was obviously still very vulnerable to attack.

"Dream Lover. I never left. I was there—"

FLEX!

This one landed on the back of her head. Imogen saw a circle of chirping birds flying over her head. Her Ivy-League brain rattled in her shattered skull.

"—a fly on the wall. Buzzing. Listening to every single word, every single thought."

"No!"

Toby's eyes shone brighter. His lips drew back into a snarl. Imogen thought he looked like a feral dog, like the ones in Mexico she'd only seen in pictures. Nasty. Foaming at the mouth. Rabid.

"Yes!"

"You know," a voice called out from the main chamber of the Great Hall.

Sandra.

"If you gave me a little help here, Imogen…"

Imogen's eyes went to Sandra.

She went to FLEX, but Alex pinned her to the ground as Toby made a beeline to Sandra, who clung to the tiny patch of floor for all she was worth. He stood over her, grinning triumphantly.

"You've lost, Aunt Sandra. There's nothing you can do now. It's time to end the game, once and for all. Every game has its ending."

Toby held up his hand, positioning it over Sandra Miller. She struggled to gain the higher ground, but to no avail. She knew the dogcatcher had cornered her, and she was as good as bound for the pound in the sky. Not far away, Imogen squirmed on the floor, trying in vain to break free of Alex's psychic grip, trying to make her aching mind FLEX. But the pain was too intense. The headache had her limping like a car with a blown-out tire. She'd need a spare if she was going to have any chance of re-joining the game.

"Say goodbye, Aunt Sandra," Toby said fiendishly, savoring

every word. "I'm going to love killing you."

But then, before Toby could FLEX his mind, focus his thoughts, another voice filled the hall. It came out of nowhere, but in the same direction where Alex had Imogen pinned—the endless hallway.

"Hello, little brother," the voice said.

A figure stepped out of the darkness.

It was Mary Miller, clutching a bloody knife in her hands.

"I've waited a long time for this."

Damned Fine Coffee

"Here, d–d–dear," Flo said, handing Imogen a steaming pot of fresh coffee. "Drink up. You'll need this."

Imogen brought the scalding hot pot of Joe to her mouth and downed it. Rivers of hot coffee spilled down her chin and dripped onto her bloodied shirt, but Imogen didn't stop until she'd gotten every drop out of the seemingly bottomless pot.

"That'll help... with your head," Olivia said. "I love your new look."

"When... when was he here?" Imogen asked Olivia, wiping her mouth with the back of her clawed hand.

"Not long ago."

Imogen figured Toby had drained the last of Olivia's energy just before he broke free of Sandra's grip.

"I'm sorry, Imo. I couldn't stop him."

"That's okay."

"How's it going on the other side?"

Imogen laughed.

"Not so good, Livs. But I have an idea. You in?"

"Ab–so–fucking–lutely!"

An instant later, Flo was at the counter, refilling the coffee maker.

"I'll put on a fresh pot."

Sibling Rivalry

"Jesus Christ, Joanne," Toby shouted into the darkness, but Joanne Garriga heard nothing. Her body had been torn to shreds, letting the thing inside of her out, and what was left of her lay splattered on a nice section of a darkened corner in the corridor. "I told you to keep her locked up!"

"Why, little brother," Mary said, inching closer, licking the blood off the blade with her tongue. "If I didn't know any better, I'd say you were scared."

"Joanne?"

Toby called into the dark hallway, but no reply came.

"Need a hand, Aunt Sandra?" Mary asked.

"No, I think I can hold on a little longer. Kill that little fucker, Mary, my special girl."

Mary launched herself at Toby, swinging the blade wildly.

Toby FLEXED.

And FLEXED.

And... FLEXED some more.

But nothing happened. Absolutely nothing.

Imogen, distracted by the unexpected turn of events, had inadvertently given Alex her mouth back.

"Toby? What's going—" Alex began but was interrupted.

Revived by Flo's elixir—the world's greatest cup of coffee,

loaded with enough caffeine to give an elephant a heart attack—Imogen sent Alex flying across the room. Alex crashed into the wall, splatting like a bug on a windshield. She shrieked, both in pain and surprise.

Alex screamed, "Toby!"

But Toby had his hands full, literally, with the undead Mary Miller, who had been waiting for this moment for a long, long time. She slashed at Toby, cutting into his monstrous palm, his forearm, his face. Hot blood splattered onto Mary's face, each new splatter making her howl even louder, even wilder.

Toby FLEXED.

Nothing.

Mary laughed knowingly.

"You have no power here," Mary shrieked, quoting *The Wizard of Oz*. "Don't you get it, little brother? You can't hurt me with your little mind tricks. I'm an NPC."

"What the fuck is that?" Imogen called, crossing the hall, walking on the empty floor like Jesus walked on water.

"NPC. Non. Playable. Character." Sandra cackled. "You took her out of the game, Toby. And you knew the rules. We can't interact with them anymore when they're 'out'. But I put her back in."

Mary howled and slashed at Toby, the blade cutting and slicing into him with ease.

"Toby," Alex cried, struggling to get to her feet, but Imogen threw her against the wall again, even harder this time.

"YOUUUU CAN'T HURT MEEEEEE, LITTLE BROTHER-RRRRR," Mary screamed with each thrust of the knife.

Toby fell onto his back. He FLEXED, hoping for a miracle, but none came. No one listens to the prayers of the damned. He shielded his face with his arms, feeling every slice of the knife tearing away at his meat suit, and cutting even deeper—deep down to where his true image hid.

"You can't hurt me, either, Toby," another voice called from the darkness.

"Grandma?" Toby and Alex asked at the same time.

Mary halted her assault. Imogen turned to the corridor, but held Alex in place.

Cast-Iron Cassie stepped out of the darkness, shaking her head.

"My, my, my. Look at the mess you've both made. You've been naughty. And you know what we do with naughty children?"

Toby grunted, sliding himself across the floor. Mary plunged the knife into his shoulder, holding him in place.

Cassie grinned. "We kill them."

Naughty Children

Cassie moved to Toby and Mary.

"I see you've got this one, Mary. You shouldn't be here. You're not really one of us, but I suppose you've earned your pound of flesh."

Then, Cast-Iron Cassie continued on to where Imogen had Alex pinned. She stopped to nod at Sandra.

"Sandra," Cassie said nonchalantly.

"Cassie," Sandra replied. "No, that's okay. I'm fine. I'll just hang around here. Don't help me out or anything."

"Don't be such a whiny baby, Sandra. You know how much I hate whining," Cassie said, without turning back to Sandra. "And you must be her. Imogen Rockwell. Daughter of Agnes Miller, and a Daughter of Lilith."

"You're... Cassie Miller?"

"She is," Alex said, intruding on the moment. "And she's a—"

"Quiet, you," Cassie said, once again sealing up Alex's mouth. "You always had such a smart mouth."

"Are you... 'out' as well?" Imogen asked.

"I am. Fucking Junior skewered me with reindeer antlers. Can you believe it? ME! Taken out by goddamned Christmas antlers!"

"It was pretty funny, Cas." Sandra laughed, still somehow clinging to the floor, but unable to get a solid enough grip to pull herself out. "I guess I don't need to do this—"

Sandra FLEXED, and a moment later she was standing beside Cast-Iron Cassie, Imogen and Alex.

"Took you long enough, Sandra," Cassie said, shaking her head.

"Well, it was dramatic, wasn't it?"

"You with the dramatics," Cassie laughed. "Now, what do you say we take out these two little shits, once and for all?"

"I like that idea," Mary Miller muttered, flicking her fingers over the handle of the knife.

"Oh, my dear little Mary," Cassie said, turning to Mary Miller. "Sweet, crazy little Mary… you're not invited."

FLEX.

Mary Miller exploded into countless pieces. Toby was covered in bits of the person who'd been his sister in the game so long ago, the game that they were all still playing.

"What happens if we… take them 'out'?" Imogen asked.

"Well, the game ends," Sandra said.

"You save the world, and we reset the game," Cassie added. *Croatoan.*

"Yes, and no," Sandra corrected Imogen. "You let me in, kiddo. What can I say?"

Imogen sealed her mind, throwing up lock after lock until she felt no trace of Sandra Miller poking around in there.

"I have to say, Imogen. I like the way you think," Sandra said, winking slyly at Imogen. "That word has a lot of power. With intention, it can reset the game. Give the winner the power to create a whole new world. Fashion it how they see fit. Reset the players. Give them new lives, new roles. Scatter the Millers in the wind. But it can also open a door to other games."

"There are... more than one?" Imogen asked, incredulously.

"We are... legion, Imogen. There are infinite games being played right now. This is just one of them.

"Are there... more of... ME out there?"

Sandra smiled but said nothing.

"There are more things in heaven and earth than are dreamt of in your philosophy, Imogen. Billy Shakespeare understood. He saw beyond the veil. He saw the infinite worlds out there. The infinite possibilities. Drove him a little mad, I think. We had to throw him a bone, so we made this world, where he's the most often quoted writer of all time."

"And not Marlowe," Cassie added.

Imogen thought for a second. The game was so close to ending.

But there was something off. Something missing.

"You said... winner."

Sandra nodded her monstrous head.

"Indeed. Winner."

"That means... there can be—"

"Only one," a booming voice called out, not from within the darkened corridors of the hall, but from the fiery pits of Hel.

A massive, clawed hand reached out of the fire. Then another. Slowly, the beast pulled itself out. Four long, curved horns adorned the top of her head. Tufts of red hair framed her long, narrow, pale face. Trails of black tears stained her face under her pitch-black eyes. And instead of eyebrows, there was a long row of what appeared to be dark beads or jewels. They sparkled in the firelight.

As she pulled herself out of the Pit, the trail of her long, black, see-through dress slithered on the floor like a serpent, THE serpent, the one in the Garden. Underneath her gown, her pale skin glowed. Her muscles tightened and relaxed with every breath as she walked. Her full breasts swayed with every stride.

"Hello, Mother," Sandra said, smiling.

Lilith, the Queen of Hel, had come home.

In Her Image, Part 1

"You've been naughty, my children. So very naughty," Lilith hissed.

"Mother, I—," Sandra went to say, but Lilith whipped her head to Sandra, and Sandra fell quiet. Her face drooped, like a child who'd just been scolded in the food court at the mall.

"What have you done? The game is out of control."

Alex said quietly, "I think we just need to—"

"Just need to WHAT, Alex? What is it you think you need to do?" Lilith roared. The earth trembled. The sky burst into a bright ball of flame. A symphony of cries came forth from the Pit. And music... familiar music.

The gates of Hel are open.

You can never go home again.

"Dakotah Dark," Imogen said under her breath.

Lilith turned to her and smiled, revealing rows of sharp, blackened teeth.

"A lullaby, to help me sleep. It calls to you, doesn't it?" Lilith asked Imogen.

"It does."

"Mmm," Lilith said, eyeing Imogen. "That's because you're special. You're not like the others. Mmm. You belong to Agnes. Where is she?"

"'Out'," Cassie replied. "She was... afraid you'd be mad, so she's..."

"Mmm," Lilith said, running her long, green tongue over her black front teeth. "Agnes always was so weak. I ought to have put a stronger spine in her."

"What are you going to do, Mother?" Toby asked, his eyes never looking directly at Lilith.

Lilith was on him in a flash. She wrapped her talons around the whole of Toby's face. A steady stream of thick, yellow drool spilled onto him.

"Keep that word out of your mouth," Lilith snarled. "I am not your mother."

Lilith squeezed her hand around Toby's head.

"I could crush you right... now."

She tightened her fingers around his head and squeezed even harder. Toby groaned. The sound muffled by Lilith's massive, long fingers.

"How many times must you be told, Alex? We don't make MEN."

Something came to Imogen then—

the Daughters of Lilith.

All the Millers with the gift were female.

"He's not a real boy. Pinocchio."

That's why Toby was an energy vampire. He wasn't really a Miller. He was a cluster of energy created by Alex. A companion. Toby was the Monster to Alex's Dr. Frankenstein. And maybe now that she'd built the perfect Monster, they wanted to end the world before the game reset and Toby went back to being nothing more than tiny, random particles of energy.

"And you... BOY," Lilith growled, spilling more saliva onto

Toby. "You have a debt to settle, yes? Did you think if you won the game, you'd not have to pay?"

Toby squirmed under her grasp.

"You don't reach into Hel, take something out without my knowing and not replace it."

"Mother, no," Alex cried. She moved to Lilith and Toby, but Lilith kept Alex in place.

"Those are the rules, my dear one. The game has rules. And I'd say you've broken nearly every one, my children."

Lilith looked up and down at her daughters. Eyeing them intensely, one by one.

"Except for... YOU," Lilith said, stopping at Imogen.

"I... I..." Imogen stammered.

Another thought came to her head.

"Am I... like him?" she motioned to Toby.

"Not real," Lilith clarified.

Imogen nodded, and Lilith shook her head. The serpent at the end of her dress slithered up beside Toby and hissed.

"But... they made me... us?"

Imogen indicated Toby and Alex, remembering how Agnes had once been barren, and the Bobbsey Twins had played god.

"You were taken from another game. You were always my offspring. But in this game, you were 'out'. And they brought you back in, from another game."

"Croa—"

Imogen started, but Lilith stretched a long finger over Imogen's lips.

"Don't say that word unless you mean it."

"Now, what to do with you, my naughty little children?"

Lilith turned her head to Toby and smiled.

"But first, Pinocchio. I believe Charon is waiting for you—"

Toby screamed, fought back against Lilith's powerful grip on his head. He thrashed and flailed, kicking and punching at her hand, but her grip only tightened. The serpent wrapped itself around Toby's legs and dragged him toward the Pit. Toby screamed louder as Lilith released his head.

"Say goodbye to your little friend, Alex," Lilith commanded.

"No, Toby," Alex cried. She tried to move her legs, but she was stuck in place. "TOBYYYYYYY!"

The serpent dragged Toby to the edge of the pit, releasing his legs. Toby stood, and made to run back to Alex, who made to run to him. But before Toby's legs could follow the impulse to flee, a long hand reached out of the Pit and grabbed a hold of Toby's leg.

As the arm reached up higher, Imogen saw the figure was dressed in a black robe. The hood obscured its face, or it just didn't have a face. It held Toby with one terrible hand, and in the other it grasped a long, old-looking wooden pole.

A shiny coin appeared in Lilith's hand, which she tossed to Charon, the Ferryman of Hel. Momentarily releasing the pole, he caught the coin. He nodded to Lilith, and the coin vanished. A second later, his hand once again gripped the pole.

Toby screamed as Charon dragged him down deep into the Pits of Hel, where he'd ferry him down the River Styx to meet his fate.

Alex cried, covering her face with her hands. By now, her meat suit was shedding, and her own monstrous form was nearly fully revealed.

"And now... what to do with you, my naughty, naughty children? Mmm?"

The serpent slithered its way between each of their legs, as though it were catching their scent. It stopped at Imogen and wound up her leg, which still wore bits of the human meat suit.

"Mmm," Lilith purred. "Let's play a game, shall we, my naughty children?"

The Great Hall, which was really the Mouth of Hel, slowly transformed, inch by inch, into the Miller house on St. Augustine Place.

The house of horrors.

Staycation 3.0

It was a steel cage match, and the steel cage was the Miller house, but the house changed every round. Turning round like a giant Rubik's Cube, redesigning itself. First, a Dutch Colonial. Then, a ranch house, and finally an absolute fun house that made the Winchester Mystery House look like a child's play set.

There were no rules, only survive the round to play against the next opponent.

Each winner of the previous round would move on until the last two daughters standing fought to the death. The winner would decide the ending—

save or destroy the world?

But there'd be surprise guest players in each round. And while they were powerless, they could still take a player "out."

Round 1.

First up in the house were Sandra and Alex.

Alex skulked in the third-floor hallway between the bed-rooms. She used the darkness to her advantage, keeping her small body low to the ground. Her size, or lack of, was an advantage. Alex could get into and hide in spaces Sandra could not. Sandra Miller was a monstrous thing. An ancient thing.

The more years she had under her hood, the larger she grew. Eventually, she'd need a world just to contain her true size.

The house was quiet. Not a drip or a creak to be heard anywhere. The house itself seemed to hold its breath. Even the mice were too afraid to scuttle across the floorboards. Alex got on her belly and pulled herself to the edge of the stairwell, poking her head between the thick balusters. Her eyes searched the darkness downstairs, but they found only darkness, and nothing slithered in the dark.

Then, suddenly, the floor creaked behind her. Light footfalls. Getting closer. They sounded louder than Toby's snoring. Alex rolled onto her back and readied herself for whatever stepped out of the darkness to reveal itself.

But the footsteps ceased, and the floorboards quit their complaining.

Alex peered into the black and waited for something to peer back, but there was nothing but the darkness. Until something stirred about a foot or so away, concealed by the blanket of black. Movement. Slight movement. The brush of fabric as something bent closer to her. Followed by heavy breathing. Labored breathing.

Alex held up a hand and prepared to blow whatever was coming for her away.

FLEX.

Her hand lit up like a dollar-store Christmas tree, and Alex saw a mangled, bloodied, and very undead Junior Miller standing over her, grinning.

"Hey there, sis," Junior grinned through a mouthful of bloody teeth.

Alex screamed as Junior lowered himself to the screaming demon disguised as a young human child.

Downstairs, Sandra Miller heard the screams. She smiled and listened, following the sound with her ears, following with her head. The darkness was heavy and thick, so Sandra felt her way around the unfamiliar suburban nightmare of a house—full of chintzy knickknacks and tchotchkes.

Her hand reached out and grabbed at the range. It clanged and clattered as she tossed a saucepan to the floor. Slowly, she rounded out of the kitchen into what felt like a larger room. There was more air in it. She could breathe more easily. A dining room, Sandra assumed. Alex's screams were louder, so Sandra knew she was getting closer to the stairwell. It very well may have been just outside of this room.

Sandra felt for the wall, and after several failed attempts, her fingers finally fell onto something solid. She laughed as upstairs Alex's screams intensified. Sandra didn't know what nightmarish vision Alex had encountered upstairs, but she was really glad about it.

"How many times have you killed me?" a familiar voice spoke in the darkness. "A dozen? A hundred? A thousand? Tell me."

"Joe," Sandra called into the dark, still trying to keep her voice just above a whisper, although she was sure Alex was too preoccupied upstairs to hear her.

"Oh, we're on a first-name basis now, are we?" Detective Joseph P. Harding said, sitting at the dining room table. The table was readied for dinner with six place settings neatly arranged around it. Harding grabbed a fork and fumbled with it.

"Fancy meeting you here, Detective," Sandra said, pressing her back to the wall. She knew this wasn't real. Harding was dead. She still had bits of him in her teeth, and occasionally she felt him kicking in her belly. But real or not, in this game, NPCs were just as deadly as opponents, so Sandra wasn't taking any chances.

She eased down the wall, carefully using her hands to guide her in the dark as though she were a monstrous Helen Keller. If she knew her Dutch Colonials, which unfortunately she did thanks to being married to an architect for fifty years in another variation of the game, then the door to the hallway wasn't much further down the wall. A few more feet. Maybe three or four at most.

Suddenly, Harding was on her.

"Going somewhere, babe?"

He stood beside her. Sandra felt his rank breath on her neck.

"Nice coat," Harding said, running his hands over her bare, foul skin. "What is that? Vicuna?"

Sandra Miller did something she rarely ever did.

She screamed.

Round 2.

Cast-Iron Cassie started the round in the basement, of all places.

"Very funny, Mother," she whispered, more like cursed, under her breath.

But even in the darkness, Cassie could make out that this was just a basement, not "the" basement where she'd been taken out by a fucking Christmas decoration. Cassie didn't even celebrate Christmas. She didn't celebrate anything, really. They were older than everything. Older than all the myths, legends, stories, and traditions their players dreamt up. Who knew, next time they might just be celebrating the birth of their Lord and Savior Josh Fucking Groban on December 25th.

She hoped not, but sometimes the players made the fucking stupidest choices—particularly when it came to presidential elections.

Cassie had an advantage. Two. First, this was a ranch house, so there was only one floor, and she was in its belly. That meant Imogen was somewhere above her. And second, there was a light in the basement. Not a lot of light, mind you, but just enough streamed in through the small casement windows. That's how Cassie knew she'd started the game in the basement, which thankfully seemed devoid of holiday decorations.

She could just wait in the basement. Lie in wait, and when Imogen eventually made her way down those rickety-looking wooden steps, she'd pounce. It was a solid plan, she thought. But what is it they said about the best-laid plans?

It wasn't long after Cast-Iron Cassie formulated her fool-proof plan that she became aware that she was not alone in the basement. She heard scuttling somewhere behind her. At first, she had written the sound off as rodents. Basements were nesting places for all kinds of vermin. But then she heard something else. Laughing. No, *giggling.* Unless rodents developed the power to LOL, Cassie knew there was someone or something else in the basement with her.

"Come out of there," Cassie ordered, keeping her voice to a hush. "I know you're there. Show yourself! Now!"

A box toppled over. More giggles.

"I said... SHOW YOURSELF," Cassie silently shouted, using more breath than voice to get her point across. "NOW!"

The scuttling stopped, and silence followed. A light passed over a basement window, and Cassie's eyes went to it. She listened as a car drove down the street past the house they were playing in.

Then, before she had time to look back to the corner of the basement where the scuttling had come from, a figure leaped out of the darkness, attaching itself to her body like a leech. It bit down, and Cassie screamed as the thing took a huge chunk out of her cheek.

"Hi, Grandma," Mary Miller grinned. "Miss me?"

Upstairs, Imogen herself lay in wait, curled up behind the oversized, over-stuffed sofa in the living room. She knew Cassie would have to come out the basement door in the middle of the hallway, which was just off the living room. As soon as Cassie ventured into the living room, she'd take her out.

But then she heard screaming downstairs, and everything changed.

The house no longer felt dormant. It no longer felt asleep. It was alive. Conscious. Making decisions. Shifting. Changing. Throwing shit at them. Imogen knew it wasn't the house doing it, but Mother. She was making the game more interesting. But she figured that might also give her an edge since she'd only played the game once that she knew of, so she was more used to the randomness of it.

The other Millers had been playing the game for eons. They were accustomed to the twists and turns. The deceptions. But with Mother once again the Game Master? Anything was possible. It might just throw the others off their game and give Imogen the edge she needed to win the whole big fucking enchilada.

She peeked over the sofa, staring out into the darkness, searching for signs of life. A rattling doorknob. Footfalls on the stairs. Some sign that her opponent was taking the bait and walking right into her snare.

Her heart and stomach sank a little when nothing happened.

No rattling doorknobs, no creaking stairs. Hell, there wasn't even the rattling of ghostly chains. Just an unearthly, unholy silence that feasted on all the surrounding sounds. By now, Imogen realized she no longer heard the screaming downstairs in the basement. She couldn't even hear her own breath.

"Hey, Imo."

But Imogen heard that, loud and clear, in her head and not with her ears.

"I'm, like, sooooooo bored, Imo," a ghastly vision of Ally said.

The creature, that was not her Ally Cat but a demented, nightmarish version of her dead best friend, sat beside Imogen in the dark, grinning wildly like a rabid cat. The thing's teeth were rotten to the root, and its breath stunk worse than a whorehouse in Phoenix in July. Its eyes were white, glowing softly in the darkness.

"I died behind a couch, you know? BOOM!"

Imogen backed away on all fours. She kicked at the creature, hitting it in the head, but it was undeterred from its course. Its grin widened to a terrible sneer. The creature jumped onto Imogen, throttling her. She was pinned to the ground. Trapped like a bug in a jar.

Imogen kept telling herself this thing wasn't her Ally Cat, but still she hesitated to vanquish it. She couldn't tell if Cassie was still screaming in the basement or not. What if she vanquished her NPC and was on her way up the stairs right now? If Imogen made a peep, she'd hear, and her plan would be foiled.

As the creature wrapped its decayed fingers around Imogen's throat, Imogen came up with a new plan. She was about to execute it when the thing said, "I wanna get a look at that

Ivy-League brain of yours!"

Round 3. Winner takes all.

An ever-changing house.

Dining rooms turned into living rooms. Bedrooms into bathrooms. Basements became attics. There was no pattern to any of it. There was no predicting when the rooms would change, or where in the house you'd end up next. The only thing constant were the rooms—the master bedroom was always the same master bedroom, the living room, the same living room, and so on.

The other change was that the house lights came on randomly, sometimes staying on for minutes, sometimes flashing for seconds, before going dark again. In this house of horrors, there was no place to hide. No room was safe.

As Imogen surveyed her surroundings, she realized right away that she was in a bathroom, thanks to her foot sticking out of the toilet. The lights flickered on, only for a second or two, and then clicked off again. Imogen realized she was in a tiny powder room. She quickly pulled her foot out of the cold water and felt for a towel. The potentially icky water didn't bother her, but she didn't want to leave wet footprints behind.

She patted her hooved foot dry and overheard a voice coming through from the Gates of Hel.

"Fucking holiday decorations, can you believe it? Did me in again," Cast-Iron Cassie said, but Imogen couldn't tell who she was talking to. She didn't know if Alex had taken out Sandra or if that chain-smoker had lived to puff another day.

Imogen poked her head out of the powder room door and looked up and down the hallway. The lights came on, buzzing brightly overhead. Imogen ducked back into the powder room, but not fully. She monitored the hallway, which was, for the moment, still. When the lights went dark, Imogen slowly pushed open the powder room door and stepped into the hallway.

Instantly, the house shifted. The rooms turning over each other like bingo balls tumbling in a bingo machine. The powder room was gone. The hallway was gone. And now Imogen crawled around an attic. A cobweb, dusty, box-cluttered attic with one sole light in its center. A lone bulb sticking out of a socket.

Imogen crawled to the socket and unscrewed the bulb. She tucked it into one of the nearby boxes and listened. Outside, the wind was howling something fierce, and rain pelted the roof, which was only a few feet above her head. The sound of the rain was both loud and distracting. It drowned out any other sounds that might travel up to the attic from downstairs.

Shit.

Imogen looked for a door, or a folded-up ladder. There had to be a way to climb or crawl out of the attic. But she saw nothing. Two small windows peered to the outside, one on each end of the attic. Imogen wondered if they could open. She crawled to the nearest window and pushed it open. Rain smacked her face. She had to admit that it felt good on her hot skin.

She pushed at the window again and it opened even wider. Wide enough for her to crawl through. She could've just FLEXED her way through to the other side, but she knew after her encounters with Ally and Cassie that she needed to conserve her juice.

So Imogen climbed through the window, the old-fashioned way, and stepped onto the ledge. It seemed an impossibly far fall, so she shimmied carefully around until she spied a balcony a level below her. A BOOM of thunder and a CRACKLE of lightning made her heart almost burst through her chest. She nearly lost her balance, but caught herself before she tumbled off, missing the balcony entirely.

She readied herself to take the plunge. The rain fell harder, soaking every inch of her malignant body. As the sky lit up with bright white light, Imogen got down real low, arming herself for the jump, and then, just as a CRASH of thunder rattled the house, Imogen jumped onto the balcony below.

Only, the balcony was no longer a balcony. It was the master bedroom. A huge room, by any standard, furnished with the tackiest bedroom set Imogen had ever seen in her life. It looked as though it'd been ordered from a catalog in the 1950s. She saw it clearly because as soon as her hooved feet touched the floor, the bedroom lights flashed on. And this time, they did not go out.

Imogen panicked as she caught sight of her reflection in the full-length mirrors on the far wall. She looked up and shook her head as she stared at her image in the ceiling mirrors, which covered every square inch of the ceiling.

Tacky.

As Imogen looked at her reflection, she suddenly saw another reflection in the mirror, moving at lightning-fast speed, heading right for her.

Alex screamed, a primal howl of warning.

Imogen braced herself for the FLEX, but as Alex got within striking distance, the bedroom became the kitchen and Alex was gone.

Somewhere in the funhouse, Imogen heard Alex growl, "SHIT!"

Imogen ducked under the cluttered kitchen table. Half-eaten bowls of cereal, toast, glasses of orange juice, and cold coffee in novelty mugs littered the surface of the table. She felt around the tabletop from her crouched position, feeling for a mug of cold coffee. Her fingers latched onto one and brought it to her lips. She downed the cold, almost flavor-free brown water in one gulp. It might have tasted like shit, but it was still the elixir of life. And she needed the caffeine to ease the ache in her head and charge up her juice.

Outside the kitchen, a floorboard creaked, followed by a hushed series of familiar cuss words. Imogen knew Alex was now just outside the kitchen door. The floor creaked again. This time it sounded farther away.

She's walking away from the kitchen. Her back is to me.

Imogen slid out from the under the table and slowly made her way to standing. She downed whatever cold coffee she found on the table and then moved as quietly as she could to the kitchen door. Gently, she put an ear to the door and listened. There was definitely something on the other side. The sound was faint, but it was there.

Carefully, holding her breath, Imogen swung open the kitchen door, hoping it didn't have a squeak or a groan in its bones. She saw the back of Alex's head. She was staring ahead into the living room, stealthily creeping down the small, narrow hallway.

Imogen moved quieter than a summer breeze and crept up behind Alex just as the lights came on. Full blast. Alex spied Imogen's shadow on the floor and rounded on her. Alex cried out, a long squeal of a war-cry. Her eyes blazed red as she bared her teeth, saliva slowly dripping down the corners of her black mouth.

She moved toward Imogen, who took a small step backwards and braced herself for the FLEX. Before either of them could move, the house shifted again; the rooms turning over a hundred times before settling again.

This time, Imogen and Alex ended up in the basement together. The heart of this Miller house. Alex lunged but did not FLEX. Imogen stepped forward, and at the same moment, FLEXED. The extra hits of caffeine made the jolt even more potent.

Alex was still howling when—

"More coffee, d-d-dear?" Flo asked, holding up a fresh pot. "Or how about a slice of pie? The best in the county."

"What... the fuck?" Alex shouted, realizing she was sitting in a booth at a diner. "Where am I? What is this?"

"I've got apple and cherry pie. But, if you ask me, I'd go with the apple. It won a prize at the fair a few years back."

Imogen and Olivia appeared on the other side of the booth.

"You can't be here," Alex said, pointing at the twins. "This isn't your place."

"But it is," Olivia said.

"We let you in," Imogen added. "And you just followed me in. But you never thought about how you'd get out."

"I've had new locks installed," Olivia said, her eyes glowing brightly.

"I'm sorry, Imo. I couldn't stop him."

"That's okay."

"How's it going on the other side?"

Imogen laughed.

"Not so good, Livs. But I have an idea. You in?"

"Ab-so-fucking-lutely!"

"We let them in, but if we let them in, like through a door, can't we just close it again?"

Olivia leaned forward.

"Close it... how?"

Imogen shrugged.

"The same way we let them in, only in reverse."

"So, we get them here, at the diner, the place Toby made for me, which we've sort of commandeered for ourselves, but they still have a backdoor into it... We get them here, close the door and—"

"Seal them up like in The Cask of Fucking Amontillado,*" Imogen said.*

Olivia squealed, "Or bury them under the floorboards like in The Tell-Tale Heart.*"*

Imogen eyed the jukebox.

"I've got a better idea. Here, take this," Imogen said, sending a huge ray of energy into Olivia. "For later."

"Be careful. I'll see you soon."

Imogen nodded.

"See you soon."

"Hey! Hey, Imo!"

Imogen turned to Olivia.

"I love you, Imo."

"I love you, Livs."

"End game, Alex," Imogen said.

Alex howled and shrieked as Imogen and Olivia slipped out of the diner, locking the doors behind them. They took old Flo with them, because how could they leave the best fucking pie and coffee in any universe behind? But they left that old jukebox.

And there, trapped inside a jukebox like a genie in a lamp

that played only Josh Fucking Groban records, lay Alex Miller. Trapped for eternity, or until Lilith decided she'd learned her lesson—if that day ever came around.

In Her Image, Part 2

"So, you won the game," Lilith said proudly.

"And that means..."

Sandra Miller stepped over to Imogen and draped a tentacle around her shoulder.

"That means... the choice is yours. Do you want to save your world, Imogen? Or do you want to end it all? Everything, everywhere. End it all."

Imogen looked to Mother.

"I don't understand. Why is it my choice?"

"Those were the stakes. At least my children followed that rule. You must announce stakes before saying the rules, and everyone must agree."

"And you agreed, Imogen," Cast-Iron Cassie said, coming up behind Imogen. "You may not have known you had a choice. Save the world, or... BOOM. But you agreed to the terms. So, here you are."

Lilith's serpent slithered up to Imogen, curling its way up the length of her monstrous body until its head rested on her shoulder.

"So, what is it you want, Imogen Rockwell?" Lilith asked gently. "What do you want to do with this world of yours?"

"Miller," Imogen said, turning to Mother.   "Imogen

Rockwell-Miller."

Sandra smiled, laughing as she clapped her hands.

"Welcome to the family, kiddo," she said, sticking a cigarette into her holder.

"I can... make it anything I want?"

"Almost," Lilith said. "There are... rules. But yes. You can make it almost anything you want. I suggest, should you decide to reset, that you start with what you know. The first time can be a little... messy. It takes practice, but I think you'll get the hang of it soon enough."

"She's a smart one," Cassie said. "Ivy-League."

Imogen looked around at her new family. Her demonic family. She was something new now, something she never even knew existed. A Daughter of Lilith, the Queen of Hel and the Creator of the Universe. Mother was older than time. She was the eyes that stared out of the abyss. Mother WAS the abyss.

Mother had been asleep, but now she was awake. And everything would be different.

No, Imogen thought, everything *could* be different.

Finally, it could be different.

"The players? What happens to them?" Imogen asked.

"They reset," Sandra said, exhaling a long plume of smoke.

"All of them?"

Cast-Iron Cassie nodded her head.

"All of them."

She could grow to love them. A part of her already did. Sometimes even monsters can do terrible things but for the right reasons. Sure, Sandra had done a bit of killing. Okay, a lot of killing. But it'd been Toby and Alex that were devouring the world, sending it into darkness. They were the reason for all of this.

But they were also the reason Imogen had discovered who she was, what she truly was underneath it all. And for that, she would always be grateful to the Bobbsey Twins—but she hoped she'd never have the chance to tell them in person.

"What do I have to do?" Imogen asked Lilith.

Why, you've always had the power to go home, my dear. All you have to do is click your heels three times and say—

"It's time to remake this world not in HIS image, but in hers," Imogen said. She closed her eyes and formed the world she wanted to see. The place she wanted to hang up her hat and stay for a spell. A world where right was still right, and wrong was still wrong. A place where sometimes the meek still inherited the earth, and a place where Josh Groban was nothing more than a second-rate Tom Jones impersonator in Las Vegas. "There's no place like home."

"I'll be keeping an eye on you, Imogen Rockwell-Miller," Lilith said, recalling her serpent to her side. "Follow the rules."

"See you around, kiddo," Sandra Miller said, before vanishing.

"Watch out for holiday decorations. That's the best advice I can give you," Cast-Iron Cassie Miller said, and then she, too, was gone.

"Now, my dear Daughter," Lilith said to Imogen.

They were alone now, and the Gates of Hel were closing slowly. It was time again for Lilith to take her seat on the throne in Hel and rule, only this time she would keep one eye fixed on her wayward children. Yet somehow, she knew, with Imogen, the rules would be respected. And followed.

"Now, my dear Daughter, say the word like you mean it."

And Imogen did—

CROATOAN!

And in a flash, the dying old world was gone, and a shiny new one stood in its place. One made lovingly in her own image.

The game had reset.

IV

A Whole New World

Like a Virgin

It was just another day, just like the one that came before it, and the one that came before that. Life bloomed like the first flowers of spring, pushing their way through the cold, hard earth and reaching for the warmth of the sun. The scars of the old world faded from view. They were still there, of course, and would remain hidden just below the surface. Gone, but not forgotten. As long as there was one who remembered it all, the scars would remain. And for the rest of her days, Imogen Rockwell would remember everything. The events played on a loop in her mind like one of those holiday specials that run continuously on television on Christmas Eve, long after they've over-stayed their welcome.

No, Imogen Rockwell would not soon forget the horrors she'd seen or the world she'd lost to birth a new one out of the rubble, out of the ashes of the old one. Nor would she, could she, forget the friends, or the family, that were now nothing more than shadows in her mind. *Sister.* Wisps of memories, whispers from a time long gone.

The end, and the beginning, happened so many years back Imogen lost count. The funny thing was that even as the world around her changed, reshaped itself in her image with every reset, with every new round of the game, Imogen herself did not change. Indeed, she was exactly as she was the day she stood at the edge of the abyss in Valhalla and claimed her victory. And Imogen knew that was how she would always be. Frozen in that moment in time, frozen like a cheap microwave dinner.

As she wandered the brave new world that she'd created, Imogen saw ghosts everywhere. Not the shadows that moved with deadly intent, nor the kind that hid the monsters and vile things that traveled up occasionally from Hel to spy on her for Lilith. She'd seen the occasional Miller here and there. Sandra mostly. Sandra who still wore her precious vicuna fur coat and a shit-eating smile that told Imogen that things were alright. For now. How long they stayed that way, Imogen realized, was up to her.

The bell above the door clanged. It sounded more like a death rattle than a welcome. The smell of aged paper, coffee, and mustiness hit Imogen's nose at once. The combination was intoxicating. Nothing... nothing else on her great green earth smelled quite like a bookstore. They were small patches of heaven where anything was possible. Places where a million stories awaited discovery. And for Imogen Rockwell, they were often places of inspiration. The game needed to be kept fresh, after all. Histories often needed a little rewrite here and there when things had gone too far in either direction, or outcomes weren't to her liking. She knew it wasn't fair, and it wasn't the hands-off approach the previous stewards of the game took, but fuck, if Imogen didn't like to see the good guys ride off victoriously into the sunset. But, as she quickly learned, life does not always go the way you want it to, and more often than not, the bad guys saw their time in the sun.

But that sunny afternoon, Imogen wasn't thinking about

good guys or bad guys. She had only one thought on her mind. Books. A book, to be exact. A special one.

"Next," the squeaky voice called out when Imogen made it to the front of the line. "Hey! Hey, lady! Wake up! Move it, will ya!"

Imogen hadn't realized she was daydreaming, back in another life for a visit, but she snapped back to the current day and time at the sound of that comical, nasal squeak.

"Right. Sorry," Imogen said as she approached the signing table. She didn't want to seem too over-eager or stalkery as she had in several previous iterations of that moment. She'd just been so happy that her enthusiasm came off ten paces shy of madness. "Hi. I was wondering, I know it's not the new one, but I was wondering… if you'd sign… this one?"

Imogen reached into her bag and pulled out a well-worn, well-loved paperback. The spine was creased, a sign the book had been read many times, and the cover had more wrinkles than Mickey Rourke's current face. *You can take the boy out of Los Angeles, but you can't take Los Angeles out of the boy*, Imogen learned.

She slid her book across the table. It moved smoothly, like a toy car gliding on a track.

"Wow," the man sitting on the other side of the table said with genuine wonder in his voice. "I haven't seen one of these… in a long time."

"It's my favorite," Imogen said.

He leaned into her, whispering, "Mine, too. But don't tell anyone behind you."

The man gave her a wink, and there was a distinct twinkle in his eye.

"There's something special about your first one, you know?

It's like you're doing it for you, not them." He indicated the line of people behind her, not in a pompous or arrogant way, but more matter-of-factly. It was what it was, as the saying goes. "This one... was for me. I wrote it in a weekend in a godforsaken motel in the middle of nowhere. Pure adrenaline. And caffeine. I had so much coffee that I thought I was having a heart attack. Dive of a place, but they had excellent coffee. Go figure."

Imogen smirked.

"You can never have too much coffee."

Again, the man's eyes sparkled, not quite with recognition, but with something.

"That's what I say. My cardiologist has a different opinion."

There were so many things Imogen wanted to say, but the man before her was a stranger with a familiar face. Sure, there were traces of the past buried inside, down deep, but in this life, in this game, they were not acquainted with each other. And rules were rules, and they must be obeyed—no matter how badly Imogen wanted to fly across the table and throw her arms around the writer.

"Who should I make it out to?" the man asked, pen at the ready.

"Imogen. Please."

"I-M-O—"

"G-E-N," Imogen finished.

"You got it, kid."

A second later, the writer had pen to paper and was inscribing the old paperback with both her name and his. Imogen could only smile as her heart beat loudly in her ears. When the thumping got so loud she thought she might just have to scream to drown it out, the writer set his pen aside and slid the book back across the table. It made its return journey just as smoothly as it had earlier when Imogen slid it to him.

Imogen took the book in one hand and held out her other to him.

"Thank you," she began, waiting until the moment their hands connected. She clasped his hand and left their connection just a little longer than would have been customary, but not long enough to ring any alarm bells. "For this."

"My pleasure, kid," the writer said as their hands separated.

Imogen turned and headed back to the front of the shoppe and the door. She reached for the rusty old doorknob, waiting for the ding of the bell, but from the back of the shoppe, the writer's voice boomed.

"Hey, kid!"

Imogen looked over her shoulder. The writer gave a quick salute with two fingers, as though saying *see you around.*

"Be good, kid."

She nodded and pulled the door open. The bright sun made her eyes squint, but it felt good against her face, like a lover's caress.

Not long after, Imogen was sitting at an outdoor café sipping her hot, fresh coffee—which was good, but not great, especially for the price. On the table sat the newly autographed paperback. She didn't know why she was hesitant to open the cover and read the inscription, but she was. She couldn't even remember the last time she'd felt so nervous. Maybe it was that first kiss by the water fountain in third grade. *Stevie Matheson.* It hadn't been the kiss that woke sleeping princesses, but it had been her first, and that made it special. You never forget your first.

Imogen set aside the cup of steaming coffee and eyed the

book one last time before picking it up and opening the cover carefully as though it were made of glass. She read the inscription, smiling ear to ear: *For Imogen. What's a girl like you doing in a place like this? Signed, J.P. Harding.*

J.P. Harding. Best-selling mystery writer and author of over a dozen books. Two had already been made into films, with two more on the way.

* * *

It was almost closing time, and the Jayden Planetarium was almost empty. For some, it was the perfect time to visit. Fewer crowds. Less pushing. And more time with the stars. Oliver Rockwell enjoyed visiting the Planetarium at that hour. He did so almost every night. Even though he was an astronomer by trade, he did not work at the Planetarium. Not yet, anyway. It was on his bucket list, and even though soon he'd have more years behind him than ahead of him, Oliver Rockwell was an optimist. A pessimistic optimist, nevertheless, an optimist at heart. Colleagues often said that Oliver looked at the world "sunny side up," and sometimes he agreed. But sometimes, on days like today, Oliver felt incomplete. Like there was something missing way deep down inside of him. He imagined that was how amputees felt long after losing a limb, like it was still there, even though they knew they could see with their own eyes that it was gone. And then it would set in—that horrible feeling of loss, of mourning. Missing something that hasn't been a part of you for a long time.

In Oliver Rockwell's case, he didn't know what it was he

missed. He'd had a good run at life so far. If it were the game, some might even say he was winning. Yes, Oliver Rockwell looked good on paper. All the boxes were ticked. As his late father might've said, Oliver had done well for himself. A nice house in a pleasant neighborhood. A nice car. Two of them, in fact. A long-devoted wife he'd married after college. They'd met in high school, and other than a brief period when they parted to "explore their options," Oliver and Diane never spent so much as a day apart from one another. Yes, Oliver had done well for himself.

And yet, every time he looked up at that night sky and watched the stars glistening and twinkling, nestled in their black blanket, a feeling of longing came over him. The universe still inspired wonder and awe in him. That went without saying, but still... something was missing. Something wasn't right with Oliver Rockwell. There was a black hole growing inside of him, and it needed to be filled.

"Ten minutes to closing, Oliver," the burly security guard said, stealing up behind Oliver. Despite the man's mammoth, button-busting size, the security guard made almost no noise when he walked.

"Thanks, George. Working the late shift again?" Oliver asked without removing his eye from the telescope.

"Yeah. Every night this week." The guard sighed. It was a great sigh. Oliver expected a "ho, ho, ho" to follow, given the man's likeness to one famous jolly old toy giver.

"Margaret must love that."

Margaret was the guard's wife. A gargantuan woman with an imposing stare, but the warmest disposition. She reminded Oliver of Teddy, the Rottweiler the Jacksons had when he was a kid. The biggest, stupidest dog Oliver had ever seen in his life, but the absolute sweetest thing. It feared its own shadow. Literally.

"Oh, Meg is making plans, alright. Bingo tonight. Trivia at the Red Baron tomorrow night. Bowling on Thursday. And tacos with the girls on Friday."

Oliver laughed.

"That's more than I do in a month."

"A month? Hell, Oliver. That's more than I do in a year."

Oliver never doubted that for a second.

"Did she pack you something good for dinner?"

"Uh, meat loaf, I think."

Oliver made a yummy sound and then said, "With mashed potatoes and gravy?"

"Loads of gravy."

"You're a lucky man, George."

The guard laughed, and Oliver swore the ground shook ever so slightly.

"Don't I know it? You got fifteen minutes."

Oliver listened for George's footfalls but heard only the sound of the man's heavy breathing as he lumbered away, probably getting his only proper exercise for the day. He called to George, eye still firmly planted on the telescope's eyepiece, "I thought you said ten."

"I don't remember saying ten. Fifteen minutes. For you, fifteen minutes. See you at the door."

"See you at the door. Hey, George?"

"Yeah?"

"Thank you."

"No problem, Oliver. You're a good egg," George said. Oliver thought he heard a slight squeak, the guard's shiny new shoes on the marble floor no doubt, as George headed for the door.

But then he heard a slight shuffle behind him. Footsteps far lighter than George's ought to have been. "We're closing soon, ma'am."

"Can I just take a little peek? I've come... quite a long way."

"Okay, little lady. One little peek, and then I have to lock up. Ten minutes."

"Fifteen, George."

"Oliver," George said.

"Fifteen minutes. She's come a long way, and I think she should get a little more than a quick look-see. Wouldn't you agree? Don't worry. I'll walk her out. I promise, we won't steal anything. Cross my heart."

Oliver crossed his heart and held up his right hand. George shrugged his shoulders and sighed in defeat.

"Fifteen minutes."

They watched George lumber through the door without saying a word.

"Thanks. I appreciate that. I really did come a long way," Imogen said.

"My pleasure. Here, look. The sky looks magnificent tonight. Not a cloud," Oliver said, making way for her.

"Are you sure? I don't want to rush you."

"I insist."

"Okay," Imogen said, lowering her eye to the eyepiece. "Wow, you weren't kidding. I've never seen a sky so clear."

"I know. It looks like a painting. 'Perfect Night Sky, in watercolor'."

Imogen laughed.

"Do you paint?"

"No," Oliver laughed, "I'm not remotely artistically inclined. I'm good with numbers, though."

"Accountant?"

"Astronomer."

Imogen smiled.

"I should have known."

"It's okay. Most people guess accountant. There's no way you could have known."

Isn't there?

"Look, there. A shooting star," Imogen said, stepping aside for Oliver to step in.

"Let me see... where... oh, there. If it were any closer, it would have bitten me. You're right. That sure is a shooting star. Come here. We can share. There's plenty of room. You really should see this."

Imogen returned to the telescope, and she and Oliver shared the oversized eyepiece, each shifting a little to make space for the other and then laughing at their courteousness.

"It's so beautiful," Imogen said softly.

"Yeah, it is. I come here every night, and I never get tired of that view."

"How could you? Someone took great care putting all those stars up there. They had to be carefully spaced so they didn't look like a jumble of light. Each design meticulously etched into the canvas. Especially that one... over there... between Lyra and Aquila."

"Father and Daughter? That one is my favorite."

"Mine, too. My dad used to take me stargazing every Saturday on this big hill just outside of our town... Snake Hill. We'd bring our little telescope and look at the stars. UFOs."

"Ever see one?"

"Once. Maybe. I still say it was a drone, but my dad swore it was a UFO. The jury's still out, I guess."

"Is he... still with us?"

Imogen closed her eyes and tilted her head so that Oliver couldn't see her face.

"No. He's... passed on."

"Oh. I'm really sorry."

"It's okay. It was for the best. He's in a better place. I go and see him sometimes. When I want to look at the stars."

"That's a really nice thought, miss?"

"Imogen."

Oliver turned and held out a hand.

"Oliver."

They shook hands, and Imogen fought back the tears with every bit of her being, with every bit of her strength. A lone tear broke through the wall and ran slowly down her cheek.

"Hey, you know, my dad used to say that the ones we love are never really gone. If we look hard enough, we can see them in the simple things. A flower. A blade of grass. And sometimes, even the stars. I don't know. It was just something he said."

"I believe it," Imogen said, wiping her cheek dry.

"Do you? Ever see him up there? Your father."

"Yeah, sometimes. Sometimes it's like I'm staring right at him."

They stood, staring at each other, for what Imogen felt was an hour, but really it was only a minute and change, at most. In her mind, a million exchanges happened all at once. Memories shared. Jokes told. Words of endearment. But nothing was said. It was only felt by the both of them.

"Well," Oliver said finally, struggling to find words.

"Well," Imogen repeated reluctantly, knowing the clock had run out.

"We'd better head down before George lets the dogs out."

"One last look?"

Oliver smiled and said, "One last look."

They gazed at the stars far longer than they should have. Imogen didn't need to ask to know his eyes were also fixed between Lyra and Aquila, on the constellation Imogen had made just for him—"Father and Daughter."

On their way out, as they stood wordlessly in front of the Planetarium, above them, Father and Daughter twinkled just a little brighter, as it so often did when Imogen found Oliver in the game.

"Maybe I'll see you again," Oliver said, holding out his hand.

They shook and Imogen said, "I think you will."

"Good. I look forward to it."

Their hands parted, and for a moment there was something more Oliver wanted to say, thought to say, but swallowed it down. Maybe next time.

"Me too," Imogen said.

"Good night, Imogen."

"Good night, Oliver."

He turned to head home, giving Imogen a small parting nod, but then Imogen called out to him before he reached the corner.

"Hey, Oliver! What's your favorite movie?"

"*Invasion of the Body Snatchers.*"

"The old one with Kevin McCarthy or the remake with Donald Sutherland and Jeff Goldblum?"

Oliver blew a raspberry.

"The black and white one. It's a classic."

Then, at the same time, Imogen and Oliver said—"You're next," quoting the movie's most famous line. They shared a laugh and then Oliver nodded again, after staring at Imogen for a time.

"Well, goodnight, Imogen. I hope you see your dad."

"Goodnight, Oliver," Imogen said. She waited until he was almost out of sight to add, "I just did."

* * *

The Mater Winery wasn't easy to miss. It was the largest and highest-rated winery in the region. If there was an award, Mater Winery won it. And it was voted number one by consumers going on six years in a row. They had "done well" for themselves. Starting out small but quickly expanding thanks to word of mouth and a little thing called the interwebs. When the masses rave about a product, one voice becomes ten and ten becomes one hundred and a hundred turns into a thousand in the blink of an eye.

Although the winery moved to a larger location four years ago, the place still had a cozy, "at home" feel to it. It was the kind of place that invited you in, asked you to stay awhile, have a drink, and maybe share a story or two.

Despite their rapid expansion and growth, they stayed the same small, off-the-beaten-path winery they were the day they sold their first bottle, which was no small feat. Their success was, and remained, largely because of their founder—Janet DeLamma.

Janet was the visionary with the nose and tastebuds for crafting unforgettable tasting experiences. According to legend, Janet came out of the womb with a taste for wine and was always a bit of a snob about what wines passed her lips. In college, she drank only the best Italian imported wines while her roommates drank box wine. Oh, the horror of it.

A year out of school, Janet made her first batch of home-made wine, an exquisite Pinot Noir that remained one of the winery's top sellers. The rest, as the saying goes, was history. Mater Winery made its first million in their first six months of operations. Their success story was an inspiration to small backyard vineyards and would-be wine tycoons everywhere.

And yet, for all her success, and all her millions, the fame, the accolades, and the labels—ranging from "genius" to "entrepreneur"—Janet remained the Janet she'd always been. Relatable, down-to-earth, trustworthy, and honest. Admittedly, her one tragic flaw was her taste in music. She had a "thing" for crooners, especially that god-awful Josh Groban. No one's perfect.

Imogen pulled her car through the massive front gate and had to make a couple of rounds to find a spot. Even on a weeknight, the winery was packed full of visitors, some of whom had traveled far to sample the latest offerings. But none had traveled the distance Imogen had. Some things are immeasurable.

She stared at Janet's photo in the lobby and smiled. In the photo, Janet wore a larger-than-life smile as she held up her first bottle in one hand and a full glass in the other. It did Imogen's heart good to see Janet again, and to see her looking so happy, so fulfilled. A million years ago, in another life, in another place and time, her Janet had been neither happy nor fulfilled. Later, after the birthing of the universe, Imogen reflected on her old life, and Janet. There'd been signs Janet was an unhappy woman, but Imogen didn't see them.

Before the end of the old world, Imogen had been but a child. She came out of the other side older, wiser, and able to see things with razor-sharp clarity. She saw the old world, her old life, in a new light. And when her eyes landed on Janet, the old Janet, she saw, and she understood the longing and the emptiness her adopted mother felt inside. The silent pain many women bear as they move through the world, often invisible under the coverings of their bodies. To look isn't always to see.

Imogen at last understood Janet's need to drown the feelings with wine. Numb the senses. Drown the sorrows. Silence the voices. Rinse, and repeat. And she did it day after day, night after night, with cheap wine. The cheapest, but at least it was not box wine. The new Janet would not approve.

A woman brushed past Imogen in a huff. Her heavy fur coat brushed against Imogen's arm. Imogen peered over her shoulder, and the woman was gone. The smell of cigarettes still hung in the air.

Imogen turned back and walked past the thin rope that kept customers out. A small sign hung above the doorway that read "Private," and Imogen knew that if Janet was at the winery, she would be somewhere beyond that rope. *Pay no attention to the man behind the curtain.* Her own wizard-ess in her very own merry land of Oz. No one was there to stop Imogen as she walked deeper and deeper into the guts of the winery until she came upon a door that led to the outside. She didn't have to peek through the glass to know that through that door, just on the other side, she'd find Janet, likely curled up on a chair, under a blanket, reading a book as music played.

As she opened the door, the first thing she noticed was the multitude of glowing lights hanging and dangling from fixed poles. Imogen imagined that at nightfall those lights must look like stars. The seating was basic but appeared comfortable. It lay protected under an impressive gazebo. A fire raged in the pit close to the couch where Janet lay reading a book. The lower half of her body lay hidden under a thick, fuzzy blanket. There was a look of peace, a serenity on her face that Imogen had never seen in the old Janet, and that warmed her heart. For a moment, Imogen felt like it'd all been worth it. The pain, the suffering, the loss. All of it. Just for this moment, to see Janet reborn, happy and fulfilled at last.

Imogen hadn't planned to linger. She'd only intended to steal a look at her mother and duck out, making a small apology along the way if she'd been discovered by Janet or one of her employees. And now that she'd stolen her glance, Imogen turned to slip out silently and wordlessly, but Janet had other ideas.

"Seeing as how you came all the way here, why not pour yourself a glass and sit," Janet said, without looking up from her book. She reached for her glass and took a small sip before returning it to the table beside the couch.

"No, I—"

"Please. I insist."

Imogen's heart raced in her chest. She'd imagined a thousand variations of this moment, but somehow never once pictured her mother asking her to pull up a seat, have a drink, and shoot the shit. It felt very grown up to Imogen, even though her age could no longer be measured in what we called years. She'd moved beyond that long ago. To think she was now both no longer a child and so much older than her mother was almost unfathomable to Imogen.

Still, the obedient daughter in her did as she was told. She sat in the chair beside the couch and poured herself a glass of wine. She brought it to her lips and savored the wine's delectable aroma before taking a hearty sip.

"Mmm. That's good," Imogen said, not intending to sound surprised.

Janet's eyes peered out over her book.

"At 350 a bottle, it better be good," she laughed.

"Three fifty?"

Janet closed her book and set it aside.

"On sale."

"Oh," Imogen said weakly. It sounded more like "yes, ma'am."

"So. Do you want to tell me who you are and what you're doing here?"

Imogen took a sip of liquid courage. She could've kicked herself for not imagining any scenario where she'd end up sitting down and talking with Janet. Always, she'd been able to eye her mom from a safe distance or creep away undetected. She hadn't spoken to Janet since... that last game. And now, the butterflies were doing loops in her stomach. The last time she felt that way was when she had "the talk," aka the sex talk, with Janet a lifetime ago. How lame that seemed now. After all she'd seen and done. How trivial those big things looked with hindsight. How the things that weighed us down, immobilized us, brought us to the brink, seemed nothing more than a small splinter in our big toe with the passage of time and reflection.

"I... just wanted to... get a peek behind the curtain. I thought maybe this door led to somewhere special," Imogen said hesitantly.

"I'd say this is a pretty special place, wouldn't you... I'm sorry, what's your name?"

Imogen set down the glass of wine.

"Imogen. Imogen Rockwell."

"I assume you know who I am?"

Imogen nodded.

"I do, Ms. DeLamma."

"You can call me Janet. Ms. DeLamma makes me sound like... I don't know. Your friend's mother or something."

Imogen smiled.

"Okay, Janet."

"So, did you come here for the tour or...?"

"No. I mean, yes."

Janet laughed.

"No, but yes? That's precise."

"I want to take the tour. See everything from top to bottom, but that's not why I came here."

"Ooh, intriguing, Imogen. Tell me then, why did you come here?"

Imogen watched as Janet took another sip of her wine. The picture looked so familiar, and yet so new. If Imogen didn't know better, they could've been sitting in their backyard on a Sunday night, talking about the week to come. Complaining. Strategizing. Sharing. Connecting. But this Janet had no connection with her. They were strangers, just getting to know each other. Whatever they were, whatever they shared before, had been wiped clean when Imogen reset the game. And Imogen's memory endured. Even after a thousand resets, she still remembered everything about her first game. She still remembered everything about Janet.

"I guess... I wanted to see you. In person, I mean," Imogen said, stumbling a bit over her words. Sure, she wanted to see Janet, but she could never tell her mother why she'd made the visit, why she always made the visit. She would think Imogen a loony if she tried to tell Janet the truth. So Imogen tucked that bit of info away and pretended everything was normal. Perfectly normal.

Janet's face scrunched up, wrinkling like a prune. There were lines there Imogen hadn't noticed before.

"Why? Why did you want to see me?"

Imogen laughed, overselling it.

"Are you kidding? You're a legend. Self-made. A woman dominating an industry primarily run by men. You don't take any shit from anyone, and I guess… I just admire that. Maybe that's why I came here. To tell you that in person."

Janet set down her wine and pushed the glass aside. Her cheeks bloomed red as she folded her hands into her lap.

"Thank you. I mean that sincerely. It's nice to hear every once in a while."

"You're welcome. And I meant every word, just so you know."

"I know," Janet said, looking right into Imogen's eyes and then penetrating deeper, but nowhere near deep enough to make it to the bottom of the well. "Your face… it's so familiar to me. But I can't place it. It feels like I have a word stuck on the tip of my tongue and I just can't get it out, you know? Do I know your parents?"

"No, I don't think so. I'm not from around here. I came a long way to see you."

Janet's forehead wrinkled as she struggled to place Imogen.

"I don't know. It's there, and just when I'm about to remember where I know you from, it's gone. It's like… something out of a dream. Maybe that's it."

"Yeah, maybe, Janet. I hope it was a wonderful dream."

"I guess I'm getting old. It happens to all of us in the end."

Sometimes. But not you, Janet. Not you.

Imogen smiled, wondering how many times they would have this conversation in the games to come. She wondered if a day would come when Janet would remember the dream of the life she once lived, and the daughter she once raised. The daughter she lost.

"So, what do you say? Do you want that tour now?"

"Yes, please. If it's no trouble."

"No, it's no trouble at all. It'd be my pleasure."

Janet's gaze lingered on Imogen far longer than was necessary, and Imogen wondered, as sparks of near recognition flared in her mother's eyes, if today would be the day Janet somehow remembered her. But, just as quickly as the moment came on, it was gone, and they were heading into the winery.

Janet showed Imogen all there was to see, and more. It was a true insider's look behind the curtain, and Imogen felt her heart swelling with pride as she watched Janet show off her baby to the daughter she'd never know. She had Imogen sample all the varieties of wine. Imogen tasted grapes, the most delicious grapes she'd ever tasted, and learned all there was to know about the making of wine. Imogen wanted their time to last longer, stretch on late into the night so they could sit out back in Janet's private oasis and talk like they used to. But Imogen knew she'd only be picking at the scab, and when they arrived at the main entrance, Imogen said goodbye to her mother. Goodbye... for now.

"It was lovely to meet you, Imogen Rockwell," Janet said, extending a hand. "Even though I'm convinced that we've met before. It'll come to me."

I hope not.

Imogen shook her mother's hand and gave her a small, appreciative smile.

"It was lovely to have met you, Janet DeLamma."

"Maybe I'll see you again. Come back anytime. Ask for me at reception."

"Yeah, maybe," Imogen said unconvincingly, withdrawing her hand as she picked at the invisible scab of her memories. "Can I ask you something?"

"Sure. Shoot."

Imogen looked up and indicated the sign with her head.

"Why Mater Winery? I'm just curious."

"What's in a name?" Janet mused.

Imogen thought about the Gemeo Project. *What's in a name, indeed.*

"Mater is Latin. It means 'mother.'"

The more Imogen reset the game, the more she realized sometimes their old lives came through in fascinating ways, like in the name of a winery.

* * *

The NYPD's cold case office was in the basement of a near derelict building in Downtown Manhattan. It smelt of stale air and stale doughnuts with a hint of stale cigarettes. A lot of detectives came through that office over the years, and some even made names for themselves, taking well-publicized cracks at the "unsolvable" cases buried in those stacks. Most of the times the files were incomplete. Evidence went missing or was just lost to time. Witnesses died off, moved, or just forgot their stories. Time did that. Scrambled your brain until up was down and down was up. Despite that, now and then, against all the odds, a gold nugget surfaced and the impossible happened—a long forgotten cold case changed its status to "solved."

While some officers viewed their time among the cold cases as punishment for some slight or pissing off their captain, not everyone saw it that way. Sometimes, the right person came along who saw the potential. A person who put faces to the names and went to bed every night with only one thought, a single word, repeating in their head—"justice."

The current custodian of the cold case room was such a detective. Smart. Determined. Inspired. She was someone who colored outside of the lines. The detective that closed cases. Brought measurable results. This detective wasn't in exile, but requested the transfer. Her superiors were less than thrilled with the transfer, but agreed, knowing that if anyone could close some of those forgotten cases, it was her. And it might've just been possible that she'd come out of the cold, dark basement making an even bigger name for herself.

Imogen stood outside the door for a long while. Her stomach gurgled, unsteady. She didn't know why she felt nervous, but she did. But after how far she'd traveled to get there, she wasn't about to let a few stray butterflies scare her off. So, she took a deep breath and knocked with determination, and maybe just a hint of reserve.

"It's open," the voice on the other side of the door called back.

Imogen turned the knob and went to push the door, but it didn't budge. She was about to give it a more forceful shove when the voice spoke again.

"The door sticks. Push it down, then forward. That's the trick."

Imogen did as she was instructed, and the door popped open, sounding like the top of a soda can. The smell hit her nose instantly. The dank library smell. It reminded her of Bryan Fry's basement, where she'd had her second kiss playing spin the bottle at Bryan's twelfth birthday party. It didn't last more than a millisecond, but Imogen counted it. The kiss was awkward, tentative. But still, all these years later, the very thought of it brought a warm smile to her face.

"Detective Craven," Imogen called out to the stacks of files and boxes that occupied every bit of visible space she could see. If there was anyone else in the room, Imogen couldn't figure out where they were or how they moved around. It felt like a video game, with every pile stacked perfectly, just waiting for the slightest nudge to come tumbling down.

"Back here. Straight and make a right. Follow the shelves. And look for the overhead lamp. I'm sitting directly under it. There's a path, even though it doesn't look like it. Still, watch that your ass doesn't bright down my house of cards."

Imogen laughed.

"I'll do my best," she said, carefully making her way through the labyrinth of boxes, photographs, folders, murder boards, and bags of evidence. Imogen couldn't help but notice some bags were empty.

Her ass nearly brought the place down a couple of times, but she didn't let on. If Detective Craven knew, she made no indication. The constant shuffling and reshuffling of papers told Imogen that the detective wasn't giving too much thought to her unexpected guest. But it didn't bother Imogen in the slightest. This visit was for her.

By the time Imogen reached the overhead lamp, her face was sweaty, and her heart was racing in her chest. All she could picture at every turn in the maze was knocking into a corner and watching as the overstuffed boxes fell like dominos. She'd made the trip one-way at least, but she wasn't sure how she'd fare on the return voyage. Imogen wondered if there were any icebergs out there in the sea of unsolveds.

"You made it, I see," Detective Craven said, without taking her eyes off the pages in front of her. "Take a seat."

"Thanks," Imogen said, carefully sliding into the chair opposite the detective. Now that she'd made it through the maze, she didn't want to back her chair into a wall of boxes.

Craven said nothing. Her eyes scanned every line of the page in her hand. Occasionally her eyes squinted, and her forehead wrinkled. A brow furrowed. At one point, she bit her lip and made a small "huh" sound. This went on for several minutes until she reached the end of the page and carefully set it aside in a folder, closing it and fixing her piercing eyes on Imogen. She reached a hand across the table.

"Detective Allyson Craven."

Imogen took Ally's hand in hers and squeezed. It'd been so long since she'd seen, let alone touched, her best friend in the flesh. And, she had to admit, it felt good. Nice.

"Imogen. Imogen Rockwell."

"A pleasure," Ally said, pulling back her hand.

"Do they call you Ally?"

Ally, aka Detective Craven, tilted her head inquisitively. "Who?"

"I don't know. Friends? Family?"

"They used to. When I was a kid. My mom called me Ally Pally. I hated that. And I had this one friend... Klarissa... she used to call me Ally Cat. But that was college, and it's a long, embarrassing story involving too many shots and a frat house, and I'm sure you didn't come here today to hear about that."

Imogen laughed, letting her face hold on to the smile.

"I had a friend. A best friend. Her name was Allison, too. Spelled with an 'i'."

"How did you know I spelled it with a 'y'?"

Imogen pointed to the placard on the desk, which read through the blanket of dust—Detective Allyson Craven.

"Ah. You have the makings of a skilled detective, Imogen Rockwell. Now. What can I do for you?"

"It's what I think I can do for you, Detective Craven."

"You can call me Ally if you want to."

"Really?" Imogen asked, surprised at the turn of events.

"Sure. I can see you want to. Do I remind you of her? Your friend?"

"Honestly, you do. A little. There are definitely some similarities. Some differences, too. But... you could've been sisters. Cousins, at the very least."

Ally smiled and her eyes sparkled just a little.

"So... what brought you to my fortress of solitude, Imogen?"

Imogen reached into her pocket and pulled out a torn piece of notebook paper. It was folded in half neatly, precisely. She put it on the crowded table and slid it across to Ally. The detective eyed it cautiously for a moment before picking it up and unfolding it with great care, as though doing it wrong would cause the paper to turn to ash and get sucked into the air purifier, whose days were already numbered.

"What's this?" Ally asked, reading the writing. "2764 St. Augustine Place? Where is this?"

"The Bronx."

"And," Ally urged Imogen on.

"And?"

"Yeah, Imogen. What's the story here? Why did you bring this to me?"

"Why don't you take a drive out there and see for yourself?"

Ally folded her hands on the table.

"And what is it I'm going to find at 2764 St. Augustine Place in the Bronx, Imogen?"

Imogen's eyes glassed over as horrible visions danced and twirled behind the black of her eyes.

"A house of horrors, Detective Craven. That's what you're going to find. A house of horrors."

This got Ally's attention. She leaned closer to Imogen. Imogen could tell from the twitch in Ally's right eye that the detective was choosing her next words carefully. Very carefully.

"Did you do something, Imogen?"

"No," Imogen said softly. "Not me."

"Then... who?"

"There is... there was... a family that lived there. The Millers. There were six of them. Well, seven. Poor, poor Fido. You need to go there. Today. Now."

"What happened to the Millers, Imogen? Did you hurt them?"

Imogen shook her head.

"Go. See for yourself. It's the game. They played the game. This case... will make you. But let me warn you, Detective Craven. If you let it inside of you, you'll never be free of it. It'll be your white whale and you'll be hunting it until the day you die."

Or until I reset the game.

A light bulb went off above Ally's head. Imogen knew she'd said the magic words because Ally suddenly looked like a hound hot on the scent.

"The game," Ally whispered, more to herself than to Imogen.

"Yes," Imogen began.

And then, they said in unison, "Stay-fucking-cation."

* * *

The place smelt burnt, like burnt eggs and toast. And coffee. It was exactly the way a good diner was supposed to smell. And Imogen was glad for it. Somewhere an electronic bell dinged, signaling her arrival to the staff. Imogen didn't see anyone, and from the looks of it, she must have gotten there not long before closing. Everything was far neater than it should have been. Ketchups, salt and pepper shakers, and sugar packets all lined up in an orderly, almost militaristic fashion, with exactness and precision.

"Sorry, hon. We're going to be closing up soon. The grill's turned off, but I can see if I can rustle up something else for you, if you're hungry," the tired female voice called from the kitchen.

Found you.

"No, that's okay. I'll take some coffee, if you've got it."

"I don't," the waitress said, and then she stepped out and stood behind the counter. "But I'm happy to make you some. I could use a little myself, I don't mind saying."

"That'd be great. And only if you don't mind," Imogen said.

The waitress smiled. Her face wrinkled just a bit, but the smile was genuine. Imogen was sure of it. She couldn't help staring at the woman's drooping, tired face. Imogen thought the woman looked older than her years, as though hardship and stress had aged her a decade beyond her time. There was a light there, but it was dimming. It happens to the best of us.

"It's no bother. Like I said, I could use some myself. Please, take a seat."

"Okay. Thank you," Imogen said, sliding onto a squat stool that looked as though it belonged under a glass case in a museum. A relic of another time and another place. But still, her ass felt like it'd just parked in the driveway of her home.

An older-looking woman came out from the back. Imogen assumed the woman had been in the bathroom. The waitress went to the counter and rang up the older woman's bill. The woman slapped a few bills on the counter and told the waitress to keep the change. Before she ducked out of the diner, the older woman turned back to Imogen and winked.

It was Cassie Miller.

The front door closed, and the waitress went over to it, then looked back at Imogen.

"Do you mind if I..." the waitress began. "I just don't want anyone else thinking we're still open, you know?'

"I don't mind," Imogen said as she watched the waitress lock the door before heading back to the counter.

The waitress looked over her shoulder, eyeing Imogen as she spooned dark coffee grounds into the filter.

"Sorry, but... do I know you? Your face... is familiar to me. I've been forgetful lately. I'd probably forget my own name if I didn't have it right there on my tag. Honestly, sometimes I have to glance down at it to remind myself."

The waitress laughed, but Imogen knew she wasn't joking.

"No. I just have that kind of face, I guess. I've never been here before."

And neither have you.

"I've been meaning to stop in for a while, though."

"Why on earth would you want to stop in here?" the waitress said, turning the coffee machine on. It hissed and whirred as though stretching after a nap.

"I've heard the pie is really good."

That brought a warm glow to the waitress's face.

"Best apple pie in the state, according to some magazine. Who knows? I don't know about things like that. Best left to the experts, right?"

"Right," Imogen agreed.

They stared at each other for a moment that bordered on being too long.

"It's just too dang quiet in here without all the customers shoveling slop into their mouths."

The waitress waited for Imogen to say something, but Imogen only sat on her stool, taking her in.

"Here," the waitress began, stopping to rummage through her apron's front pocket. After a bit of jingling, she pulled out a dull silver coin and presented it to Imogen. "Why don't you play us some music while we wait for the coffee? Juke's in the back. On the right. It's old, but it still plays nice. I'll get you a slice of that famous pie."

Imogen took the coin and, for just an instant, there was a flash of something there. She thought it was recognition, or maybe something else. The waitress's face told Imogen that she was trying to work it out.

"Are you sure I've never seen your face before? I swear I—"

The waitress's voice trailed off. Imogen waited for it to come back, holding the coin as though it were the golden fleece.

"You just look really familiar, like... really familiar. I just can't place it. I can't remember names, but I've got a knack for remembering faces. And I'd swear on a stack of *Great Housekeepings* that I've seen yours before. Haven't I?"

"Maybe it was a dream."

The waitress frowned.

"Yeah, maybe," she said, but was not convinced.

"Maybe it's all a dream. Maybe everything we see and seem is nothing more than the wild hallucinations of some... thing, somewhere. Maybe none of it's real. Maybe none of us are real."

The color drained from the waitress's face like bath water swirling down the drain.

"Sometimes," she began, swallowing. "Sometimes I dream the most vivid dreams. Like... they don't feel like dreams to me. They feel like..."

"Memories," Imogen finished.

"Yeah, memories. Like... there's all these other versions of me out there some place. Other lives. I've seen myself doing the darnedest things, I'll tell you what. But... they're just dreams. Right?"

Imogen smirked.

"I don't know about things like that. Best left to the experts, right?"

The waitress laughed.

"Right. Let me get you that pie. The coffee's nearly done. Go on and play something nice, okay?"

"Okay," Imogen said, watching the waitress lumber behind the counter, as though her body was wrapped in a weighted blanket. Her body was present, but her mind was elsewhere. Dreaming. Remembering.

The lights on the jukebox pulsed and glowed. The coin slot looked like a hungry mouth. Imogen wiped the dust off the old thing and fed it her coin.

"In the mood for anything in particular?" she called back to the waitress.

"No, anything's better than nothing. Just not that Josh Groban guy. I can't stand him. He sounds like a bunch of wailing alley cats."

Imogen didn't need to peruse the selections. She knew the jukebox and knew exactly which buttons to press.

"Hey," she said without turning her head. Behind her, the waitress set down a plate and then poured the coffee. "What's your name?"

"Isn't it on my tag? Wait. Where'd I put my nametag? Dang, Billy's gonna be right pissed at me if I lost another one."

"Check the sink in the bathroom. Maybe you left it there."

A lightbulb hummed above the waitress's head.

"Yeah. Maybe I did. I can't remember anything since... well. Just since. Anyway. Name's Florence, but everyone calls me—"

"Flo," Imogen said under the breath.

"Flo."

Imogen smiled as she pushed the chunky, faded buttons on the jukebox.

"Hi, Alex," Imogen whispered to the face staring out at her from inside the jukebox. A face whose expression was locked ina mix of terror and fury.

As Imogen sauntered to the counter, the thunderous horns announced "Macho Man" by The Village People. *Some things never change.*

"Here," Flo said, handing Imogen a clean set of silverware.

"Eat up."

Imogen made yummy sounds as she took several bites. To say the pie was good was like saying Shakespeare was pretty good at writing plays. A gross understatement. That pie had no business being there in a place like that. A small slice of heaven in a world that needed it.

"You have a name picked out?" Imogen asked, setting aside the fork that now had pie innards all over its teeth. She motioned to Flo's belly, where something stirred inside. "For the baby."

"How did you..."

Flo looked as though she wanted to say more but had suddenly been struck by a bolt of lightning and just stood there smoldering.

"This is another one of them dreams, isn't it?" she asked nervously.

"I'm wide awake," Imogen said, taking a sip of the best coffee that had ever passed through her lips. *Some things never change.*

"I don't know. I just feel... I don't know. Lightheaded all of a sudden."

"Sit down. We don't want you falling down on the job. Billy will skin you if you break another plate."

Flo laughed but then caught herself. She didn't need to say the words—*how could you know that... the broken plate... plates*—because her eyes said it all. Still, she sat beside Imogen anyway, just in case. No use testing the fates.

"I've just been so tired lately. It's like... it's sucking all the energy out of me."

"Does 'it' have a name yet?" Imogen asked warmly.

"Not really. I don't know what it is yet. I didn't want to know.

But I have a few ideas. Names, I mean. Obviously, it's either a boy or a girl. I'm not dumb."

Flo rubbed her belly. It was both a protective and soothing gesture.

"They sure are making a fuss in there. Have been ever since…"

Imogen raised an eyebrow.

"Ever since… what?"

Flo took a breath, wrapped her arms around her belly, and swallowed.

"Ever since you came in."

"Huh," was all Imogen could manage.

"I was thinking… Josiah if it's a boy."

"Josiah? Sounds biblical. A hero's name."

Flo nodded.

"I don't know. I'm not really sold on it yet. But… it's taking, you know?"

"Yeah," Imogen started. "Toby is a nice name. Not a lot of them out there."

It was Flo's turn to raise her brow.

"I bet there are more Tobys out there than there are Josiahs."

Imogen laughed, and Flo joined her. Flo's shoulders relaxed and then her face. It was as though every bit of tension was leaving her body at once.

"You got me there. But really, anything but Josh."

Flo recoiled as though she was about to throw up all over her freshly cleaned counter.

"Ew, no. It just reminds me of that stupid crooner."

"I really do hate that guy," Imogen said through a smile.

"On that, we agree. Wait. I never did get your name."

"Imogen. It's Imogen. Rockwell."

"That sure is a lovely name, Imogen. I'm pleased to meet you. Owie." Flo sighed. "They really are fussing up something awful in there."

Flo tried to laugh, but it came out sounding more like a groan. Imogen held up her right hand.

"May I?"

Without a moment's hesitation, Flo replied, "Sure. Go ahead. Maybe they'll settle down."

Imogen placed her hand gently on Flo's belly and felt the life growing inside. In that one instant, they were connected.

"Wow. You've got the Midas touch. That did the trick. Settled right down."

Imogen smiled.

"I've been known to have that effect."

She removed her hand and leaned back in her stool.

"I think 'it's' a girl. I can tell."

Flo tilted her head.

"I've been touching my belly for weeks and I can't tell anything, but that baby's gonna be a gymnast the way they're doing cartwheels in there. How do you know?"

Imogen smiled a knowing smile, and Flo got the message loud and clear.

"I just know."

Flo sucked air through her teeth.

"Alright, then. I guess this one'll be Olivia. It just feels right, you know. Like I don't even have to see to know she's an Olivia."

I found you.

"It's perfect. Like her."

Flo patted her belly.

"Yeah. I think she's gonna be a keeper."

Flo hummed a soft lullaby as she caressed her growing belly. Imogen watched as mother soothed child. As mother soothed sister.

"Can I ask you something, Flo?"

Flo ceased her music long enough to answer.

"Sure."

"Do you ever feel like you're not who you're meant to be?"

"Meant to be? What do you mean? Like I'm not living up to my potential or something? Mr. Acuda back in the fifth grade said I was gonna go places, but I think there were places on my person he wanted to go, if you know what I mean. Sick old perv."

Imogen leaned in, locking eyes with Flo in an intense stare that went down into the deepest part of Flo's soul.

"No, do you ever feel like you're supposed to be someone else? That you've been someone else."

"Shoot. I don't believe in that sort of thing, you know. But sometimes..."

Imogen leaned in even closer. She felt Flo's breath on her face as the waitress let out a mighty exhale. Minty fresh.

"Sometimes," Imogen urged her on.

"I don't know. Sometimes I dream. Like, dream-dream. They're so real. So vivid, you know? They don't feel like dreams at all. In one night, it's like I've lived a lifetime. Sometimes I'm a doctor. Imagine that. Me! A doctor. Ain't that a laugh? This one time, this one is my favorite. I was a zoologist. I was working at the Bronx Zoo. I was a real important lady. Everyone looked up to me. Everyone. I loved that life. I loved taking care of them animals. Yeah, that life... that dream was my favorite."

"What if I told you it wasn't a dream? What if I told you that you could be her again? Go back. Live that life. Live it until you're tired of it."

"I don't think I'd ever get tired of it." Flo laughed, but her face told a different story. And Imogen could read every word of it.

"I'm serious. If you could go back to that life, would you?"

Flo's face melted into one of worry and concern.

"What, and leave all this behind?"

"Do you want to?"

Flo's eyes watered and from her reaction, wiping at her tears faster than they came on, Imogen knew Flo hadn't expected to cry.

"Yes," Flo whispered as though she were giving a guilty verdict at a murder trial. "What's it gonna cost me? What's the catch? There's always a catch. Do I have to sell you my soul or something?"

"No. Nothing as awful as all that."

Imogen looked down at Flo's belly.

"I need her."

"Olivia? Why?"

Imogen leaned back.

"To make dreams come true."

Flo wiped at her eyes.

"I don't know. I don't know if I can do that. I don't know..."

"Flo... I've been looking for her a long, long, long time. I can give you the life you were meant for. Not this... existence. Getting by. Invisible. You were meant for greater things. You will live the best life... a thousand times. And when you dream, it won't be of a better life, but of all that's yet to come. I need you to say yes, Flo. Please say yes."

A steady stream of tears rolled down Flo's reddening cheeks.

"I don't know," she said, then bit her lip so hard that Imogen was surprised she didn't draw blood. "Can I see her first? Before you... take her?"

Imogen smiled.

"Of course. She'll be with you for a while. But a day will come when she's old enough, and you'll understand why I'm asking you to do this. A day will come, and I will be knocking at your door."

Flo dabbed at her face with the sleeve of her shirt.

"I understand, I think. But... but you're gonna take care of her, right? You're not in some kind of cult are you?"

Imogen thought about the Gemeo Project and couldn't help but laugh. She wondered how many lifetimes ago that was now.

"No. No cult. I promise."

Flo squeezed her belly gently, but firmly.

"I think I love her already. I wasn't sure at first. But... now..."

Imogen took one of Flo's hands in her own and steadied it. It was shaking so fiercely that Imogen was surprised it didn't snap off at the wrist and fly away, leaving a bloody trail on the diner's tiled floor.

"I love her too," Imogen said. "I love her too."

"Somehow... I know you do."

Imogen smiled.

I found you. Finally... I found you.

Imogen helped Flo off her stool and led her by the hand to the diner's front doors. Flo grabbed her coat and her bag and then insisted on locking up.

"Billy'll kill me if I forget," Flo mumbled under her breath.

They stood on the street as night fell. The blue melted into purple, which melted into black as the stars poked their heads out to say hello. Somewhere in the distance, somewhere in the far distance but still loud enough and strong enough to shake the ground where they stood, came a rumble of thunder and a bright flash of lightning.

"By the pricking of my thumbs, something wicked this way comes," Flo said, eyeing the ominous-looking sky.

"Not wicked," Imogen said, pointing to a spot far off in the distance. "Beautiful."

"I see it. It is beautiful. You know something? I'm not afraid. I thought I would be, but I'm not. Ain't that funny?"

Imogen took Flo's hand and squeezed it.

"Are you ready to be somebody else, Flo?"

"Yes," Flo exclaimed.

"Then let the game begin. Again."

A loud boom of thunder rumbled, shaking the ground, the earth, to its very core. It was a signal. A wake-up call. A sign. A second later, the sky was ablaze and bolt after bolt of lightning struck the ground. Electricity was everywhere, filling the air and penetrating deep into the ground. Flo felt it vibrate through her body, but it didn't hurt. It kind of tickled, so she laughed. And Imogen smiled.

As another boom shook the earth, Imogen turned to the sky and shouted—

"CROATOAN!"

Sometime Later: The Green-Eyed Monster

It was not the one-eyed, one-horned flying people eater that stared out of the darkness, but a green-eyed monster. The creature took many forms. It could appear as a man, a woman, a child. Hell, there were a couple of times it took the form of a family pet, but that proved a foolish choice because the thing couldn't do its thing as a dog, or a cat, or a hamster.

And its "thing" was to mate. Create life. And sometimes, take it. As it had once a long time ago in Boston. The thing liked Boston. It had been fun to wear the skin of an Irish woman with big tits. And the sex had been better than good. Sometimes it was less than adequate, and that made the entire experience feel like it wasn't worth it.

A lot of work went into becoming human. Taking on the skin of a living, breathing person. And when the sex was by the numbers, the green-eyed monster wondered why it even bothered. But when it clicked, when everything worked? Ahhh... heaven.

It was a whole new world now. The game had reset.

The thing would have to decide what skin it was going to wear next. And then, it would seek out its next victim. The succubus only prayed whoever it turned out to be was as good in bed as Jose Garriga had been.

Maybe, even better.

Time would tell.

Epilogue: We End Here - The Final Frontier

0600 hours.

The pods opened with a whoosh as a rush of air escaped the sleeping chamber. One by one they rose slowly, letting in the cold air of the space station. Even though the station was equipped with the latest, and supposedly greatest, heating system, there was no warming the chilled air of space.

"Good morning. It is 0600 hours. This is your wake-up," the computerized voice announced. "I repeat. It is 0600 hours, and this is your wake-up call. Please shower, dress, and prepare yourself appropriately. Gather in the cafeteria by 0700 hours for breakfast."

"Aw, shit," a raspy, deep voice groaned from inside the pods.

"It's too fucking early for this shit. I feel like we just went to sleep," another tired voice chimed in.

"That's because we did," a soft-spoken female voice said.

There were six of them on the station—the Odyssey Seven, an exploratory ship on a mission to map the vast space surrounding the Earth. The goal was to map the quadrant beyond the Odyssey Six, which exploded into a billion bits on re-entry. As of this morning, the Odyssey Seven was only several hundred hours from entering the quadrant.

But with nothing to do, all the prep work taken care of many hours ago, the explorers needed to pass their time. Reading, chess, checkers, backgammon and AI-driven immersive games had already gotten old for the stalwart crew. It had been the first lieutenant's idea, and the rest of the crew agreed it was a good one. More than that, it should pass the 700-some-odd hours they had left until it was time to get back to work, the real work of the mission.

"I repeat, convene in the cafeteria at 0700 for breakfast. The game starts immediately. Computer assist will be unavailable until the end of the game, but I will be listening. No cheating. I repeat, no cheating. Players who break the rules will be removed from the game. The game will continue until there is a winner. Once the game has started, it must run its course. There will be no stopping the game. I repeat, there will be no stopping the game once it has begun. Good luck to each of you. Remember the rules."

The explorers eyed each other. The game hadn't even started and competition was already in the air. It was obvious each player was mentally sizing up the other players, determining for themselves which player would be the first to break and which would be the last one standing. Each fashioned themselves a winner, but only one could win the game. Those were the rules.

The communal shower was unusually quiet that morning as each player went through their own mental prep for the game, preparing to step into the skin of another person entirely. Live that life fully and convincingly. Never break character and never call another player by their real name. They'd decided the penalties for breaking the rules, and they were harsh. Severe, even. And there was only one way to win the game—

survive.

One by one, they shuffled into the cafeteria, greeted by the smell of bacon, eggs, pancakes, coffee, and orange juice. It smelled better than it tasted, but there was little point in being finicky when you were light years from home. You took what you could get unless you wanted to starve, like the medic had done on Odyssey Two. The crew ended up eating her when their rations ran out thanks to a computer glitch. Only two explorers made the return trip.

Five of the six piled food onto their plates, already consumed with their characters. Mannerisms, facial expressions, walks... had all changed. They were no longer captain, medic, engineer, navigator, and programmer but mother, son, uncle, grandmother, and daughter. And when the final explorer burst into the cafeteria like a water balloon falling on a pin, the family unit was complete.

In the corner, the jukebox powered on. A Josh Groban song pumped through its tinny speakers.

"Honey," the father smirked, "I'm home. Now turn that shit off!"

Bonus Content

Want more Homecoming?

Download the exclusive bonus content and dive into the following:

- Bonus story: *Green-Eyed Monster*
- The Jukebox from Hell's playlist

Just tell us where to send it!

https://BookHip.com/NXAPKMQ

Acknowledgements

I am glad you're here with me. Here at the end of all things.

We meet again.

Pull up a chair and let's have a little honest to goodness chat. A lot has happened since we last met, and I want to share some of it with you.

First, THERE MAY BE SPOILERS AHEAD! I'm typing this now because chances are I will allude to some of the events in *Homecoming* somewhere in this acknowledgement, but I'm not entirely sure where any of this is going. I guess we'll find out together!

My point is this: don't be that guy or girl and jump to the back of the book to read the author's notes, looking for your name, without first READING THE BOOK. Bad! If that's you, no judgement — no, really! — but do yourself a favor now, flip back to the first page and start reading from there. We'll all still be here waiting for you when you catch up. I promise.

Now, back to the good stuff.

If you follow me on social media, you already know a few things about me. I'm a bleeding-heart liberal with an intense loathing of the current president and his administration, I have two dogs I adore, I'm addicted to coffee, and I've had a very difficult two years. Specifically, from Christmas 2024 until the time of this writing.

Why, you ask?

My older sister passed away just after Christmas, and the aftermath has been a tidal tsunami of anger, grief, helplessness, more anger, more grief... and so on. You get the picture, right?

I'm telling you this not to get sympathy cards and emails, although those are lovely and welcome, but to explain the state my mind has been in since we last sat here together shooting the shit.

To be blunt, it wasn't in a good place. It wasn't *home.*

I had several false starts to *Homecoming.* I knew the story. I knew the story when I started *Lockdown.* It was always leading here. Always. But *telling* the story proved to be the hard part. I finished one and a half drafts of the book before I gave up for a while. It just wasn't working for me. Not the story, but the telling. I felt I owed it to you and the story to tell it the way I saw it in my head and not try to put it in a fancy box with bows and ribbons.

Still with me?

Good.

Now, if you follow me on the socials, you also know that in October of 2024 I started working in earnest on a novel called *The Mourning House.* It was a massive undertaking, telling a story about an Irish family spanning over forty years.

From the first page, I knew two things:

1. It was good. Scary good.
2. This novel was going to be *lonnnggggg.* Like, John Irving long.

And it was.

In its final state, *The Mourning House* is 750 pages. Yes, 750 pages.

It took me four months to complete, and halfway through, my sister left this world.

In my sadness, I knew I had to finish the book. I had so much time already invested, not to mention words. The most difficult pages were already written, so I just needed to bring the story to a close. It took another 300 pages to do that, but I did it.

And then I returned my attention to my other family, the Millers. I had to close out their story, and I had to do it properly. Once I had Harding's opening chapter complete, I hit the ground running. Like *Staycation,* I wanted *Homecoming* to be lean and mean. And it is.

But there's more to it, too, isn't there?

I was surprised how much saying goodbye to the Millers tugged at my heart. As I neared the end of Part One, I decided to write the epilogue before moving on to Part Two. Give myself a definite landing pad. Before you ask, yes. The story was always going to end this way. I knew every word of the epilogue before I wrote it.

From the moment I introduced Olivia and Imogen in *Lockdown*, I felt more of a bond with Imogen than I did with Olivia. But I knew Imogen felt something for her that I did not. Killing Olivia off wouldn't be easy, and it wouldn't be a true death. They ARE Millers after all, right?

In the end, I think much of the epilogue is me saying goodbye to parts of my life that are now forever gone since my sister passed, and in those final pages, I was hoping to see her again. It may be a little selfish on my part, but, damned if it doesn't work and yet again turn *Staycation* on its ear.

An emotional ending to a story that had its origins in an idea about kids eating their parents? Just give me all the awards already, will you?

For my devoted *Staycation-ers,* I will say this to you now: in this book, there are definite references to Stephen King. But not the ones you think. I bet my life on that. Just because Part One takes place in a motel, excuse me... "'otel'"... doesn't mean I was thinking of or nodding to *The Shining.* I'm not and I never was. Every single haunted hotel story for the next thousand years will be judged against King's *The Shining,* and I say... good for him, and shame on you. That book is about a haunted family, and an alcoholic writer. It's not about a haunted hotel.

Dracula by Bram Stoker was the first book I ever read. Yes. It was a children's abridged edition, and it was only about 60 or so pages, but the words belonged mostly to Stoker, it told the highlights of the story, and the artwork was wicked cool.

I was hooked on horror.

Stoker introduced me to horror, but King made me think I might be able to write a few horror books of my own. And that's what I've done. He's influenced every modern horror writer whether they want to admit it or not. I admit it, proudly. He's the reason I'm a writer. And I will, from time to time, give the man a nod. I think he deserves that much for all he's given to the genre and his legions of fans (see what I did there? If you don't, did you even read *Homecoming?* Go back now! Read it).

As for the King reference in *Homecoming?*

Shoot me a message on socials, send me a smoke signal or an email if you think you have it figured out. If you figure it out, you'll be rewarded. This offer is good for the first 12 people who put the pieces together.

You will have to go all the way back to *Staycation* to piece it all together. It's always been there, and no one has ever mentioned it.

Happy hunting!

I want to say, here at the end of all things, that I am so glad you took this ride with me. Your enthusiasm, support, kind words, encouragement... have meant so much to me, especially when I was out of silver linings and sat here wondering why I bother to do any of this, why more people aren't reading my books.

You're the reason. Yes, YOU.

I wanted *Homecoming* to be the ending you deserved, and I hope you think it is. If not, well, you're shit out of luck. That's the way the story goes, and that was the fate of the Millers. And Joanne. And Josh Groban.

No, I will never stop ragging on him. If you know, you know.

But don't despair, my fine friends.

Endings aren't forever. They're simply goodbyes... for now.

Maybe one day soon we shall meet again, right here.

You never know. I guess we'll just have to wait and see.

Now, as far as thank you's...

The list is short. I've thanked most of you already, and I can't begin to name all the names of card-carrying *Staycation*-ers. I'd feel like shit if I forgot someone. So just know that if we shared any exchanges on social media, if you sat in during any of my live feeds, signed up for my newsletter, etc... I appreciate you, and I thank you from the bottom of my heart for making me feel like a writer. I cannot begin to tell you how that feels after a lifetime of dreaming about it.

Hint: it feels so much fucking better than I ever imagined.

Andre and Natasha. I have no words for how much your

support has meant to me. You believed in me from day one, when no one else did. You were there when I was days away from hanging up my pen and giving up on this dream.

You made my dream come true, and I will always be grateful to you both for that. I have loved every minute of our working together, and I am privileged to call you friends and family. A million times... thank you. The best is yet to come. Trust me.

My alpha and beta readers: the Melissas, Loralee, and my partner in crime, Dana. Thank you for your honest reactions, responses, and sage advice.

A second shout-out to my wife and partner, Dana, thank you for your patience on the days when the writing was hard, and your encouragement when it came easily.

To my oldest friend and biggest champion, Irin... what can I say that I haven't already said? Thank you. For everything.

This book is not dedicated to my sister, but she is in its pages, nonetheless. Noelle, wherever you are, I hope you like it. Until we meet again.

And I must thank my M4L editor, Melissa, again, for your wonderful work, advice, and insights. It has been a pleasure working with you. My words are better because of you. Until next time!

Lastly, thanks to all the readers who've trashed *Staycation* and *Lockdown*. You've made me giggle so hard, I farted. I plan on giving you many more books to trash, so clear your calendars.

Other than that, I think I've got you all covered.

Again, thank you... for everything. For buying my books. For coming on this wild ride. And staying on it. For telling your friends about it. For sending me your far out (and wrong) theories. For making me feel like a rock star when I felt like shit.

I owe you more than a book.

Well, we're back where we started. Ride's over. Time to get off.

But feel free to get back in line and ride the ride again. I bet there's a lot you missed the first and second time around. Not all the secrets have been revealed.

Until we meet again, be safe, be healthy, be as happy as you can be. We all deserve it.

And please, be kind. Everyone deserves that much.

May the road rise to meet you.

RJ
May 2025
Asbury Park and Denver

Enjoy this book?

We hope you enjoyed this release from M4L Publishing.

Reviews are the most helpful tools in getting new readers for any books. We don't have the financial backing of a New York publishing house and can't afford to blast our books on billboards or bus stops.

(Not yet!)

That said, your honest review can go a long way in helping us reach new readers. If you've enjoyed this book, we'd be forever grateful if you could spend a couple minutes leaving it a review (it can be as short as you like) on the site you purchased this book from.

Thank you so much!

About the Author

RJ CLARK began his professional career as a child actor and model, following in his famous uncle's footsteps, Stanley Clements. RJ's face was seen nationwide in the U.S. Army "Stay in School" print ad campaign. He also appeared regularly on daytime television, and worked on numerous film and commercial projects before inevitably returning to his first true love, writing.

As a screenwriter, RJ's screenplays won first prize or placed in the top 5 of nearly every major national—and international—competition worth mentioning. His novella, Two for One launched the indie literary magazine "The Instagatorzine," broken into two parts across the magazine's first two issues.

A native New Yorker, RJ attended NYU, holds a BFA and an MFA. He has lived in all five boroughs, but now calls historic Asbury Park, NJ home with his wife and dog, an Aussillon named Venus.

While RJ no longer works in the theatre as an actor, he provides accessibility services for deaf patrons at live per-formances throughout the country. He is passionate about theatre being for all, and enjoys being able to introduce new shows to deaf or hard of hearing patrons.

When not writing, you're most likely to find RJ either playing guitar along the Jersey Shore, taking photographs of cool dogs and musicians around Asbury Park, voraciously reading new books, working on new music, or traveling the world.

A few of RJ's most favorite things include black coffee, chocolate, Stephen King, peanut butter, Pringle's, Truman Capote, tabletop games, the Universal Studios Monsters, horror movies, and David Tennant.

Follow RJ online:

Facebook: RJ Clark Horror Writer
    Staycation Group (Facebook): Staycationers, Unite!
    TikTok: @rj_clark_writer
    IG: @rj_clark_writer
    Threads: @rj_clark_writer
    Website: www.rjclarkwriter.com

More from M4L Publishing

Homecoming *RJ Clark*

Lockdown *RJ Clark*

Staycation *RJ Clark*

Dead Girls Don't Cry *RJ Clark*

Salvation *Andre Gonzalez* and *Audrey Brice*

Nightfall *Andre Gonzalez* and *Audrey Brice*

Resurrection *Andre Gonzalez* and *Audrey Brice*

Replicate *Andre Gonzalez*

The Burden *Andre Gonzalez*

Insanity *Andre Gonzalez*

Erased *Andre Gonzalez*

Humbug *Andre Gonzalez*

Sweethaven *RJ Clark*

Timber Beast *A.K. Hughey*

Alice *Audrey Brice*

Wish *Courtney Konstantin*

Quixote *Stephen Wertzbaugher*

Arturius *A.K. Hughey*

Steamboat *Courtney Konstantin*

Strangled *Stephen Wertzbaugher*

Dethroning Oz *Audrey Brice*

Scorned *Z.S. Diamanti*

Followed Away *Andre Gonzalez*

Followed East *Andre Gonzalez*

Followed Home *Andre Gonzalez*
A Poisoned Mind *Andre Gonzalez*
Snowball: A Christmas Horror Story *Andre Gonzalez*

www.ingramcontent.com/pod-product-compliance
Lightning Source LLC
Chambersburg PA
CBHW071212210726
48293CB00002B/399